I0555792

# The Probability of Murder

## The Sophie Knowles Mysteries Book 2

## by Camille Minichino

Charlotte was gone forever and her bag was in my possession. I thought back to her facetious comment about it would be all mine if she didn't reclaim it.

Who else's business was it now? What if there was something in the bag that would help the police find her killer?

I could think of a long list of reasons to open Charlotte's bag, not the least of which was that I was curious. What had she deemed necessary to lock up in a flimsy nylon bag?

Not that she'd been that security conscious. The tiny padlock was identical to a set of six I'd bought for myself. They were TSA-approved and simply provided some small measure of protection against random unzippings around airports or hotel rooms.

I fished around in my travel drawer and pulled out a small key that I knew would fit Charlotte's lock also.

Back in my office, on my knees again, I inserted the key, removed the padlock, and took the zipper pull between my fingers. At each step, I paused, reconsidering.

This was Charlotte's private property. Did her death take away her rights? Did I have any claim to snooping in her bag just because she was no longer around to protect those rights.

Finally, I came to a decision: open the bag and determine whether the police should see the contents or I should simply get busy, wash Charlotte's clothes and put them in the box I kept for a charity pickup.

I pulled the zipper across the top of the bag and eased the side away.

Inside the bag were no gym shoes nor socks nor sweats nor a magazine nor sunglasses nor a bottle of water.

It wasn't a gym bag at all, in fact.

# Chapter 1

Another Friday, another party in the Benjamin Franklin Hall lounge, the most rocking place on the Henley College campus. Putting Henley, Massachusetts on the map.

Pity the poor humanities majors, with no building to call their own, no colorful mathematicians and scientists to celebrate. Today the honoree was mathematician August Ferdinand Mobius.

"The wicked superhero," cracked the computer genius Daryl Farmer, a freshman all the way from California. "How old is the dude? Like, two hundred and seven?" Daryl stood, with one hand in his jeans pocket, the other on his hip. Apparently the guy was unconcerned about aggravating his statistics professor, who could manipulate his grade. If I were so inclined.

"Two twenty-one," I said, amazed at how close he'd come.

"Wish I had a blow-up of the dude for the wall on my side of the dorm."

Nerdy, sarcastic guys like Daryl were a new addition to the former women-only college. I liked them.

Daryl did have a point about the abstruse personalities my Mathematics Department came up with when it was our turn to choose a theme for the weekly celebrations.

The parties in the Franklin Hall lounge were sponsored by its occupants, in ascending order, by floor: the departments of mathematics, physics, biology, and chemistry. We took over the otherwise drab uncarpeted room on the first floor and displayed posters and equipment that evoked the Woman, or Man of the Week.

I loved teaching math. I didn't even mind the extra work

involved in chairing my department this year. But there was no question that the gatherings were more fun when one of the sciences was in charge.

Since classes, and the parties, started eight weeks ago, the get-togethers they'd sponsored involved safety glasses, asbestos gloves, magnets, and, almost always, things that plugged in and flashed on and off. We'd seen colored smoke, fire, and liquids that changed hues before our eyes. Stiff competition, the only drawbacks being the unhealthy smells when the Biology Department took the lead and the risk of an explosion when it was the Chemistry Department's day.

Our fun meetings had grown from seasonal, to monthly, and now weekly. The idea was to motivate the math and science majors to read beyond their textbooks and their mandatory class assignments and interest them in the historical backgrounds of the celebrities in their fields.

"Bring them in with food; keep them here with the excitement of learning," said my optimistic colleague, Fran Emerson as we took seats next to each other for the Mobius presentation.

We faculty were cheered by an SRO crowd today as most weeks, refusing to believe the free snacks and soft drinks that lined the conference table were the main attraction. Glancing at the paper plates in the hands of many students, overflowing with cheese, crackers, fruit, and enough brownies for their own dorm party, I could tell some food budgets ran out by Friday afternoon.

A senior physics major took it upon herself to bring us to order, using a bell and clapper from the storeroom to get our attention. Students made a last minute dash to the goodies on the conference table and eventually took seats on chairs or on the floor and fell silent.

Today the petite sophomore Chelsea Derbin, a match in height to my five-three, was up, ready to wow us with a talk about one-sided surfaces. After a short talk on the life and times of Mobius, she led the group in the construction of a Mobius strip.

"Take a strip of paper and twist one end before gluing the ends together," she instructed, as she demonstrated.

"Way to go, Chelsea," Daryl said.

Chelsea did her best to ignore him. "See," she proclaimed as she ran her marker around the newly formed surface. There's just one side now! How cool is that!"

"What can you do with it?" Daryl challenged, from his lofty perch as the star student in our recently created computer science program. Daryl's question seemed more intimidating, perhaps due to his imposing physique and a look that was more mature than many of the young men who were now part of the Henley student body.

Though Daryl could be annoying, this was the kind of participation and intelligent questioning I relished, not just from the new male students, but from all of them. It had been a tough road overcoming the resistance from both administration and alumnae to going coed. I wanted to think it was worth it.

I was still getting used to seeing names like William and Zachary mixed in with the Megans and Kaylas. I didn't even mind that I couldn't tell simply from the roster if Lindsey, Blair, and Devon were girls or boys.

Chelsea's eyes grew wide at this new challenge from Daryl. She bit her lip and finally squeaked out, "You can cut this different ways and get a bunch of intertwining loops?" Chelsea's ending with a question gave the lie to the excitement and confidence she tried to pour into her delicate voice. Usually one to wear flowery print dresses, today Chelsea had chosen jeans and an oversize sweater. The better to hide in?

Chelsea looked at me. "Dr. Knowles?" she said, a plea for help. Her enthusiasm over Mobius strips begetting more Mobius strips wasn't catching on among the noshing crowd in front of her. I'd hoped Chelsea, a small-town girl from the Midwest, had gotten over her timidity this year, but I could see she'd hit her limit this afternoon. She was a nervous wreck, even more so than I'd anticipated. Much as I hated to, I stepped in.

"What can you do with that beaded necklace?" I asked Daryl, grateful for the rise in popularity of unisex jewelry.

Daryl balanced his salt-laden snack plate on his knees and fingered the brown and ivory shell pieces. "These are beautiful heishi beads with a lot of meaning. I got it directly from a Native American woman sitting on a rug in New Mexico. It doesn't have to be functional."

Aha! A perfect opportunity to make a parallel with mathematics.

"And it might come in handy someday if you need a miniature lasso in a hurry?" I said.

Daryl smiled and I sensed he knew where I was going. "Yeah, I guess so."

I cleared my throat in preparation for my timeworn speech about the beauty of mathematics, the meaning it brought to universal patterns, and its usefulness in describing the physical world.

In the nick of time, a lovely distraction appeared at the doorway. My boyfriend, medevac helicopter pilot Bruce Granville, who never bored eighteen-year-olds when he gave talks about his job. It wasn't fair that he had dark good looks plus larger-than-life stories to tell.

I wasn't the only one to notice. "Your hunky guy is here, Sophie," said Fran.

I'd recently inherited the department chairmanship from Fran, who now directed the computer science program. Her new bob and black designer jeans—her idea of casual Friday dress—made Fran the youngest looking grandmother I knew.

I caught Bruce's eye through the crowd and sent him my best smile, which carried the promise of a great weekend.

The novelty clock on the wall, with its "pi" notation, read four-thirty. Bruce had appeared with military precision, appropriate to a former Air Force man, at sixteen thirty to claim me from the drudgery of classroom life.

Known to all the Franklin Hall faculty and many of the students, Bruce greeted them as he made his way through the room to me. That he was wearing his well-aged bomber jacket from his dad's army days added to his appeal and snatched the stage from a grateful Chelsea.

"Time to go. Thanks, all you guys," Chelsea said, with relief in her voice. She gathered her meager demonstration equipment—scrap paper, scissors, and a marker— and turned off the boom box that aired her syncopated background music. She'd given it her best shot. I gave her a reassuring word, about the next time, and so on, but she rushed by me, saying, "Restroom." I had an idea why. I hoped I hadn't pushed her too hard to take charge of today's show-and-tell.

"Let's give a shout out to Chelsea," Daryl said to her retreating back.

"Woo hoo," sang a small chorus of her peers, those who weren't already connected to their smartphones.

Meanwhile, my handsome dark-eyed date was closing the gap between us, chatting with people as he did so.

"Do you know what's going on over at the library?" I heard Bruce ask Fran. She shook her head. "Nothing I know of."

"The place is surrounded," he said.

"Surrounded by what?" I asked, joining them.

"There's a fleet of cop cars in front of the building," Bruce said. "The main library gate's closed off. I had to park across the street and walk in through the tennis courts."

That was strange enough. Then I became aware of ringing cell phones in all corners of the room. The sound wasn't that unusual since the official end of the party also meant cell phones could be turned back on, but there seemed to be an inordinate number of calls coming in today, their varied ringtones creating a mathematically complex cacophony.

"Could it be just campus security having a meeting?" Fran asked.

"Nuh-uh," Bruce said. "I doubt it. Unless it's an emergency drill. I saw an ambulance headed into the gate, plus all the patrol cars from town. Official Henley PD. You know, protect and serve." Bruce saluted and Fran laughed.

Bruce sounded facetious about the competence of the Henley Police Department, but he wasn't fooling anyone. As a pilot with MAstar—Massachusetts Shock, Trauma, and Air Rescue—Bruce was on good terms with the state's law enforcement agencies. Fran and a select few of those gathered at the party also knew that he was best buds with one of HPD's detectives, Virgil Mitchell.

I overheard snippets of conversation from students speaking into their cell phones. A few were texting. I felt left out.

"I'm walking over there right now," I heard from one student.

"There's a fire truck on campus, too?" from another, apparently being clued in by someone at the library site.

"No way," from a female Jordan.

"Way," from a male Reece.

Daryl, the blue-eyed blonde with an appreciation of Native American crafts, spoke into his phone, then announced to the assembly, "They're taking someone out of the library on a gurney."

Unfortunately the Ben Franklin lounge windows faced away from the campus, so we didn't have a line of sight to the alleged emergency scene outside the Emily Dickinson Library.

Bruce and I fell in with the flow of people streaming toward the front door.

"We're out of here soon, no matter what, right, Sophie?" Bruce asked me.

As much sympathy as I felt for whoever was on the gurney, I hoped nothing would interfere with the getaway in Boston that we'd planned.

"To Boston, the home of the bean and the cod."

"Where the Cabots speak only to Lodges," Bruce responded.

"And the Lodges speak only to God," I finished.

"Ten minutes, tops, and we're on our way," Bruce said, squeezing my hand.

I squeezed back. "What's to keep us here?"

# Chapter 2

My mind was more on Boston than the Henley campus as Bruce and I filed out the front door with a dozen or so people. The rest of the crowd took the elevator to the basement, presumably to use the exit closest to the library. We stepped out into a chilly, darkening afternoon with just the right amount of fall snap in the air. My favorite season, with classes in full swing and the taste of pumpkin and cranberries always near at hand.

Bruce and I had both been out of town at conferences lately, which ate into our time together, above and beyond Bruce's tricky seven days on/seven days off schedule at Henley's airfield.

"After dinner tonight there's that midnight showing of *The Eiger Sanction* in Cambridge," Bruce reminded me as we made our way toward the library where it seemed the entire Henley College population had gathered.

"A seventies movie. Can't wait," I said, in that way that he knew meant, "If you insist."

Bruce was also scheduled to leave on Sunday morning for a climbing trip to New Hampshire. He'd be available only through spotty cell phone reception and maybe through rangers when the visibility allowed. Not my favorite arrangement, but he was passionate about his mountaineering hobby. With an exciting, risky job piloting helicopters into accident scenes on the ground, you'd think he'd take up chess to relax, but not my guy. Hanging off the side of a mountain was his way of unwinding.

The next twenty-four hours, give or take, were ours, however. We were headed north for an excursion where we'd be roughing it at a four-star hotel overlooking the Boston Common. My duffel bag was in my campus office, packed and ready to be transferred to Bruce's SUV.

I couldn't wait for a dose of special togetherness before Bruce left to scale the heights with two of his buddies. The fair-weather summer and early fall tourists would be long gone and we'd have the north shore's beautiful wharf areas to ourselves.

In return for watching that nearly forty-year-old Clint Eastwood climbing movie, I'd made Bruce promise to spend an hour with me at the Museum of Science where a new mathematics exhibit had opened. I hoped to get inspiration for the math department's next turn as entertainment committee for a Franklin Hall party. As much as I was a fan of Mobius and one-surface structures, my goal was to have props that were more titillating than strips of paper.

The closer we got to the library, the more jarring the scene in front of us became. An unsettling feeling came over me as we watched the ambulance take off, shooting out of the main campus driveway, patrol cars blaring behind it. I could hardly believe the number of cell phones that were raised high to document the event. Did someone really want a photograph of another person's misfortune?

"It's going to take forever to get to the hospital by the roads," Bruce said. His standard half-joking plug for using air transport, particularly his own MAstar, for medical emergencies.

The lights of the remaining police and campus security vehicles, about a hundred feet away, swirled red and blue as chatter from police radios and onlookers rose up and reached us.

I looked at Bruce. Without speaking, we considered our next move. Option one was to take off as planned, immediately, without a backward glance. Our curiosity could be satisfied later tonight or tomorrow by a phone call to Fran or any other member of the Henley College community. Or we could even wait until Monday morning. Option two—

"We should at least find out who's in the ambulance," I said, knowing Bruce would agree. It was his life's work after all. And my campus.

"Sure, just a quick Q and A," he said.

I nodded. "And then we're out of here."

"It's probably no one related to the campus," Bruce said.

"Yeah, some walk-in off Henley Boulevard," I said. "It happens a lot."

"You don't have the tightest security at that entry point."

"Retired cops. What can you expect?" I asked.

"I won't tell Virgil you said that," Bruce teased.

"Anyway, he'll never know. There's nothing here that a homicide detective would care about."

"Nah."

We sounded convincing.

As we approached the building, I saw the faces of the students and staff closest to the police tape, which wound its way to the open library doors and inside the main lobby area as far as I could see. I guessed most of the onlookers had been in the library for the start of this drama. I could tell from their reactions that it was no stranger who'd been carted off campus with such ceremony.

"Since when does a medical emergency require crime scene tape?" I asked Bruce, nervousness coming to the fore.

He shook his head slowly, processing the scene in his mind.

"Dr. Knowles, do you know what's happening?" Daryl Farmer, the most vocal boy at the party—they were too young for me to think of them as men—came rushing up to me. "It's Ms. Crocker. I heard someone say she was shot or something. I think she might be dead."

"Charlotte Crocker? The librarian?" Bruce asked.

Charlotte Crocker, the librarian. Charlotte Crocker, my friend. I stopped short, unable to move. Charlotte Crocker shot? Dead? It wasn't possible. I pushed the absurd phrases out of my head.

Charlotte and I were gym partners, lunch partners, shopping partners. She'd been Henley's reference librarian only two years, but had made her mark on students and faculty.

I'd finally met her only family less than a week ago. Charlotte and I had taken her nephew to tour the MAstar medevac facility where Bruce worked. Noah, a senior at a Boston college, was interested in being a helicopter pilot. Charlotte was excited about the day, seeming every bit as curious about what was going on at the airfield as Noah was. It was clear she doted on him.

Childless herself, Charlotte also doted on every young person who came across her path, and our Henley College students were the beneficiaries. I hated the idea that she'd been taken away with a serious illness, or injured on our campus. That she might have been shot made no sense at all.

"Yeah, she was really nice," Daryl said, as if responding to my thoughts. "She did so much work for us, no matter how busy she was. She practically wrote our papers for us, you know? And she counseled a lot of the girls. She was your friend, too, wasn't she, Dr. Knowles?"

Bruce looked at me. He could tell I wasn't ready to speak.

"Thanks for letting us know," he said to Daryl. "We'll check it out."

"I wonder who could have done that? Hurt Ms. Crocker," Daryl asked, slow to take a hint.

Bruce put his arm around me, turned from Daryl, and said, softly, "I'll call Boston."

I reached to my shoulder and grabbed his hand, wishing his MAstar bird could sweep us back in time and take us up and away from the scene in front of me.

Under normal conditions, I'd love the briskness of the day, and my long-sleeved turtleneck and fleece vest, my interpretation of casual Friday dress, would be enough. But since I'd heard Charlotte's name in connection with the intrusive emergency vehicles that seemed to have taken over the campus, I'd become shivery cold and regretted leaving my jacket in my office. I could have used it, plus a coat, scarf, and fur-lined gloves.

After the second shiver, I found myself weighed down by Bruce's bomber jacket.

"Thanks," I muttered and felt Bruce's comforting hand through the thick leather.

"We're going to check this out, okay?" he said. "It could be nothing. It doesn't take much to get a rumor started in a place like this. You know that."

Yes, it could be nothing. A college campus, essentially a closed community, was a perfect setting for creating fiction. I'm overreacting, I told myself.

Never mind that the roar of the fire engine's motor, even in its idling state, and the indistinct chatter of cops and academics made it hard to stay calm.

Daryl was only a freshman. How could he be sure it was Charlotte Crocker who was hurt? He'd barely met her. And who said her injuries were that bad? I was once sent away in an ambulance after a simple fall. I'd tripped on my raincoat going up a flight of stairs at a mall a few years ago, cracking my nose, sending streams of blood over the slippery tile steps. Security had swooped down on me immediately and rushed me to the nearest hospital, sirens roaring, lights streaking through the air. Genuine concern aside, what corporation—or school—wants a lawsuit these days?

Probably something similar had happened to Charlotte. We'd joked about how the college needed to upgrade the rickety old half-wood, half-metal ladders in the library stacks. She might have fallen while reaching for an ancient tome.

If it had even been Charlotte.

People around me kept mentioning a gunshot, but did they even know what a gunshot sounded like? And, besides, that was information-by-cell-phone. Definitely hearsay and, therefore, unreliable. Nothing I should pay attention to.

As I wished away the idea that my friend had been seriously hurt, Bruce led me closer to the Henley police cars and the detectives who'd begun to talk to the onlookers. We zigzagged past uniformed cops with pens and note pads who were pulling students and staff aside, talking one on one and in small groups.

Fran Emerson and many of the students who'd been at the Franklin Hall party had apparently passed us after we left the building. Fran motioned me to join them off to the side, but I shook my head and let Bruce lead me in closer to the police tape. Bruce had never answered my question about the yellow and black tape. Was it used only when a crime had been committed?

When I reminded him now, he shrugged. "Probably it's routine," he said. "Crowd control."

I bought the answer, gratefully. The imposing brick administration building, immediately to the east of the library, had emptied out. Upper management had gathered and stood together on the steps.

The academic dean and her administrative assistant stood at the top of the stone steps. Below them, as if they were posing for an overhead shot for a Henley College recruiting brochure, the levels were lined with other officers and staff members, all in professional dress, unlike the professors. In my peripheral vision I picked out Martin Melrose, our three-piece-suit financial manager, and two vice presidents.

The lower steps were populated with secretaries, cleaning service staff, and mailroom employees. It was as if someone had told them all to line up according to their salaries.

I wondered if the event rated summoning Olivia Aldridge, Henley's president, home from her alumni tour of the west coast.

After fifteen years on campus, I knew almost everyone on the steps, but this afternoon I managed to avoid eye contact completely. No one in the administrative tableau was talking anyway; all were staring straight ahead at the drama unfolding on our beautiful fall lawns and pathways.

By now Bruce and I had reached the narrow path between the library and the administration building. I felt a wave of panic when I realized where Bruce was headed—toward his best friend since college, Henley PD homicide detective Virgil Mitchell, a few yards ahead.

My knees went weak. Not just an injury? A homicide?

"They took someone away in an ambulance?" I said to Bruce. "If someone is dead, they wouldn't put her in an ambulance, right?"

"Henley sends everyone when there's a nine-one-one call," he said. "And we don't have a separate coroner's vehicle, so ...." He shrugged, not wanting to state a possible conclusion, but he didn't need to.

"Do you want to stay back here while I talk to Virge?" Bruce asked. Then, as a smile crossed his face, "Of course you don't."

Virgil, all two hundred fifty pounds of him, left a group to the care of a woman in uniform and approached us.

He and Bruce did a knuckle bump, which I'd never seen between them. Maybe it was code for a greeting mired in sympathy. A condolence rap.

Virgil took my hand, another first. "Sophie, I'm sorry about this. People are saying you were one of Ms. Crocker's close friends on campus."

My whole body seemed to buckle. *Were.* I'd heard *were.*

I felt Bruce's arm tighten around me, holding me up since my spine was useless. "What happened?" I asked Virgil.

"Tell me about Ms. Crocker, Sophie. Anything you know about her that can help us?"

"Help you do what? Is she …?"

Virgil led us past the array of staff on the admin building steps, where the principals had stopped posing. Most were chatting in place as two uniformed officers headed in their direction.

Dean of Women Paula Rogers, who'd been making an effort to be my friend this fall, had broken away, and came up to me. "Sophie, what's this about? Did you expect this? I mean, to be questioned?" she asked, ignoring both my protectors, the beefy Detective Virgil Mitchell and my very fit boyfriend.

Something about Paula put me off from our first meeting. I hadn't been eager to develop a friendship with her and I certainly wasn't going to start now by answering her silly questions.

Virgil ignored her. Bruce gave her a charming smile and turned me away from her. I could have kissed both of them.

Virgil and I settled on a bench on the vast lawn at the center of the campus. Bruce squatted in front us. In a couple of weeks, right after Thanksgiving, an enormous Christmas tree would be erected and decorated near this spot. Would we even remember today?

With nothing new to see, students, presumably with police permission, drifted past us on the way to the campus coffee shop or to the dorms that lined the eastern edge of the property. The small clusters of students were more animated than sad or concerned, I noticed. I wanted to stop and lecture them: *this is not simply excitement for a Friday night. You can't just go on your dates now as if nothing's changed.*

But as professors often do to gain perspective, I projected

back to Sophie Knowles, college student, twenty-five years ago, understood their need to move forward, and partly forgave them. Besides, I wasn't completely convinced anything serious had happened.

Not for another minute, anyway.

"Sophie, you probably know." He paused. "There's been a homicide," Virgil said, dispelling any lingering hope I had that the emergency vehicles had responded to a sprained ankle or a possible concussion from falling books.

I took a deep breath. "Charlotte was killed?"

"I'm afraid so."

I looked toward the library, in the direction of the sunset. There seemed to be a sudden and drastic shift to a nighttime sky.

# Chapter 3

I had mixed feelings about leaving the campus. Part of me wanted to flee and come back later to the revelation that the entire ambulance event had been a fiction. The other part wanted to stay behind, in case the obtrusive vehicle did come back: "It was a mistake," the EMTs would say. "This lady is fine."

As it was, I had little choice but to comply with Virgil's request to meet him at the police station downtown for an interview.

"Where all the recording and authenticating equipment is handy," he'd said.

So formal. I hadn't liked the sound of it.

I sat in the passenger seat of Bruce's SUV, as the Henley skyline came into view. Not that it was all that impressive. The golden-domed city hall, our tallest building, was in the center of town, flanked by a couple of less than imposing government headquarters. Within the last few months, the Henley police department had finally been relocated to the complex.

Entering a brand new, attractive building, the newest in town, did little to make me welcome the experience. Virgil had respectfully requested that I meet him downtown for the interview.

I saw a group of mostly campus people in the hallway, all seeming less nervous than I felt. I nodded to all the secretaries and service people as I followed close behind Virgil. I acknowledged all, but made sure my look was somber enough to discourage any attempts to engage me.

My efforts fell flat on Paula Rogers, who nearly tripped me in the process of reaching me. Paula, whom I'd met first in

Ariana Vogel's beading class, before she was hired as dean, had mistakenly thought I loved beading as much as she did. How could she know I'd enrolled in the class solely to keep Ariana, my best friend, happy? My longsuffering childhood gal pal, and owner of A Hill of Beads, had that much coming from me.

"You're here, too?" Paula said to me.

I thought it was obvious but held my tongue. "Uh-huh," I said and tried to put Bruce between us as we walked toward the waiting area.

"Did you notice how not everyone is here? We all gave our vitals back on campus. I wonder how they decided who they were going to question further. Let's get together tomorrow and compare notes. I know you have the scoop on this," she said. "And I'll bet you'll need some TLC by then."

Before Paula could close the loop on a chummy get-together, our moneyman, Martin Melrose, elbowed her out of the way.

"Do you know anything about this?" Martin asked. "Why'd they pick us to come down here?"

I had my own question: Why did Martin and Paula think I knew anything more than they did? Maybe because of the Bruce-Virgil connection, I decided. I saw Paula in town now and then, at beading classes, and my interactions with Martin had been a little more frequent now that I had the math department budget to worry about. But it wasn't as if I ever sought either one of them out or socialized with them off campus.

"Do you think we're all suspects?" Martin asked, more nervous than his usual fussy self. "I don't really have an alibi except I was home all night and on campus all morning. I'm thinking we should get the school attorneys involved."

Another question: Who was the scraggy young man I'd never seen before? Too old to be a student, he leaned into Martin, appearing to be whispering in his ear, coaching him as Martin asked me questions.

Not that I cared that much, but the young man, shabbily dressed, with a significant birthmark on his neck and part of his cheek, pulled Martin away before I needed to respond. Was he a suspect? Did he have an alibi?

Did I?

The whole episode was like a confusing dream where people you know mix with complete strangers, and there's a whole back story you haven't been made privy to.

"Ready, Sophie?" Virgil asked.

"Yes," I said, but I didn't think I'd ever be ready for the full impact of what I knew was coming.

Virgil couldn't have been more solicitous, holding the door for me, pulling out the surprisingly new metal chair, all but patting me on the head.

"Are you warm enough?" he asked, stepping over to the thermostat by the door. "Look at this. We can adjust the temperature of each room individually." You'd think he was demonstrating state-of-the-art technology, but I understood that he was proud of his new digs as well as concerned about me.

"I'm fine," came from a part of me I didn't recognize.

I was always ill at ease in the police station, however. Old and rundown, or shiny and new; it didn't matter. I wished I could reach into my purse and grab a puzzle to work. I always carried a plastic or metal manipulable to twist apart, and a few word puzzles of my own or someone else's making. Solving them and creating them gave me equal pleasure and tended to focus my energies away from anything unpleasant. I couldn't think of when I'd needed to manipulate a puzzle cube more, or when it would have been less appropriate for me to reach into my purse and choose one to place on my lap.

When a young officer set a bottle of water in front of me, I was ridiculously suspicious in spite of her nice smile. Was she after my fingerprints as a suspect? The thought was beyond hilarious since Vigil had easy access to even my DNA if he wanted it. All he had to do was lift prints or a hair from my house on one of the many evenings he and Bruce and I shared a pizza and a movie. Martin's silly questions had done a number on me.

The officer left and Virgil and I were alone, across a small metal table from each other, far from the comfortable chairs in my dark-toned, soothing den that I loved. The newly painted pale green walls of the interview room were a distant cousin to anything I'd call pleasant.

"Coffee?" Virgil asked. "I'm afraid we don't have any of those great donuts we're famous for. And, to be truthful, the coffee here's no better than in the old place."

"I'm fine," I said again, more normal, grateful for the friendly connection he was trying to reestablish. Emboldened by his gestures, I ventured a question. "When did all this happen, Virgil?" I looked at the bottle of water on the table in front of me. It seemed too much effort to remove the cap. "How did she die?" I asked, hearing myself finally admit to the fact of my friend's death.

"Do you know a Hannah Stephens?" Virgil asked me, getting down to it, and ignoring my reasonable queries. Probably every reporter from Henley to Boston, forty miles away, knew more than I did at this point, but Virgil had gone to cop mode.

"Hannah Stephens? Yes, I know her."

"How well?"

"Just to say hi to. I don't have her in class. She's Charlotte's student aide, an English major."

"So, you never had lunch with her or counseled her, anything like that?"

"No, nothing like that."

I resented that Virgil got to ask me more questions before I had any details about Charlotte's murder, a simple fact that I'd practically had to drag out of him back on campus.

I surveyed the venue. A clean (for now), stark room with a table and two chairs. A boxy unit by the thermostat that screamed out: recording devices here! Maybe even a gun cocked and ready. We were in homicide detective Virgil Mitchell's house now and I knew the faster I played it his way, the faster I'd be out of here and able to get some answers on my own.

"No one seems to have seen Ms. Crocker since last night when she closed up around nine o'clock," Virgil said. He paused. "Did you?"

"After nine last night? No, I didn't. Did anyone see her today? You think she was shot last night?"

"When was the last time you did see Charlotte Crocker?" Virgil asked, his head turned slightly, his eyes making contact from the sides.

"Excuse me?"

All the pepperoni pizzas we'd put away together counted for nothing when I was asked a question like that, and in the manner of every television detective on primetime. For the moment my rational mind took a vacation and I heard Virgil's question an accusation. I gulped—loudly, I thought—and pushed the feeling away.

"When was the last time you saw Charlotte Crocker?" he repeated, slightly less hostile. If he'd ever really been hostile, except in my mind.

"On Wednesday, I think. We went downtown for lunch."

"You didn't make a habit of calling or seeing each other every day?"

"No, not necessarily. We emailed or texted sometimes."

"Across the yard?"

"That's how we do it now."

Virgil raised his eyebrows. Uh-oh. I hadn't meant to sound condescending. Virgil was only a couple of years older than I was, Bruce's age, but his mindset was different, not hanging around kids all day, as I did. At least not the best and brightest kids, outfitted with the latest in i-technology, like almost all the Henley students. I taught them math but they taught me a new app practically every week—last week I downloaded a site that would point you from your location to the nearest restroom, in any city— and new ways of communicating. They were more connected than Virgil would ever want to be.

He flipped through pages in his notebook. "You went downtown for lunch on Wednesday. Any special reason?"

"We didn't need a reason to get off the campus." I smiled, then settled back into the somber mood I wasn't ready to give up. "We were both inside buildings all day."

"What did you talk about?"

I shrugged. "What girlfriends talk about."

"The new governor?" Virgil prodded.

"For a minute or two. "

Virgil laughed. "That's about right."

Charlotte and I had bonded soon after she moved here from California two years ago. We'd met at the gym downtown around the same time we first saw each other on campus, and slid into an easy friendship. Certainly not of the closeness I'd shared with Ariana since we were preteens, but Charlotte and I saw eye to eye on politics, books, and campus issues. We parted ways on only one issue—reluctantly, I smiled again—fashion. Charlotte wore classic, fifties preppy. I'd adopted the popular student look: layered pieces, bordering on steampunk, aka the Victoriana-meets-Goth look.

I could see that Virgil was waiting for more specifics about my last lunch with her.

"Charlotte was planning to visit an old friend in Florida for Thanksgiving," I offered.

"Another two minutes to talk about that?"

I wasn't trying to be difficult; it was simply hard to remember what we discussed.

I decided to relax for a minute and be honest with Virgil. "This is like when I come back from a two-hour coffee date with Ariana, and Bruce can't figure out what we could have talked about for that long, and I can hardly tell him. Except that we didn't finish. Women friends always run out of time before we run out of things to say. It was the same with Charlotte and me."

"I see."

But he didn't. I doubted he and his buddies sat and chatted more than five minutes before doing something—playing cards or racquetball, lifting weights, fishing. It was hopeless to think he'd understand how Charlotte and I interacted.

I'd never allow such sloppy reasoning in my math classes, but these were extenuating circumstances.

I remembered something Charlotte and I had talked about. "There's a new book club forming at the public library in town. Charlotte and I discussed joining the group and we brainstormed books we'd like to see on the list." I felt proud I'd thought of something specific.

"Okay, that's good," Virgil said, and made a show of writing it down. "Did you text her today at all or any time since nine o'clock last night?"

"Uh, I don't think so. I was busy with classes today, and then the party. August Mobius, November seventeenth," I said.

"We're a little early, but close enough." How pitiful. Reveling at a party about a mathematician from two centuries ago while Charlotte was ... "When did you say she died?"

"I didn't. But I'll tell you now that Ms. Hannah Stephens, the student aide we talked about, left her boss in the library just before nine o'clock last night. She went back into the stacks around four pm this afternoon to shelve some books. She found Ms. Crocker's body on the floor up against the bookshelves."

I drew in my breath. I didn't want to hear any more and Virgil sensed that. He unscrewed the cap on the water bottle and pushed it closer to me. I accepted it gratefully and swallowed short bursts of cool liquid.

I hated the thought that Charlotte had been lying helpless on the library floor while I concerned myself with a sophomore's presentation and my plans for the weekend. I wanted to ask Virgil if it was a quick death, then realized he wouldn't tell me even if he knew this soon, then realized I didn't want to know. Tears formed and I quickly switched to a blank screen in my mind.

After a grace period, Virgil continued. "Do you remember what you were doing last night, Sophie?" Virgil looked away immediately after he asked for my alibi, thus missing my shocked look. "I have to write it down."

I felt my muscles relax as I heard his apologetic tone and felt his hand briefly on my shoulder. "I was home, doing the usual, reading, puzzling."

"Phone calls?" he asked.

I nodded. "Bruce, to set up plans for today and the weekend. Ariana, to chat."

"You didn't speak to Ms. Crocker?"

"No, not last night."

"Can you think back and remember the last time you and Ms. Crocker spoke or emailed or texted?"

"I can check my phone."

"That would be a big help. Not right now, okay? I have a few more questions then I'll leave you to go through your phone and write down the times of your last few communications."

"Okay."

What else could I say? Nothing I could remember or jot down would bring Charlotte back. This interview had done nothing to ease my pain about Charlotte's death.

And what about my own safety? If Charlotte was vulnerable just because she was in a campus building after dark, many of us, faculty and students, were at risk. I stayed late often, working in my office long after everyone else had gone. Sometimes it was easier to stay where all my class prep resources were than to try to stuff everything into my briefcase, inevitably leaving something behind. For the most part, home was for relaxation and for my puzzling activities, and, when Ariana prevailed, my beading hobby.

All my hobbies—everything, in fact—seemed trivial at the moment.

"Just a few more things, if you don't mind," Virgil said. "Was Ms. Crocker seeing anyone that you know of?"

I started at first. The question was out of sync with my thoughts. "Seeing anyone" was lumped with trivial matters in my mind, but I understood why Virgil was asking. "As in, a boyfriend? No, not that she shared with me."

"Or girlfriend?"

"No, not in that way."

"You think you would know, either way?"

I nodded. "I think I would."

I didn't tell Virgil that Charlotte made it a point to never talk about her love life, if she had one, past or present, male or female. She waved away my initial queries about boyfriends or exes, and I begged off ever bringing it up. I had Ariana for that kind of conversation.

"Did Ms. Crocker have any vices? Anyone she might have owed money to? A gambling debt, maybe?"

Vices? I laughed inside. Charlotte was about as straitlaced as the stereotypical librarian. She'd fretted over a speeding ticket she'd gotten on a trip to Vermont last summer. She'd attended traffic school for several long, boring sessions just so the violation wouldn't appear on her record or affect her insurance.

Had she owed money? Another smile came as I pictured a connected guy sending a goon to collect from Charlotte, finding her in her tweed skirts and silk blouses with ties at the neckline. "She did like playing the lottery, if you call that gambling."

"I do."

I bristled. "She wasn't in danger of losing her house or her car or anything. She played maybe a couple of dollars a week." I wet my lips with a small sip of water. "That's not a crime, is it?" I asked, concerned about Charlotte's good reputation, in life and in death.

"Nothing wrong with the lottery," he said, embarrassing me with his indulgence. "It pays my salary. Brilliant solution to the commonwealth's budget problems, huh?"

"I forgot about that aspect." I'd read somewhere that Massachusetts apportioned a certain percent of the lottery funds to government salaries.

"Forty percent goes to fire, schools, and"—Virgil pointed to his chest—"yours truly."

Nice to have the details. "A worthy cause," I said, attempting a grin.

"Lots of scams, too, though," Virgil said.

"I suppose so."

"I hope your friend was never the victim of one of those scams. You know, like believing a letter that says"—Virgil made quote marks with his fingers—"'you've won big, just send us some money and we'll release your megabuck winnings'."

"Who would fall for something like that?"

Virgil rolled his eyes and shook his head. "Way too many people. You'd be surprised. Friend of mine, his brother, college educated and all, lost ten thousand dollars in one of those scams. He still can't believe a million bucks is not on the way to him via a bank in a third-world country."

"I had no idea."

"I've seen scam letters supposedly written by a soldier in Iraq, just to tug at your heartstrings, and another one that claimed it was from the Secretary of the Treasury. The victims come in here, but there's not much we can do once you've sent your hard-earned cash off to a stranger."

"It's amazing that people can be so gullible," I said, to sound more interested than I was.

Virgil seemed wrapped up in the topic. I wondered if someone close to him had been a victim. I hoped I hadn't insulted one of his friends or relatives.

"Another question is, what kind of person pulls a stunt like that? Making a living off duping people?" he asked. He gave me a curious look, as if I knew the answer.

"A bad person, I guess."

Virgil slid a lined note pad toward me. "I'll leave you to go through your phone logs and I'll be back in a few, okay?"

"Okay."

When Virgil left the room, I replayed our conversation. A bad idea, since I couldn't go back and edit my responses. Why hadn't I been more at ease, more help to the investigator of my friend's murder? Why had I felt on trial myself? Was it my imagination or had Virgil been in pure cop mode most of the time?

There were no answers the second or third time I went over our meeting in the new Henley PD interview room.

I rotated the pad Virgil left on the table for me and took out my smartphone. I scrolled through my log and started my list of recent calls, emails and texts to and from Charlotte.

I wondered when things might really be okay again.

# Chapter 4

Bruce made valiant attempts to bring life back to normal as we drove away from the police station in his SUV.

Unbidden, he stopped at a new chocolate shop in town. He caught the door just as the clerk was about to turn the sign to "closed" and returned to the car with two mochas and a bag of cookies. I wondered what kind of offer, or threat, he'd made to the scrawny kid in charge of closing up.

The man knew the way to my heart.

Writing out the list of the conversations I'd had with Charlotte over the last week had taken its toll on me. Forced to relive every minute of our recent contact, I'd grown morbidly philosophical.

Would we have texted about the bland food in the Mortarboard Café, the campus coffee shop, if we knew one of us would not live through the weekend? Would we have spent even a moment whining about the faulty self-checkout system at the library? I know we wouldn't have compared notes on the relative cost of gasoline close to and farther from campus.

Fortified by caffeine and sugar, two of my favorite food groups, I gave Bruce a summary of my interview with his cop friend.

"Does Virgil play the lottery?" I asked.

"Not that I know of. Why do you ask?"

"He started this curious ethical discussion about the lottery, all the scams there are, how the money from the lottery keeps cops on the beat and the Commonwealth of Massachusetts in the black. You'd think the infrastructure would collapse without it."

"Maybe he's right."

"It doesn't matter. It was just curious, considering why I was there."

"Maybe he was just trying to make you feel comfortable, talking about something off-the-wall."

"It didn't work."

Suddenly worn out, I sank back into the seat. At the next light, Bruce studied my face with his trademark squinty focus and offered to drive me directly home.

"We can pick up your car tomorrow," he said.

"I'm not as bad as I look," I said, shaking my head. Too many logistics, and there was a good chance that I'd want to wallow alone and not leave my house for a couple of days. "Just drop me at my car and I can drive myself home."

"I'll follow you home, then."

"I need to stop in Franklin Hall first."

"I'll wait."

Sometimes I was glad for Bruce's persistence and this was one of those times.

My task at Franklin Hall was to revisit the scene of the party and make sure things were put away and neatened, in case old Woody, our friendly, trusted janitor had buckled under the extra workload. The math and science students were dependable, taking turns as cleanup crew, but the arrival of the city of Henley's entire emergency crew had significantly changed the Friday afternoon rhythm.

I knew my own rhythm would be thrown off indefinitely. Time would help, but the best feelings would return only when the police had found my friend's killer. I wished I could do something to help them.

Bruce and I entered the pitch-dark basement of Benjamin Franklin Hall just before eight o'clock. Smells from chemistry on four and biology on three always permeated the air when the doors and windows had been closed up even for a couple of hours. I imagined drips of nasty stuff seeping down, polluting the clean floors of math and physics on one and two. Down here below street level, the atmosphere was worst of all since there was nowhere else for the ghastly molecules to go.

The old building seemed to creak under our weight and I was doubly glad of Bruce's presence. I flicked on the lights as we made our way to the elevator.

When the doors opened on the first floor, I was surprised to see a light at the end of the hall, leaking out from under the door to the lounge. Woody wouldn't ordinarily close the door while he was working, nor would the frugal old man leave a light on.

Bruce instinctively put his arm out and walked in front of me, the way parents do when they're about to stop short and don't want their kids taking a header through the windshield.

But years of living with students and knowing their habits told me what was happening in the lounge after hours. My only fear was that the "culprits" wouldn't hear us and thus suffer terminal embarrassment.

As we walked toward the lounge, I coughed so loudly that Bruce stopped and turned to face me. "What's happening?"

"I'm sounding an alarm," I said.

His confusion was short-lived as Chelsea and Daryl, the guy who'd challenged her Escher-like one-surfaced loops, stepped to the door of the lounge, still arranging various parts of their clothing. I was glad that academic differences hadn't kept them from a budding relationship. Or maybe it was in full blossom.

"Oh, hi, Dr. Knowles and Mr. Granville. We're just, like, cleaning up," Chelsea said, though the long conference table we'd used for this afternoon's buffet was still piled with the detritus of the Mobius party.

"How nice of you," I said.

"It's so sad about Ms. Crocker," Chelsea said, running her fingers through very long and tangled chestnut hair. I didn't blame her for being eager to shift my attention from the shoes next to the brown plastic couch. I knew she was an easy mark if I chose to tease or taunt anyone, but I was in a mood to let her off the hook.

"Yes, it is sad," I said.

"Yeah," Daryl added. He patted all sides of the small patch of blond hair on his chin as if it were the most rumpled part of his overall look. "Have they caught the guy yet?"

"How's her family doing?" Chelsea asked.

"I don't know anything yet," I said. I realized I knew very little about Charlotte's family. I decided to call her nephew in Boston, Noah, if I could find his number.

"Well, if you see them or anything, tell them we're really sorry," Chelsea said.

"Thanks, I will. I'll be in my office if you want to store any of these leftovers for next week." I had no desire to talk about Charlotte with students who had other pressing things on their minds.

"We'll just take everything back to the dorms, if that's okay," Chelsea said.

"No problem. Have a great weekend," I said, as if one were in store for me, too.

The couple's faces took on expressions of joy, pleasure, anticipation, a very cool evening to come. I couldn't name it, but whatever the emotion, it butted up against my feelings of loss, for Charlotte, for everyone who would not have a very good weekend.

I turned and nearly ran down the hallway.

"That was too much of I don't know what," I half-explained to Bruce as we sat in my office. "How can anyone be happy right now?"

"I get it. Let's just do what you have to do here, quickly, and go home. How did those kids get in anyway? And why'd they pick this building for their romp?"

I was glad to have something to smile about. "Students are very resourceful when they need privacy. The couch in the lounge may be the best they can manage that doesn't cost money."

Bruce nodded understanding, his eyebrows raised in an expression that said he finally got it. Perhaps remembering his own college days? Another time, I'd have teased him.

"This year, with men on the campus, things are even worse," I added. "The girls are crowded into Clara Barton and Paul Revere dorms, so the guys can have a whole building to themselves. The boys are in the middle dorm. Nathaniel Hawthorne."

"Girls to the left; girls to the right," Bruce joked.

"And you can imagine how much jockeying around goes on. The math and science students are lucky"—I spread my arms to indicate all of Franklin Hall—"they have their own building. Every Franklin resident knows Woody's schedule. He leaves the basement door open while he wheels the trash out from various locations and during that twenty or thirty minutes a marching band could enter the building."

"So much for security. You might want to rethink that campus safety and security plan."

I sighed. "No kidding."

I threw folders into my briefcase. A mere gesture, since I doubted I'd get much done this weekend.

My eyes landed on a green and gold duffel bag in the corner. Charlotte's. I remembered now that Charlotte had given it to me on Wednesday after lunch. It was a different one from the navy blue bag she regularly took to the gym. Though I was happy to do her a favor, I remembered being confused by the reason she wanted to leave the bag with me.

"I'm going to visit a friend in a convalescent hospital that's not in the best part of town," she'd said. "I'd feel better if I didn't have anything tempting in my car."

"Isn't this just full of your gym clothes?" I'd asked.

"More or less," she'd said.

"But I guess a break-in artist wouldn't know he was stealing dirty laundry until he'd already broken in."

"Uh huh. That's why I'd like to leave it here. And, just think, if I don't come back for it"—she'd pointed to the duffel—"it's all yours."

"Thanks a lot," I'd responded.

Now I regretted how I'd hesitated to grant what turned out to be my friend's last request.

Bruce picked up Charlotte's green and gold duffel along with my briefcase and my own red and gray duffel that served as supplementary overnight luggage.

"Feels like her rock collection is in here," he said, pretending to be bent from the weight of Charlotte's bag.

"You always say that," I reminded him.

"Because you gals always carry way too much."

"Remember that the next time you want to borrow my nail clippers."

Here we were fooling around as if my friend hadn't just been murdered. I stifled a sob, but not before Bruce heard it.

Bruce led me out of the building with a look that said he wasn't willing to negotiate. "I'm driving you home," he said.

This time I didn't argue.

It felt better than ever to be off the campus and on a stool at my country kitchen island. Bruce made himself at home with my pots and pans and the meager contents of my fridge. I'd planned to grocery shop after our getaway in Boston. Still, I knew Bruce would work his magic and there'd be a spicy concoction for our late dinner.

I drained my now lukewarm mocha and ate another chocolate cookie for an appetizer. Comfort food always helped.

While he peeled and chopped remnants of veggies, and stirred something aromatic on the stove, Bruce tried to distract me with talk of his upcoming climb. On Sunday, he'd be off to a mountain in New Hampshire with Kevin and Eduardo, two flight nurses from MAstar.

"Have you ever thought of paying the small fee and just taking the tram ride to the top? The view's the same, right?"

Bruce smiled a no comment, and I remembered how he felt about people who rode the tram. He insisted that climbers shouldn't have to share the same peak with those who were carried up in luxury.

"This'll be Kevin's first major climb," he said, proceeding on his own track. "He doesn't know it, but he's going to be our belay monkey."

"Is this a test to see if I remember what that means?" One of the first things Bruce had taught me about climbing was that "belay" was not a verb form of "belie." I took the bait and the opportunity to show off. "Kevin is going to feed you guys the rope at the beginning of a pitch, and a pitch is sort of a section of the mountain, one rope length long, and you climb one section at a time."

"Not bad."

"I also remember that climbing in New Hampshire is where your friend Larry fell and broke his wrist in three places and dislocated all the bones in the palms of his hands."

"There you go, exaggerating. Larry broke only three of eight bones in his right wrist. He's been climbing different routes on that peak since he was in college. He got sloppy is all."

"That's comforting."

Why Bruce thought this topic was a good distraction was beyond me. An image of him two hundred miles away and one thousand feet up, on the side of a mountain, with dried fruit for meals was not what I needed in a time of stress. But he chattered on.

"This will be Kevin's first multi-pitch alpine-like climb, so it will be fun for Eduardo and me to teach him a few things." Bruce smiled playfully and tossed a carrot in the air before setting it on the cutting board. I hoped he didn't have something similar in mind for Kevin.

"I wish you weren't going," I said.

Where had that come from?

Bruce was understandably concerned at my remark. It wasn't like me to dissuade him from indulging a hobby he loved. You couldn't ask a guy who'd done a tour in Saudi Arabia and now landed helicopters on the freeway for a living to sit out all other adventures. Besides that, in times of stress, my preferred state was solitude.

He turned off the stove and came over to me. "Really? Because I'll cancel the trip right now."

I quickly waved away the idea. "No, no. I don't know why I said that."

"I don't know why I didn't think of that right away." His beautiful dark eyes turned sad. "Here I am joking around and you've just lost a friend."

Now I felt really bad. Guilt-tripping my boyfriend. Hours of planning and expense had already gone into the climb. I had to buck up and send him on his way.

"I'm going to feel worse if you miss this trip," I said. "Thanks for offering, though. I'm fine."

Bruce sighed and I could see that he was weighing his next move. I hated that I'd put him in a no-win situation with a silly comment. "Soph—"

I held up my hand. "I promise I'll get Ariana to come over if I feel like having company."

Bruce finally grinned. "Beading as therapy?"

"Hey, it works sometimes."

Anything was worth a try.

I'd convinced Bruce to go home to his place after a delicious casserole dinner. Even in my anxious state, I'd been able to eat enough to show my appreciation. Melted black diamond cheese will do it every time.

I wasn't going to be very good company anyway. One of us moping around my house was enough, and I knew Bruce could use the extra time to pack and prepare the equipment for his trip.

Boys and their toys. Bruce owned duplicates and triplicates of each important piece of equipment, selecting certain sizes and brands, depending on the kind of climbing he anticipated. Much of the gear he left behind was stored in my garage, since his own was substandard and barely housed his car, he claimed.

The amount of gear he carried on each climb astounded me. I could name a few pieces, like the belaying device that attached to a climber's harness and controlled the rope, special self-boring ice screws, and strange-looking clips called carabiners. And who couldn't identify pitons, steel spikes of different lengths and thicknesses, that appeared in every movie-climbing scene? I flashed onto Roger Moore clutching the side of a straight up-and-down mountain face in one of Bruce's favorite James Bond movies, the titles of which were interchangeable to me.

I worried about Bruce's center of mass shifting, what with his backpack plus all the odds and ends hanging from his harness.

"Everything's attached and racked very carefully," he'd assured me. He favored me with a demo of where each screw, each piece of nylon webbing, each layer of extra clothing was assigned its location, packed in the order in which he might need it while standing on a tiny ledge, or in other situations I preferred not to hear about.

Now, sleepless at one in the morning, I wished Bruce were here. Fortunately, I had the good sense not to call and invite him over. He'd made good on his promise to get Kevin to help ferry my car here before morning. They'd put my Ford Fusion on the street at the end of my walkway, to keep from waking me up with a noisy garage door opening, I figured. I could, therefore, drive to his house across town right now.

Not a good idea.

I wandered around my small cottage style house, picking up puzzles here and there. First I worked on puzzles of my own construction, for my freelance work. I had a brainteaser due to a puzzle magazine in a week.

Or, more exactly, my aka, Margaret Stone, had a delivery deadline. I'd been using my mother's maiden name for my second vocation, at the request of the college administration, particularly the academic dean, who wanted me to keep my professional research identity unsullied by frivolous pursuits. While I'd resisted the edict at first, I now found it fun to have another persona.

I finished the puzzle, formatted it for submission, and started two more beginning-level teasers involving puns on the names of the days of the week and months of the year.

When those problems didn't make me sleepy, I went to work as a solver myself. I sat in my den and polished off two diagramless acrostics. I cracked the code of a difficult crossword called "Reverse the Terms," waving my fist in the air and hooting at figuring out the answer to the clue "Laundry Room Short."

"Fire in the Iron" I shouted to the empty rooms.

A few more successes like that—"Hand in the Bird" for the clue "What a Turkey Stuffer Has"—and I switched to cryptograms from an old book Ariana had found for me on one of her many yard sale excursions. The cryptoquote that resulted made me smile: "The mind that is anxious about the future is miserable."

Had Seneca been thinking of me?

Puzzled out, I considered working on a bracelet I'd started

in Ariana's "Hill of Beads" shop, but decided I needed daylight to work the tiny glass beads. Ariana would have rolled her eyes at my excuse.

I left my den and plodded into the kitchen. Maybe more food would induce sleep. I took the remains of the dinner casserole from the fridge and sat at my counter pulling burnt cheese, my favorite part, from around the edges. I wouldn't tell Bruce his creation tasted better cold.

A few cookies later, I headed down the hallway toward my bedroom, regretting that it was too late to call Ariana to tell her how good her peanut butter fingers were.

I passed my home office on my left and saw my duffel bag near the doorway. Bruce had dropped off the load—my briefcase, my red and gray bag that had been destined for Boston, and Charlotte's bag, with her gym clothes. All three were lined up, their contents all less important than they were even twelve hours ago.

Might as well unpack my bag, however; maybe the exercise would tire me out.

I flicked on the light and knelt down to unzip my bag. Something shiny on Charlotte's bag caught my eye. A small silver padlock hanging from the main zipper of her green-and-gold duffel.

Strange. Why would anyone lock up sweats and sneakers, clean or dirty?

*Not my business.*

I pulled my vacation clothes out of my own overnight duffel and carried them to my bedroom. Upscale sweats for the long ride and one relatively nice pair of pants for the Friday night dinner that never happened. I put my duffel back in a low corner of my garage with the rest of my luggage, as usual leaving in it small bags with duplicate cosmetics, and other essentials for the road, like my favorite travel slippers. I'd need everything soon again for our Thanksgiving weekend at Bruce's cousins' place in Connecticut.

I looked over, past my car, at what we called Bruce's corner of my garage, where he stored extra gear that wouldn't fit in his tiny storage space. I generously allotted one whole wall where he could display some special pieces, like an antique ice ax his father had given him. I frankly didn't see the difference between the forty-year-old ax and the brand new one next to it. They both looked lethal, with the saw tooth heads and pointy tails that could dig into hard ice.

The shiny padlock on Charlotte's bag called to me. I kept thinking about it, as if it were a logic puzzle I hadn't been able to solve.

*Not my business.*

On the other hand, Charlotte was gone forever and her bag was in my possession. I thought back to her facetious comment about it would be all mine if she didn't reclaim it.

Who else's business was it now? What if there was something in the bag that would help the police find her killer?

Maybe Charlotte kept an address book in her bag, or even her cell phone. I could use it to contact some of her friends and family and notify them of her death. I had no idea even how to reach her nephew, perhaps her only relative. Noah's telephone number could be in the book that I was now positive I'd find. I'd done a cursory checking of my own records for his information earlier this evening and had come up blank. I knew the police would track all this down, but wouldn't Noah like to hear from his aunt's friend also?

I could think of a long list of reasons to open Charlotte's bag, not the least of which was that I was curious. What had she deemed necessary to lock up in a flimsy nylon bag?

Not that she'd been that security conscious. The tiny padlock was identical to a set of six I'd bought for myself. They were TSA-approved and simply provided some small measure of protection against random unzippings around airports or hotel rooms.

I fished around in my travel drawer and pulled out a small key that I knew would fit Charlotte's lock also.

Back in my office, on my knees again, I inserted the key, removed the padlock, and took the zipper pull between my fingers. At each step, I paused, reconsidering.

This was Charlotte's private property. Did her death take away her rights? Did I have any claim to snooping in her bag just because she was no longer able to protect those rights?

But Charlotte had been murdered. That changed things and involved different questions, didn't it? Was all of her property, even her laundry, now part of a homicide investigation? Did that mean that I should get in my car right now and drive it to the police station? I couldn't use the excuse that they'd be closed at this hour. But how silly would I look, delivering dirty tennis clothes to the police in the middle of the night?

Finally, I came to a decision: open the bag and determine whether the police should see the contents or I should simply get busy, wash Charlotte's clothes and put them in the box I kept for a charity pickup.

I pulled the zipper across the top of the bag and eased the sides away.

Inside the bag were no gym shoes nor socks nor sweats nor a magazine nor sunglasses nor a bottle of water.

It wasn't a gym bag at all, in fact.

It was a money bag.

I could hardly breathe. It took three attempts to get my breath back to normal.

The bag was full of bills. Stacks of old used bills in several denominations. The bills had been tossed in, only a few packaged together with rubber bands. There was no orderly arrangement of crisp new bills, such as I'd seen in briefcases and duffels in heist movies and television crime dramas. I riffled through the currency, as if I were tossing a very expensive salad. I saw hundreds, fifties, an occasional twenty-dollar bill, nothing less.

I sat back on my heels.

I ran through the Ws. Whose money was this? Where had it come from? Why did Charlotte have all this cash? What should I do with it and when?

The bag had small zippered compartments at either end and along the sides. I swallowed, took a breath and explored each one. All were empty except the smallest, at one end of the bag. Only a couple of inches deep, the pocket held several slips of paper, each with names and numbers. I counted seven separate pieces of notepaper, torn from a small book and clipped together. Not exactly the complete address book I'd hoped for, but it was a start.

Perhaps the money belonged to these particular friends and Charlotte was keeping it safe, as she'd eventually asked me to do. My gut told me such an innocuous explanation wasn't realistic, but neither was one that involved prim librarian Charlotte Crocker as a cat burglar. I fought against the nasty images that came to mind of Patti Hearst, John Dillinger, Bonnie and Clyde, Willie Sutton. If Bruce, the movie buff, were here he would have rattled off the best heist movies. And he'd have known which actors—De Niro, Affleck, Wahlberg, Pitt, Clooney—went with which movie.

I wished he were here to joke about it. I reminded myself that it was my own choosing that he wasn't, so I switched off the pity track and went to work.

I shuffled through the notes and found one that read "Jeff/Noah," followed by a phone number. I'd call Charlotte's nephew, Noah, in the morning. I guessed Jeff was a roommate. Noah might know exactly what this money bag was all about.

"That was just like Aunt Charlotte," he'd say. "She never trusted banks and kept every penny of her savings in cash in a duffel bag."

"There are a lot of pennies in the bag," I'd say, and we'd both have a good laugh over dear Aunt Charlotte.

A wave of tiredness came over me, as though my mind and body had created enough alternate stories and made enough decisions for one day. I zipped the bag shut and pushed it behind my couch, now realizing why it was so heavy. Bruce hadn't been kidding.

Without standing upright, I lifted myself onto the cushions and sank into the soft burgundy fabric. I pulled a favorite afghan, knitted by my mother in many shades of purple, over my body.

Just before I fell asleep, with an image of Boston's Great Brink's Robbery of nineteen-fifty in my head, it occurred to me that maybe I should have put the bag on top of the couch and myself behind it.

# Chapter 5

I woke up to the sound of my neighbor's truck. He worked construction on weekends and often served as my alarm clock. But why was I hearing him roar off from the couch in my den, fully clothed, and not from under the lavender comforter in my bedroom? I sat up, disoriented, certain only that it must be nine on Saturday morning, since Jay kept a rigid schedule.

I wrapped the purple afghan around my shoulders as my mind grappled with strangely angled puzzle pieces that seemed to be from different boxes. A campus scene, close up on a library with blood-spattered books on its shelves. A hotel on the Leonard Zakim P. Bridge over the Charles River, both hotel and bridge waving in the fall breeze. A mountain climber in full gear, hanging off a steep cliff with only a one-finger grasp on the rock. A montage of American and foreign currency in many colors, and blood-spattered, like the books in the library.

The experience was disturbing, as if I were dreaming while awake.

When my phone rang, it was a relief, something real and focused. I reached behind me to the end table, picked up the receiver, and checked the screen. Even better, it was Bruce, and I wouldn't have to feign cheeriness.

I muttered something close to "Hey, good morning."

"Are you doing okay?" Bruce asked. "Kevin and I got your car home last night. I tried not to wake you."

"I didn't hear a thing."

Not because I was sleeping the sleep of the just, but because I was in a fog regarding my friend's duffel bag.

"So are you okay, really? I know you like to be alone when

you're stressed, but this is different. And I can blow off this trip in a minute."

I let out a hoarse laugh. "Let me guess. You told Eduardo that you didn't go to Boston after all, and he arranged to move up the climbing trip."

"Uh ...," followed by a guilty groan from Bruce.

"And you've packed all your cams, ice axes, and pitons and you're on your way to his house. You'll pick up Kevin in Medford and be crossing the border to New Hampshire by"—I pulled back the sleeve of the turtleneck I'd worn yesterday and all night, checked my watch, and added a couple of hours travel time—"well before lunch." I took a breath. "How'd I do?"

Bruce chuckled. "You're very good. You know me too well. But I could still hang back. Eduardo can manage Kevin just fine by himself."

I remembered that this was to be a teaching trip for Kevin. "But you're the best teacher, right?"

"Well, sure." He paused. "If you need me to stay home, say the word, Soph. Kidding aside, you know I mean it."

I did know that he was serious. I loved that I could count on Bruce.

I glanced down at Charlotte's bulging duffel, peeking from behind my makeshift bed. I pulled it toward me and with one hand wiggled the zipper open part way. Unfortunately, the contents hadn't morphed into simple shredded graph paper or a few pairs of dirty socks during the night as I'd hoped. It was still a money bag, full of wrinkled American bills.

"There's no reason for you to stay home," I said.

The calls started coming around ten, when every adult should be up and about on a Saturday morning.

Ariana was first. "Bruce just called and told me about Charlotte," she said. "I'm coming right over with bagels, cookies and other assorted baked goods from the Vogel kitchen."

"I'm okay," I said, hoping she wouldn't believe me, and glad that Bruce had arranged for the perfect stand-in.

"Cinnamon or sesame today?" she asked.

"Sesame with a cinnamon spread, please," I said.

What would I have done without loyal friends who understood my subtext?

Waiting for Ariana, I fielded several calls, including one from Paula Rogers, wanting to stop by and chat about "the event" as she called it. Her behavior in the hours since Charlotte's death, on campus and then at the police station, looked like she was jumping at the chance to replace Charlotte on my list of friends. Daryl Farmer, Chelsea's latest, also called, just to say, yo, could he help in any way?

Sometimes I questioned whether it had been such a good idea to vote in favor of listing cell phone numbers in the Ben Franklin directory. I'd become the clearinghouse for information for students and faculty both.

Fran, my colleague in the math department, would have had the number anyway since we'd been friends from my first day at Henley.

"Do you need anything, Sophie?" Fran asked. Besides her full teaching schedule, Fran provided part-time day care for her two grandchildren. Good pal or not, I wasn't about to add to her load.

I lied for the umpteenth time and promised to call if I thought of anything she might do for me.

I decided the best way to avoid more calls was to tie up my line. I extracted the slips of paper from the pocket of Charlotte's duffel and found the one for her nephew, Noah.

I punched in the number, with its Boston area code, and asked the male who answered if I could speak to Noah.

He'd picked up right away, but I seemed to have awakened him.

"Huh? Who're you calling for?" he asked.

"I'd like to speak with Noah," I said again, more clearly, then quickly remembered the "Noah/Jeff" combination on Charlotte's note. "Is this Jeff?" I asked the sleepy guy.

"Uh-huh."

"This is Professor Sophie Knowles from Henley College. I'm a friend of Noah's Aunt Charlotte."

"Who?"

"I'm Noah's Aunt Charlotte's friend."

I spoke each syllable deliberately this time. It must have been earlier than I thought. I should have remembered that college kids kept strange hours. I'd have done better calling him at two this morning.

"Oh, oh, yeah, hey, Aunt Charlotte." He laughed. "Sure, this is your nephew Noah. What's up?"

Strange. "This isn't Aunt Charlotte. It's Dr. Knowles. Sophie Knowles. Remember me from the visit to Henley airfield, to the air rescue facility? My friend, Bruce Granville, is the medevac pilot."

"The ... uh ... pilot?"

How many field trips had Noah been on in the last week? Maybe he'd already heard about his aunt's death and was in shock. I tried a different tack. "Noah, have the police contacted you?"

"Uh-oh, no?"

I didn't recall that Noah spoke principally in question marks.

"I'm sorry to say I have some bad news about your aunt."

I did my best to gently explain what had happened, as if death by violence could be softened. I'd hoped to be able to get through this call without tearing up, but the thought of Charlotte lying dead in her beloved library for nearly a whole day before Hannah found her was more than I could handle. I was dangerously close to crying and upsetting Noah, confusing him further.

"Wow," he said, when I finished. Not as overwrought as I'd expected. Certainly not as overwrought as I was. Just curiously surprised, as if his favorite young rock star had died suddenly.

"I know your mother's passed on, Noah. I'm assuming you're Charlotte's only relative. I can accompany you if you want, when you come to claim her body."

I heard an unmistakable groan, and then silence.

I was afraid Noah had fainted.

"I can give the police your number instead of waiting until they find you. I'm sure they'd like to talk to you."

In fact, I had no idea how the police went about locating relatives of murder victims. Was there a database somewhere with all known kin of everyone? My page would be pretty empty, being the only child of only children.

Another groan from Noah.

"Are you okay, Noah? I'm sorry to give you this news over the phone, but maybe it's better than—""

A heavy sigh came over the line from Boston, loud enough to interrupt me. "Okay, look. I'm not Noah, okay? I'm Jeff."

"You're Noah's roommate?" Silly question, but I was at a loss to understand why he'd let me go on so long.

"There's no Noah, okay? My name's Jeff Connelly. I'm a junior psych major at BC and I work in the campus snack bar. I met that lady, Charlotte? She was looking through the notices on the bulletin board and found the one I put up saying I'd do odd jobs."

"Charlotte hired you to do a job?"

"Yeah. I put my work hours down on the ad, and she came to the counter and asked for me."

"What did she want you to do?"

I heard a hemming and hawing. "Look, I'm sorry about this Dr. Knowles. I can't believe the lady's dead."

"Jeff, if that's your name, it would really help if you could tell me why she hired you."

"Okay, yeah. The lady, Charlotte, offered me two hundred bucks to pretend to be her nephew. I just had to spend the day with you and her in Henley. It wasn't the kind of job I had in mind when I put up the ad. I was thinking more like yard work, you know, but I figured, hey, I'm a psych major, right? Role playing might make a good term paper or a research project someday."

I'd moved to the kitchen where I'd been multitasking, putting water on for coffee and getting plates out for Ariana and me. Now I dropped onto a chair in the breakfast nook and tried to process what Noah/Jeff was telling me.

"Charlotte Crocker paid you to pretend to be her nephew? For just that day? Did you go anywhere else?" Too many questions. "Sorry, answer any of the above, Jeff."

"Yeah, well, nowhere else. All I had to do was make like I was interested in helicopters. And I got a couple of meals and my expenses paid, too."

I thought of how many starving students the money in Charlotte's bag would feed. Two hundred dollars wouldn't make a dent in the fortune I'd uncovered. I rubbed my forehead with my fist. Massaging my brain.

"Why would she do that?" I asked, resigned to the fact that an unknown college kid in Boston might know more about my deceased friend than I did.

"Why'd she need me? I asked her that. She said she wanted some information about private flights from the airfield out there. Nothing to do with that medevac facility your boyfriend toured us through. And she wanted to take someone like me, living far enough away so no one would recognize me. And maybe she was impressed by, like, I'm a psych major."

Impressive, indeed.

But it made sense, finally. I remembered Charlotte's showing more interest in the overall Henley airfield facility than in MAstar. She didn't ask how the flight nurses who flew with Bruce were trained, or how many calls a week came to them, or any of the usual queries people had when they toured the grounds or even simply heard what Bruce did for a living.

As I thought back, neither Charlotte nor Noah had shown much interest at all in MAstar.

I pictured the sprawling airfield on the edge of the town of Henley. MAstar was only one of many aviation-related businesses. Sharing the field were both nonprofit and for-profit companies. In my five years with Bruce, I'd become familiar with pilots' clubs and associations, civil air patrol staff, touring services, hangar rental procedures, and the equivalent of body shops for planes.

And a wealth of opportunities for private travel arrangements.

When Charlotte wandered off to check out the other airfield facilities, I'd been surprised but not suspicious. Of course, I didn't know she'd created a fake nephew, either.

"It seems like a complicated set-up just to book a flight," I said.

"No kidding. She said it was some kind of confidentiality thing. This way no one would wonder why she was going out there."

She'd used a trumped-up tour of MAstar to scope out the possibilities for a private flight. A getaway.

She'd used Bruce. And me.

A wave of anger swept over me. I forgot for a moment that Charlotte was the victim of a homicide. I felt betrayed. I didn't expect Charlotte to confide in me if she wasn't comfortable doing so, but to plan and execute an elaborate hoax? I remembered how generous Bruce and his coworkers at MAstar had been to us, explaining the procedures that took a crew up in the air to a safe landing on a freeway, and a quick transport to the nearest hospital with the requisite services. They'd shown us their dorm-style rooms and their night vision goggles. They thought we were interested in their lives and work.

Generally, Bruce didn't enjoy touring people through MAstar. He even griped when they had to clean up for their annual Family Day, when the spouses and children of his colleagues showed up expecting balloons and soft drinks. But he'd willingly arranged the day for Charlotte. Bruce's coworkers had treated Charlotte and Noah as special guests. Because of Bruce. Because of me.

I shook myself out of the "me" phase though it would be a while before I'd forget the subterfuge. Maybe Noah could still help me salvage something useful from the wasted day.

"Is there anything else you remember, Noah? Uh, Jeff? Did she say where she wanted to go on the private plane?"

"I didn't ask. I mean, she was paying me, and I didn't want her to think it mattered to me. She didn't look like she ran a drug cartel or anything, and I didn't figure her for an arms dealer, so ... "

I pictured a shrug on the other end of the line.

"I understand."

"Hey, I'm really sorry your friend is dead. But, uh, am I in trouble? I spent the money already. If I had to, I guess I could come up with it."

"I don't think that will be necessary, Jeff. But I think the police will still want to talk to you."

"Yeah, sure. I hope I didn't do anything wrong. I mean, I just figured she was trying to surprise somebody, you know?"

That she did.

To make a good impression on Ariana, owner of the town's bead shop and my closest friend, who didn't need impressing, I set out a bracelet I'd been working on for Bruce's young niece. I added a few beads to it in case she remembered exactly what state the project was in the last time she saw it. The pattern called for a fringe of beads attached to the short end of a rectangular piece of fabric. For the past week or so, I'd been picking away at the design, trying to follow the instruction "Be creative!" instead of counting out the colors in perfectly symmetric rows.

I thought I might arrange the beads according to the Fibonacci series, starting with red, then another red, then two green, three blue, five yellow, eight purple, and so on.

Ariana had said, simply, "That sounds nice."

Ariana arrived bearing the promised bagels and spreads, plus pastries of her own making. She was dressed in happy rainbow hues, not solely for my benefit, but a pleasant example of her usual dramatic look. I noted several layers of tank tops and a shawl over wide silk pants. I was in my customary Saturday morning gray sweats, though it was close to noon.

She pointed to the unfinished bookmark at the edge of my counter. "Do you really work on this when you're not expecting me?" she wisely asked.

I wisely didn't answer.

We sat at my kitchen counter with hot herbal tea for her, coffee for me, and an enormous basket of breads that Ariana had baked. She'd divided the goods into "healthy" on the right and "delicious" on the left. A dozen bagels of mixed flavors were in a separate bag.

I didn't blink before reaching for an unhealthy éclair, one of Ariana's specialties, and biting into it.

"Thanks," I said, allowing myself to focus on the burst of flavor from the unbeatable combination of chocolate and cream. For a minute, my head didn't hurt.

"Why didn't you call me right away?" she asked. "It's terrible to lose someone you had such a bond with."

Not as much of a bond as I'd thought.

"It sort of just happened and I'm still trying to figure out what to do."

In fact I needed to decide whether to show Ariana the money bag in my den. I hadn't wanted to spoil Bruce's trip by giving him further reason to worry about me and any decisions I had to make, but I did need to talk to a real person face to face before going to the police. I smiled as I thought of what Virge would say about my real human/cop distinction.

Fortified by the great triple threat of caffeine, sugar, and dairy, I led Ariana into the den, sat her down, and unzipped Charlotte's duffel bag. I opened my palms, fingers pointing to the opening, stopping short of uttering "Ta da."

Ariana's eyes widened. She leaned in closer. "Mother of God."

It took a lot for Ariana to return to her roots in Catholicism. Usually she invoked lesser deities like Airmid, the Celtic goddess of healing, or the Slavic Belobog, master of light, source of happiness and luck.

I took out the sheaf of notes in the duffel pocket, with Noah's now on top, and explained the Noah-Jeff drama.

"Mother of God," Ariana repeated. "She was a fugitive."

I'd thought as much but hadn't let myself say the word. Ariana had no such qualms.

"I'm not sure about that," I said, to challenge the thought a little more. "You're assuming she stole this money?"

"Who else has a bag of cash like this?" she asked.

I gave her the alternative theory. "We read about this all the time. Eccentric people who keep their cash in mattresses or stuffed into socks."

"I know what you're saying. Usually they're a hundred and ten years old, have never thrown a newspaper away in a hundred years, and live alone with four hundred cats and fifty birds."

"Sweet."

I recognized Ariana's way of distracting me and getting a laugh—be so careless with numbers that I'd cringe and forget what the real topic was.

She bent over the bag and ran her hands through the stash

as if she were sifting through expensive glass beads. "Seriously, this money is connected to something evil. I can feel it. You kept it here overnight?"

"It was pretty late by the time I found out that it wasn't Charlotte's sports clothes, clean or dirty."

"Did you count it?"

"Nuh-uh. Should we do that?" I asked.

"No, never mind. You need to get rid of this immediately."

"I know and I'll take it to the station later today."

"We should take it out to the garage or even outside right now. It's very bad to have this in your living space."

"You mean someone might come looking for it?"

Ariana's eyes, which had returned to normal, widened again. "I never thought of that."

"Then what were you thinking?"

"Just that the bag shouldn't be just sitting here, emanating bad vibes and sending them throughout your home."

Oddly, I knew what she meant, in a Feng-shui kind of way.

I needed to mentally organize all the possibilities for the source of the money in Charlotte's bag.

"Let's go through the options," I said to Ariana. "Say she was obsessively worried about another Great Depression or a natural disaster that turned the world's economy into cash-only."

"Or she was driving along and found the bag by the side of the road," Ariana said, indulging me.

"Or she had a hundred-and-ten-year-old aunt who kept the cash from her deceased husband's pension checks."

"The aunt died and Charlotte inherited the money."

"What if Charlotte was innocently holding the bag for someone she didn't realize was a robber?" I asked.

"That would be your situation," Ariana said.

"Good point," I said. And a sobering one. I allowed myself a "why me?" moment before moving on. "Shall we assign probabilities to each scenario and see what falls out?"

"Let's skip the numbers for now. Instead, we should figure which one is more likely to have led to her murder."

"Someone might simply have known about the hoarded money and killed her for it," I said, still insisting on an explanation that might spare Charlotte's good name rather than put her in a class with Specs O'Keefe.

"That doesn't fit with Charlotte's leaving the money with you, unless she had some warning that it was an attractive nuisance that could get her killed. And then, wasn't she putting you, her friend, in danger?"

"I guess it doesn't line up with her scoping out a clandestine flight, either," I said.

"We're back to, she has the money illegitimately and we need to get rid of it." Ariana spread her arms, sermon-wise, to make her point.

I finally had to agree with Ariana's position—it made the most sense that the bag of money had a bad beginning. I tried the bank robbery image again, this time with Charlotte in a mask, but bills from robberies were always shiny and new in movies. And the picture of Charlotte with a burlap bag over her tweed jacket and neutral crew neck sweater simply didn't work for me.

But, in spite of two years of friendship, not much about Charlotte Crocker now fit my view of her.

Anything was possible.

# Chapter 6

To appease Ariana, we put the bag—green on both the outside and the inside, it had turned out—in the trunk of my car, instead of in the same air space as ours, and set out for the police station. We agreed that I'd drop Ariana at her shop so she could take care of business, then I'd transport the bag to Virgil. When I was finished, I'd call and pick her up, at which time we'd resume our meal of coffee and sweets.

The whole Charlotte Crocker murder case would be out of my hands.

The day had turned overcast and I wished I'd never had to leave my bed. Or my couch.

As I drove, I found myself checking the rearview mirror. Had I been foolish not to take this bounty to the police as soon as I'd opened the bag last night? If Charlotte was looking into a secret, hasty departure, that meant she could be, as Ariana thought, a fugitive. She was fleeing someone, that was certain, or she wouldn't have gone through such hoops to keep her flight a secret. Was it someone who was entitled to all or part of the money in my trunk?

"All that cash," Ariana said, wistfully, as if she were making a list of ways to spend it. "Where would someone get it?"

"Not a clue."

Ariana snapped her fingers. "Maybe she won the lottery."

I looked at her, open-mouthed. "The lottery," I said.

"I was just joking," Ariana said.

"Maybe not." Why hadn't I considered that right away? "Funny you should mention it," I said. "Charlotte was an avid lottery player." On second thought, I shook my head. "I'm sure I would have known if she'd won this big. She played with a few other people, off and on campus—Martin Melrose, the college treasurer, for one."

"I know who you mean. The little man with thick glasses and a bow tie."

"That one. They pooled their money for some games. But even when they win only a few dollars each, they're so excited, they broadcast it all over. She couldn't have won all that money and kept it a secret."

Ariana pointed her thumb in the direction of the trunk. "And the Commonwealth of Massachusetts doesn't give out cash in those amounts, either. Sometimes if it's just a scratch game, the store will give you the couple of bucks, but if you win big, it's a check. In fact, if it's really big, you get it in installments over many years. If you want it all at once, you pay a huge tax penalty. At least that's what my tax man said."

I looked at my new-age friend, with her current blond-verging-on-transparent hair and shimmering rainbow outfit, and heard her talk about bucks and winning big. "You know all this how?"

Ariana blushed. "I read it in a magazine at the hairdresser's."

"A likely story."

Ariana and I had taken a pass on counting the money, cursed as it was. We put together a guess from quick looks at the predominantly hundred dollar bills and the money trivia I knew. I remembered a fairly useless "fact" that one million one-dollar bills weighed a little over a ton, and one million dollars in one-hundred-dollar bills weighed about twenty-two pounds. We had something in between. My bathroom scale wouldn't accommodate a wide duffel bag, but between us two amateur weightlifters, Ariana and I estimated that Charlotte's bag weighed about thirty pounds.

"Accounting for the fact that there are fifties and twenties and not all hundreds, I'd say—"

"One million dollars," Ariana finished.

"Give or take."

Funny how doing arithmetic always helped me unwind.

"I'm surprised you didn't insist on counting the money.

Don't you want to know the exact number?" Ariana asked.

"It doesn't really matter."

"But you love numbers. You know how many other Sophies there are in the United States."

"Yeah, I do."

"And what rank is it among all the female names?"

"Number four hundred and sixty-three."

"And what rank is my name?"

"Number eighty-two, with one 'n', fifty-two with two 'ns'."

"See?"

"This is different."

"It sure is." Ariana shivered, though that may have had more to do with her wearing a flimsy shawl on a chilly fall morning than with the accursed money sending cold vibes from the trunk of my car.

Ariana's shop, A Hill of Beads, had had a makeover in the last couple of months and I still wasn't quite used to the new, streamlined look, neater and cleaner than the disheveled, dusty old aisles, at least for the time being. Organization, which she saw as the enemy of creativity, wasn't Ariana's strong suit.

Through the front window, the passerby could see a dizzying array of shiny raw material for accessories of every kind. Counters with box after box of beads, separated by color and size. Strings of beads hung from racks and sample necklaces on headless forms lined the counters. See-through bags of findings, pin backs, and filigree reminding the crafter of the amazing number of things you could make or decorate with beads.

As much as I loved numbers, I was glad I didn't have to count Ariana's inventory of beads.

Before she left my car, Ariana reached over and gave me a good luck hug. She whispered a few syllables in her latest charmed language and I teased her about it, as she'd expect.

I felt I was making progress—I didn't feel too guilty kibitzing with Ariana as if it were a normal day and I wasn't headed for the Henley police station with a heavy bag of cash owned by a recently murdered friend. I could hardly wait to be rid of the whole load.

But another idea took over as I pulled away from the curb. I looked around and, conveniently, spotted a copy shop across the street.

It called to me.

Before I knew it, I was standing at an industrial-size copy machine, spreading seven small pieces of paper on the glass surface under the cover.

I was less ready than I'd thought to be done with the finer points of investigating Charlotte Crocker's murder.

Guilt returned in full force as I sat on a bench in the police station, waiting for Virgil. I held Charlotte's green and gold bag on my lap, a heavy weight. Even heavier, from the guilt, was my purse, hanging from the arm of the bench, and now containing the piece of paper from the copy shop with the images of Charlotte's seven notes, complete with ragged edges from where they were torn from a book.

I talked myself both into and out of the idea that I'd done something illegal by copying the notes. I simply wanted to be sure that all of Charlotte's friends—I doubted now that she'd ever had any relatives at all—knew of her misfortune. I thought of her friend in Florida where Charlotte had planned to spend Thanksgiving. Surely she needed to be notified immediately.

Good story. If there even was a friend in Florida, unless she'd hired one.

The odds that Charlotte had pulled only one con, hiring Noah, were about the same as the odds that I'd win the lottery if I bought my first ticket today.

With a little more thought I came up with another rationalization for copying the slips of paper. The police were busy; they couldn't be expected to offer condolences to these people who were special enough to be in her duffel with a load of money. I could help with that.

For the third time, I unzipped the bag part way, checking that indeed it was chock full of bills. Ariana had sufficiently convinced me of its evil nature that I wouldn't have been surprised if I found it had all turned to ashes. Glowing ashes at that.

Reflexively, I looked down at my purse every time a uniformed officer passed in front of me. What was the real reason I'd copied the names and numbers? The closest I could come to answer was that, somehow, giving up complete control of Charlotte's case hadn't been an option.

Charlotte had gone from "friend" to "case" in a matter of hours, I noted.

The flowers in the fabric print of my purse seemed to radiate heat and warm my leg. In my oversensitive state my purse seemed to be glowing from the ink on the copy paper. When I lost my sense of reason and gave in to fantasy, I did it in a big way.

I couldn't have felt worse if I'd skimmed a few hundred off the top of the money bag I'd unlocked. No wonder most criminals were caught; their guilt must give them away every time.

I thought how Charlotte would never carry a fabric purse like mine. I had them in all colors and prints, to match the season—today's was basically brown, with tiny green leaves in a William Morris-like design—but my elegant friend used only classic, dark leather bags. Except for the low-end duffel now on my lap.

*Whirrrr. Whirrrr. Whirrrr.*

The sound of helicopter blades rang through the hallway. This time, it wasn't my imagination that all eyes turned to me.

A call from Bruce to my cell. "Sorry," I said to all within earshot, trying to shrink my already small frame.

"We're walking in," Bruce said. "Just checking how you are."

I pictured the three guys in their approach shoes, a cross between a trainer and a walking boot, making their way from where they parked the car to the base of the climb. Unlike simply crossing a parking lot in front of the supermarket, the approach to the base of a mountain could be an arduous trip in itself, with rough terrain. It could be as long as my entire morning run. When I did a morning run, that is. This approach would take only about an hour, Bruce had said, as if it were no more trouble than getting the mail at the end of a driveway.

"Don't back step the rope," I said to him, showing off my short glossary of climbing terms.

"Uh, right," Bruce said, and I knew I'd revealed my ignorance of context. Too late, I realized I'd simply told him not to entangle his foot and fall upside down.

I started to sign off with Bruce, ready to worry about snowstorms at high altitudes. If I was lucky, he'd be able to connect by cell, but nothing was guaranteed on a mountain and I'd come to believe that Bruce liked that feeling. "Conquering planet earth," I'd called it.

A shadow crossed my lap. I looked up to see Virgil, his bulk somehow threatening today, as if he were wearing a long, black hood and carried a scythe.

"It's Bruce," I said, showing him my cell phone. "He's off on a climb with Kevin and Eduardo."

"Yeah, I know. No accounting for some peoples' idea of fun, huh? Harnesses and hitches."

Virgil had also picked up some climbing vocabulary, though he was as likely as I was to strike out for a mountain to scale.

The astute detective sensed the weight of the duffel as I tried to rise from the seat gracefully while clicking off my phone.

When he took the bag from my hands, I flinched. If he noticed, he didn't mention it.

"Heavy," he said. "A present for me?"

"Sort of."

For the second time in less than a day—sixteen hours, to be exact— I sat in an interview room across from a Henley PD homicide detective.

Virgil didn't show as much surprise as I'd expected when he saw the contents of the duffel bag, certainly not as much as Ariana or I had. It was as if he'd known all along that I'd be bringing it his way.

"You're not surprised?" I asked.

"You've had this since when?" he asked. My effort to catch him off-guard and answer a question hadn't worked.

"Charlotte dropped it off in my office on Wednesday afternoon."

"And you didn't open it?"

"I didn't even touch it before last night." No reason to sound defensive, I realized. "I figured it was her gym clothes and that she'd collect them sooner or later."

"Has anyone else handled the bag since it's been in your possession?"

I thought for a minute. "Bruce. He carried it to my car yesterday evening. But he has no idea what's in it. He just plopped it in my den."

"And left for the hills."

"Right." Though Bruce drew a great distinction between the hills and the mountains. I pointed to the bag, now dominating the small table. "I haven't told him what's in there. I don't want him to have any distractions while he's hanging by a thread."

"I hear you. That's it? No one else touched the bag?"

Ariana popped into my mind. Had she actually touched the bag? Yes, I remembered her sifting through the bills, awestruck, invoking the Mother of God. How dumb of me not to keep my friend from contaminating the evidence. Or myself. But at the time the forensics implications hadn't sunk in.

"Ariana," I confessed, clearing my throat. "She may have touched the bills."

Virgil knew Ariana so he'd have no reason to suspect her of pocketing a few bills, if that was his concern. Still, he blew out a breath and said, "That's unfortunate."

"Sorry. I wasn't thinking."

He spread Charlotte's notes in front of me. I could have sworn they were warm to the touch from their stint on the copy machine. I'd had the urge to trim the left hand edges, messy from being ripped from a short spiral binding. "I don't suppose you know anything about these notes?" Virgil asked.

Other than that one of them referred to a kid she hired to play her nephew as she scoped out an escape route. And that copies of all seven sheets now resided in my purse.

"Nothing I can think of."

A pang of guilt shot through me, but once the sort-of lie was out, I couldn't take it back. I had no idea why I was reluctant to tell Virgil the story of Charlotte's ruse at the airfield. I chalked it up to an inexplicable need to keep my snooping to myself and not to add to the bad marks against Charlotte's good name.

I felt I was falling into a trap Charlotte had set, and one that would get more tangled before it cleared up.

I was more anxious driving away from the police station than I'd been on the way in. A bad sign that said a lot about my spirit of honesty and cooperation with the Henley PD. Why hadn't I given the Henley PD every scrap of information I could, to help them solve this case? Did I really think I was better off on my own, calling Charlotte's contacts?

I realized that Virgil or someone on his investigative team would soon be calling Noah/Jeff. I wondered if the young college student would be savvy —dishonest?—enough not to mention that I'd called him and learned about Charlotte's scheme. I considered calling Jeff and persuading him to omit any mention of our conversation. It would be to his advantage, I'd remind him. After all, he'd been withholding information by not contacting the police immediately when he found out his employer had been murdered. Unless he already had called them.

I decided that calling Jeff wasn't a good idea. If I were found out, it could seem like I was tampering with a witness, the only charge I knew that came close to the offense.

I never thought I'd be the guilty party when I had to memorize Shakespeare in high school English. *Oh, what a tangled web we weave when first we practice to deceive.*

One thing for sure, I had to get busy myself and try to make sense of the notes I'd found in Charlotte's loaded duffel bag. Since I'd gone to the trouble of copying them, I might as well use them.

First, I had to get rid of Ariana.

I clicked on her smiling picture in my smartphone. "Is there any way you can do without your car for a while?" I asked her.

"You need some time alone?"

"Uh huh."

"No problem," she said. "I'll get Luke to take me by and pick my car up later. He owes me for ... well, never mind. I left a box of that tea I told you about on your counter. Brew some for yourself, okay? It'll relax you."

"Okay, thanks."

I felt better, knowing that Luke, Ariana's latest in her "younger man" phase, would be happy to spend some time with her. The new meaning of "cougar" came to mind.

It was nice that not every decision left me guilt-ridden.

Home in my own kitchen, unobserved, I eschewed the box of tea, with its symbols of peace and tranquility on all sides, and made myself a cup of espresso, double strength. I took the brew into my office along with the hot-off-the-press page of names and numbers.

I'd arranged the notes on the glass of the copy machine in a hurried, haphazard way that now irritated me. I didn't miss the irony as I cut the notes to their original size and arranged them on my desk.

This was an interesting puzzle, I told myself. It had nothing to do with violence or the death of my good friend.

I moved the notes about on my desk, hoping to find a pattern. Three were clearly names and phone numbers. I placed them one under the other:

"Jeff/Noah,

Marty," and "Garrett," were each followed by ten-digit numbers. Marty was in the five-zero-eight area code that covered Bristol County, Garrett in Boston's six-one-seven district. Since I knew that Jeff/Noah was someone involved, albeit indirectly, in Charlotte's escape plan, could I assume that Marty and Garrett were also? I wrote it down as a possibility.

The other four notes had names—Jane 1, Jane 2, John 1, and John 2, clearly code names, followed by strings of numbers. Two were strings of ten numbers, of the form xx-xx-xx-xx-xx. Another was a string of the form x-x-x-xx-xx-xx. The final string had only one single-digit number and four two-digit numbers, x-xx-xx-xx-xx.

It was a good thing I was right at home with number puzzles like this. I knew Ariana would have been dizzy by now. Either that or she would have found some numerological significance having to do with good or bad fortune.

The first thing that came to mind for the four notes that weren't telephone numbers was the lottery, something that would have been last on my list if I didn't know about Charlotte's hobby. I assumed the state lottery had a website and made a note to check it to see if the arrays on the notes fit the format of the numbers people drew. Or were given. Or bought. Or however lottery numbers were distributed. I'd never risked even a dollar on a gamble like that.

I wasn't quite brave enough to telephone strangers named Marty and Garrett yet, so I started with the strings of potential lottery numbers.

I went on line and learned way more than I wanted to know about the Massachusetts State Lottery Commission, created in 1971, run by state treasurer so-and-so, and bringing new deals to you and yours every day. Amazingly, I could have done my holiday shopping then and there, with season's lottery tickets for everyone on my list. I couldn't think of anyone who would be happy to get them.

Except Charlotte.

One more beat and I thought of someone else: Margaret Stone, my mom, whose name I took as my own for my puzzle-making career. For most of her adult life, she kept to bingo and horse races, but I'm sure she could have been persuaded to try the lottery if she thought it could be done as a group sport. I'd heard the itch to gamble skipped a generation, and it fit our family profile.

I couldn't resist the chance to see how much money the town of Henley had received from the state since the establishment of the lottery. All I had to do was run my mouse over the dollar signs that made up the image of Massachusetts until I found Henley, and the number would pop up. I did it. Eight million and change! That paid the salaries of a lot of cops and firefighters.

I could find no simple explanation of how numbers were submitted or what it cost to play. A host of different—"exciting"—games were offered, on line and in person, but unless you knew what you were looking for to begin with, you'd be at a loss on the site, as I was.

I suddenly had a different image of proper librarian Charlotte Crocker, wearing a polyester outfit she saved for the occasions, standing in a dusty convenience store, scratching off gummy adhesive with her perfect nails, excited to see the winning number, asking the clerk for her winnings. Or maybe the winnings were in the form of store credit and she walked away with a free soft drink and beef jerky. Not the Charlotte I knew.

The scene, concocted *ad hoc*, brought a confusing image to my mind and a smile to my face.

The lottery website needed help. Between ads, popup windows, and animated cartoon characters beckoning me into a world of fun and flashing lights, it was hard to find out just what a set of numbers looked like. I nearly clicked on "email the webmaster" when I saw a pull-down menu hidden among the loud promos.

I finally found what I needed by going to a list of recent winning numbers. Comparing the strings of digits on Charlotte's notes, I saw that two were from a game called "Power Ball," one was from "Megabucks," and the last from what was termed the thrilling new game, "Megaball."

So what? I asked myself, before anyone else could. I now could reasonably say that Jane1 and John2 played Power Ball, Jane2 played Megabucks, and John1 played Megaball. Again, so what?

Before I clicked off the site, having learned far too little of anything useful, I was pulled in by the photograph of a middle-aged, red-haired woman, smiling out at me and the world. She'd won Boston Bruins tickets for life. I wondered if she was happy with that prize or was stuck with it and would try to trade them in for membership in Boston's Museum of Fine Arts.

I found myself wondering what I'd choose if asked. Free puzzle books for life? As a contributor, I already received complimentary subscriptions to as many as I could feasibly read. A fancy new car? I was happy with my reliable Ford. Without risking a penny, I'd recently been awarded a small grant that gave me membership in several special libraries on line and in Boston.

I did need blue placemats to match a bowl Ariana had made for me during her brush with ceramics. And matching napkins would be a nice touch. Nothing else came to mind.

Either my life was full and perfect as it was and I didn't need a lottery win, or I was unambitious and boring.

# Chapter 7

I abandoned my lottery research project and settled down with a much-too-small portion of shrimp fried rice from a recent, I hoped, takeout dinner splurge. I flipped through a puzzle magazine while I ate, further postponing contacting the people who belonged to the telephone numbers on the notepaper.

After the last kernel of rice, I got down to it and started with Marty, the five-zero-eight, a local boy. I punched in the full number. It was Saturday, so I wasn't surprised to hear the click to voicemail after three rings.

I listened to the message, by a vaguely familiar female voice.

"You have reached Henley College, Henley, Massachusetts, and the office of Martin Melrose, Controller and Director of Student Financial Services. Our office hours are … "

What?

I clicked off with a gasp, as if I'd dialed the netherworld and needed to erase any trace of my caller ID immediately.

Three-piece-suit, bow tie, coke-bottle glasses Martin, familiarly known as our treasurer? I knew he and Charlotte both played the lottery, but why would a piece of paper with his phone number be in a duffel bag surrounded by literally, dirty money? And who called him Marty?

I looked at the number again. The area code was the same for much of Bristol County—Lakeville, Bridgewater, Fall River, and a host of other towns, and Henley College didn't have a unique exchange. I'd had no reason to believe I was calling my own campus. It had probably been years since I'd had the occasion to call Henley's main landline. The few times this fall I'd called Martin Melrose's extension, it had been from a campus line, requiring only the last four digits.

Eventually I stopped arguing my case for not recognizing my treasurer's number.

Martin was part of a group of people, not all on campus, who pooled their money to increase their chances of winning. I knew Martin held the purse, so to speak, and maybe his number was in Charlotte's bag simply because they had group business to discuss. In any case, I needed to talk to him and to the others in the pool.

Statistics was among the math classes I'd been teaching for years, so, when Charlotte mentioned increased odds of winning among those belonging to the lottery pool, I'd been curious about how it worked.

There were many variations, Charlotte had explained, but with hers, each member drew a different number, and if any one of the group won, all shared in the prize.

"So, if my ticket wins, say, one hundred dollars, and there are five in the group, I get only twenty?" I'd asked.

"That's right," Charlotte had said.

"Even though it was my money that bought my ticket?" I'd asked, a bit skeptical.

"Yes, but if I win one hundred dollars on a ticket I bought with *my* money, you also get twenty dollars," Charlotte explained.

I finally understood that, although pooling didn't increase my chances of winning with my ticket, it did increase my chances of getting any money back at all.

The explanation did nothing to make me want to play.

I was eager to speak to one member of the pool, Martin Melrose, but I didn't have his home phone number and it wouldn't do to leave a message at the office like, "Marty, I found a bag of cash belonging to Charlotte Crocker and wondered if it had anything to do with your lottery pool."

To save us both an embarrassing moment, I'd try him again on Monday morning instead.

In the meantime, there was still Garrett, of six-one-seven, Boston. Maybe he was a participant also.

I punched in the number and heard an Asian accent.

"Shop At Ease. This Kwang Ho."

I recognized the name of a chain of convenience stores in the Boston area. Bruce and I had often stopped at one located off the turnpike while heading into the city.

"Hi, is Garrett there?"

"Garrett? He skip out."

"He's out for a break, or for the day?" I asked.

"He out for good."

"Did he quit?"

"Walked out like that." I pictured Mr. Ho snapping his fingers, but I couldn't swear to it. "Never come back."

"Was he fired?"

A dial tone followed.

Thanks, I muttered, and punched "Redial," harder than I needed to.

"Shop At Ease. This Kwang Ho." The same voice.

"Can you tell me where Garrett might be or how I can get in touch with him?"

"I tell you. Garrett took all stuff and not even say goodbye."

I knew there was no time to untangle the grammar before the next hang-up.

"Where is your store located?" I asked quickly. An easy question that shouldn't provoke Mr. Ho to blow me off again. My hope was that, if I visited the store in person, I might find an employee more articulate and more cooperative than Mr. Ho.

"Bailey Landings, edge of town."

"What's your street—?"

A dial tone.

I had a feeling that if I redialed one more time I'd get voicemail.

Bailey's Landing, close enough to Mr. Ho's Bailey Landings, was a small town northeast of Henley, about an hour away. I'd been through it on my way to visit a friend in Quincy.

I went online to check out the exact address of the Shop At Ease market and found four of them in Bailey's Landing. I printed out directions to all of them. My car was equipped with a GPS, but I always took a hard copy backup. Only kids who grew up in the digital age were really in a position to save the trees.

I reviewed my progress. I'd gotten up to speed on what the number sequences for different Massachusetts lottery games looked like, and I'd begun my tracking of the phone numbers in Charlotte's bag. Trivial when I looked at honestly.

Besides Martin Melrose, the hottest lead was now a convenience store clerk named Garrett. I was already bored with the lottery numbers and needed a break before tracking down the Janes and Johns who were potentially winners of Megaball or Gigaball or whatever they were called.

I pulled on my favorite Irish knit sweater, anticipating a perfect fall crispness in the air around Massachusetts Bay. The off-white sweater was one of my mother's first knitting projects when I was in high school, and I never wore it without picturing her, small-framed like me, sharp-eyed, and a powerful force for good in my life. I missed her every day.

I thought about asking Ariana, who loved water vistas, to come along for the ride. The combination of her upbeat personality and excellent baking talent guaranteed it would be a more pleasant ride than if I visualized Kwang Ho for an hour.

*Buzzz.*

My doorbell. Probably Ariana, come to claim her car. I could invite her in person.

Out of habit, I checked the peephole in the front door. I stepped back quickly at the sight: Henley PD homicide detective Virgil Mitchell. From the look on his face, he hadn't come for a friendly game of poker.

I licked my lips and straightened my sweater, as if the school photographer had arrived for a candid, and opened the door. So far with Virgil I'd exhibited fear and intimidation, then surprise and evasiveness. How should I be on this third visit with my friend, the cop?

I opened the door.

"Hey," I said, still undecided on my persona of the moment, except to give him a weak smile.

"Sophie Saint Germain Knowles," he said, brushing past

me, not waiting for an invitation to sit at the table in the breakfast nook.

How could Virgil have remembered my full name, used by my mother when she was about to chew me out? I doubted it was because he, like my math teacher father, was enamored of my namesake, Sophie Saint Germain, an influential, self-taught French mathematician whose work spanned the seventeenth and eighteenth centuries. Not only did I doubt it, I knew it wasn't true.

"You're channeling my parents?"

A smile broke out on his face, then quickly faded. "I talked to"—he drew quote marks in the air—"Noah."

"Coffee?" I asked, heading for the stove. The venue was mine this time.

"Sure. While you're thinking of a response."

Virgil was frustrated, and rightly so.

I moved Ariana's cookies from the counter to a spot on the table in front of Virgil, filled my French press with an aromatic blend, then took a seat across from him. The autumn reds, yellows, and oranges on the placemats, which had seemed so festive lately, now seemed frivolous and unnecessary. I rolled them up and pushed them to the side, leaving bare wood as décor.

"I was going to tell you," I said.

Virgil breathed a heavy sigh and, before I knew it, tears welled up and spilled down my cheek. Whether they were for Charlotte or for the loss of my parents or the confused state I was in, I had no idea.

The last thing I wanted was for Virgil to think I was trying to manipulate him with the crying damsel routine. I quickly left the table, went into my hallway bathroom and pulled myself together with a few tissues and a very deep breath.

I was back in less than three minutes, just in time to prepare the coffee.

"You've been holding out on me, Sophie. Why would you do that?" Virgil asked, with no reference to my little setback. "Where's the old logical, level-headed Dr. Sophie Knowles, math professor? The one who has a favorite prime number of the month or something like that. Where'd she go?"

"That's a good question, Virgil." I almost said, "I'm not myself," but I'd made enough snarky comments to others who made that claim that I stopped in time. "I just know I want to help somehow."

Virgil waited until he'd swallowed a large bite of cookie. "That's not your job. That's why you pay your taxes, so people like me can get paid to do police work."

"Calling people Charlotte knew and telling them about what happened didn't seem like police work. It was a harmless way to do something for my friend."

"Until you talked to Jeff."

I nodded, humbled. "When Jeff told me what Charlotte had done, my first reaction was anger that she'd deceived me. But then I guess I felt I needed to protect her good name. I know it was stupid."

"What it was, was dangerous, Sophie. I can't tell you everything, except please step back and try to ... " Virgil threw up his hands, for want of a verb.

I poured our coffee and decided to help him out. "Get on with my life." Another phrase I'd sneered at more than once.

Virgil put his palms up and nodded. "Thank you. You took the words right out of my mouth."

I sat down. "Did you figure out what the other notes are about?" I asked.

Virgil gave me an exasperated look. He twirled his index finger in the space between us. "What did we just decide here?"

"Even the old, sensible Sophie was a curious citizen, Virgil."

"Okay, then how about this, citizen Knowles. I'm not at liberty to say." Now who was calling up clichés? "But I want to make it clear that there are some dangerous, underlying ..."

I came to his rescue again. "Criminal elements?" A term from my little-known hobby of watching crime dramas. "Is this about drugs or something?" I didn't think so, but I wanted to open my mind to allow Virgil to fill it.

Virgil shook his head, not a "no" shake, but a "what am I going to do with you?" shake. "Just trust me on this. You don't want to get in the middle of this. Mourn your friend as you knew her. And let us do our job."

"That's easy for you to say. Your friend wasn't shot."

"Where did you get the idea that Ms. Crocker was shot?"

"That's what was going around on the cell phones at the library. She wasn't shot?"

Virgil shook his head. "We haven't released all the details yet. It's interesting to see what the rumor mill churns up when it has no input."

All this time—which seemed like weeks and weeks—I hadn't thought to verify the gunshot rumor. I was annoyed, mostly with myself.

"Can you at least tell me how she died, Virgil?"

"She fell from the ladder that's attached to the bookshelves. The one that slides back and forth along the shelves."

I drew a quick breath. "So it could have been an accident?" Thus, making us all feel safer, I thought.

Virgil looked at me and, to his credit, did not remind me how long he'd been a homicide detective, starting in Boston many years ago. He didn't play a numbers game and tell me how many crime scenes he'd witnessed, how many cases he'd solved.

"The area showed signs of struggle," he said. "And so did her body."

I groaned. "How awful."

"We think the guy came in while she was alone and wanted something from her. When she wouldn't give it to him, he tried to force it out of her. She resisted and tried to get away by climbing that movable ladder. It ends at the loft that runs above the bookshelves. She was probably trying to get there."

I knew it well. "But there are stairs for that purpose. The ladder is just to reach the high shelves in the bookcases."

"She maybe couldn't get to the stairs and hoped to climb over the railing from the ladder. All the killer had to do was shake the ladder off its track, and …. " Virgil shrugged the rest of the sentence.

It had almost been easier to imagine a clean shot to my friend's chest. Terrible, but over in a flash. Now I was left with a long scenario of fighting, wounds, bruises, blood, drawn-out fear, and a painful fall. Unless I could curb my imagination. Virgil had said "struggle," I reminded myself, not "blood-letting."

*Whirrrr. Whirrrr. Whirrrr.*

My cell phone ring intruded. Gratefully accepted, to put an end to the scene in my brain. The phone rang and vibrated on my counter, spinning around its center of mass, which I always found a little creepy.

"Bruce," I said to Virgil.

"You'd better take it. You never know when he'll get a connection again. He doesn't exactly travel in cell tower country. Tell him hello."

I picked up the phone and clicked on. The motion stopped, as if I'd killed a parasite that lived in my phone.

"Hey," Bruce said. "You okay?" He sounded far away and high up, but that was probably my imagination at work.

"I'm the one at home with gas, electricity, and central heating, so, yeah, I'm okay."

"I mean, you know …"

"I'm fine. Virgil's here and says hi."

"Virge? Anything wrong?"

"No. Just some routine last questions about … yesterday."

"Good. I'm glad you have some company. I don't like the way you sound and I'm kicking myself for leaving."

"I sent you," I said.

I also wanted to correct Bruce's impression of the police visit, inform him that his cop friend had brought more trouble than comfort, but I didn't like the idea of sending Bruce up a mountain thinking he should have canceled the trip.

"It's a quick trip," he said. "We should be up and back without a hitch."

"How's Kevin doing?"

"Ready to get started. We'll hike down in the dark to give him the full experience."

"So you'll be at sea level to sleep."

"In the comfort of a luxury campsite."

"An oxymoron."

Bruce laughed. "The guys are waving at me to hurry up. There's one excruciatingly slow group up there ahead of us.

Amateurs. But most everyone else is off the mountain now, so it's a good time."

"What do they know that you don't?"

"I miss you."

Vigil's hulking presence cramped my style, limiting my use of endearments. I resorted to, "Me, too. Are the weather conditions good?"

"So-so. You know, it's always a gamble."

A gamble. A bolt of intelligence struck as I flashed back to my first interview with Virgil. He'd been the one to bring up gambling. He'd asked if Charlotte had any vices, like gambling. When I mentioned the lottery, almost as a joke, he'd run with it, talking about the system at length, introducing the idea of scams, going on and on about scammers and victims of scams.

If I were a betting sort, I'd have bet that Virgil had known all along that Charlotte had been a victim of a lottery scam. I thought of the bag of money, the layers of US dollars in Charlotte's duffel bag. Was that the mark of a victim? Or was Charlotte herself a scammer with a load of cash?

"I'm signing off, okay?" Bruce asked.

I hoped he hadn't said anything important in the last second or two.

We exchanged quiet "love yous" and I returned to Virgil with new curiosity. I took my place across from him and leaned over my folded hands.

"You've known all along that Charlotte was involved in a lottery scam haven't you? Since when? Since she was hired two years ago?"

Virgil took a sip of coffee. The mug seemed small in his giant hand. "That's police business, Sophie."

Which was nicer than "That's none of your business, Sophie," and certainly not a denial.

"She was my friend and I thought I knew her, Virgil. You knew something was up before she was murdered and you didn't tell me? We hung around together and you didn't warn me that she was about to be murdered."

I knew I was being extreme, but I wanted to provoke Virgil to action.

It seemed to work. Virgil stood abruptly. If I didn't know him so well, how much more gentle he was than men half his size, I'd have been worried. He reached into his jacket and pulled out a folded stack of letter-size pages.

"I'm out of here," he said, and handed me the sheets.

I took the sheaf of papers and unfolded it. The Henley Police Department logo screamed out at me.

"What—"

"Thanks for the coffee," he said, and was out the door.

# Chapter 8

An hour later I was in my den, still reading through the papers Virgil had given me. What was the real police term for these documents? I knew it as a rap sheet, singular, but this was a multi-page record. Maybe originally it was one long piece of paper. I'd also heard "yellow sheet." Or just "sheet.

Pull his sheet," one cop would say to another on television.

The name of the state from which the pages had been sent, maybe faxed, had been drowned out by the thick, black Henley PD header. The contents of the file were clear, however.

My friend, Charlotte Crocker, was a convicted felon. She was a scam artist.

Except she wasn't even Charlotte Crocker.

On the first page was a mug shot. A different, younger Charlotte Crocker stared straight ahead at the camera and at me, over the name Carla Cooper. She wore a knitted burgundy poncho and long earrings that ended in rainbow-hued peace signs. Her light brown hair looked thin and straggly, her eyes bloodshot. The date and the outfit were out of whack with each other, as if this were a Halloween costume twenty years after the hippies took to suburbs and switched to business casual.

The string of digits that made up her ID number, on a black card that she held up, reminded me of a lottery number from one of the mega-games I'd just learned about. I wondered if she'd ever thought of placing a bet on the number.

I thought of the irony—my so-called friend had led me to believe she was so upset about that one speeding ticket she'd gotten, and all the while she had a record of violations that would have kept a small town cop in Vermont busy for months.

Everything was wrong about the police photographer's image of the woman I'd considered a friend. From the arcane hippie look to her snarly expression to the fact that she had a mug shot at all.

I remembered a day we spent together with Ariana just before school started in the fall. A typical girlfriend day for the three of us, with shopping and lunch and nonstop talk of books, movies, men, the problems of the world, and the hint of gray that was sprouting now that we'd left the big four-oh behind.

I tried to recall something unusual about Charlotte that should have given me a clue that the real Charlotte was a felon. I remembered a passing remark she'd made that day, somewhat wistful.

"I wish I'd known you both twenty years ago," she'd said, and hugged us.

Apparently she considered us a good influence on her, but two decades too late.

She'd made a similar comment, more recently, that might have tipped me off about an impending tsunami, but I couldn't dredge it up.

If I stretched it, I could think of a phone call or two that she took in my presence that left her momentarily upset. But all that was hindsight. At the time, she seemed as even-tempered and trustworthy as they came.

I focused on the sheet. I could hardly count the list of aliases, all with birth dates within a few years of either side of Charlotte's real (but who knew?) birth date of 1966. Carolyn Crouse was born in 1963 in Seattle, Christine Coulter in 1970 in Miami, Catherine Chesterfield in 1968 in Cleveland, and so on, through several more aliases and dates and places of birth.

I'd read that many people who change their identities keep their initials. I supposed that was handy—any monogrammed luggage or bathroom towels wouldn't have to be replaced each time a new persona was adopted. Or in case the person forgot and started to sign something, at least the first initial would always be correct. It occurred to me that probably none of these names, including Charlotte Crocker, was her real name.

Another wave of anger came over me as I realized how

incredibly naïve I'd been. I heard a low growl and was shocked to realize it had come from me.

How could she, whatever-her-name-was, have faked her pleasant sophistication, her generosity and helpfulness to Henley College's students? Whoever she was, Charlotte must have had some training in library science to be as good as she was at her job. Clearly, it hadn't been enough to satisfy her.

But, she wasn't necessarily trained at all, I realized in a moment. I remembered reports I'd hardly believed at the time, about a guy who flew commercial airplanes on a fake license, and another man without a day of medical training who was head of a surgical unit at a hospital. A story came to me that seemed silly at the time, of a man who posed as a government official and sold the Eiffel Tower.

None of these scams seemed silly today.

I was sure there were other examples. Henley's hiring and firing procedures were no more fail-proof than those of the Federal Aviation Association or the American Medical Association.

Had Henley's students—or I—been in danger all the while? Was Charlotte about to work her scams on us? Was her killer after us, too?

I got up quickly and made a tour of my house, checking all the windows and doors. Fresh autumn air would have to be sacrificed until further notice.

I plopped back onto the couch that had served as my bed last night and took up the police documents again.

There were two more pages in the set, each listing charges and convictions of one or another of the C. C.s. I read the details of the statutes violated, the class of the crime, bond information, sentencing, where time was served. The words swam in front of me. Fraud. Theft. Malicious destruction of property. Misdemeanor. Felony. Assault. Willard County. Shaw County, Plummet County. I counted the stamps: Time Served. Paroled. Did Not Appear.

A glossary of criminal justice terms. All related to my friend.

I folded the package and stuffed it in a cabinet under my counter with my never-used pie plates.

Even with the new information at my disposal, I had more questions than answers. Why had Virgil given it to me? Was he trying to scare me off? How long had he been investigating C. C.? Or, I thought snarkily, C-squared, to depersonalize her even further. Was C. C. on the run, a real fugitive, or was she legitimately out of prison with a legitimate bag of money and fleeing a bad guy who was after her?

I needed a spreadsheet to map the possibilities.

It was scary enough to think that C. C.'s murderer was out there and may be targeting someone else right now. Maybe our treasurer, Martin Melrose, also a member of C. C.'s lottery group was at risk.

And that wasn't all. I reeled at the extent of her criminal enterprises, cataloged on the rap sheet, which went far beyond the lottery.

All unsuspecting students were at risk. I was at risk.

Until I knew exactly why Charlotte was killed and by whom, no one who knew her was completely safe. I didn't want to know what Virgil, or anyone else, would think of my reasoning.

I wandered around my little cottage, straightening scarves and doilies, picking up a stray glass or mug here and there, sharpening my pencils. Normal things. I sat down to check for messages on my office phone, something I didn't ordinarily do on weekends, but this was no ordinary Saturday.

I had messages from freshman Daryl Farmer, Dean of Women Paula Rogers, Charlotte's assistant Hannah Stephens, my favorite Mobius stripper, Chelsea Derbin, and several of my student majors, all wanting to help in different ways, as if I were the go-to person for all things related to the murder on campus.

Daryl offered that he was a pretty good hacker and might be able to get into Charlotte's files for clues to her murder. Paula's contribution was a dinner invitation to a fine restaurant "where you can be pampered." And grilled for information, I added to myself. Hannah missed her boss and wanted to talk to me and grieve together. Chelsea thought I needed "a gift basket with chocolate and nice smelling soap" that she put together and could deliver whenever it was convenient for me.

The last message was from none other than Henley College's

president, Olivia Aldridge. The president wanted to know if I'd be willing to help with a memorial service to be held on campus in a week or so. I'd be the perfect person, since Charlotte and I were so close and I'd know what she would have wanted. In fact, Olivia ended, why didn't I go ahead and take charge of it. She'd be happy to go along with whatever I came up with. And while I was at it, would it be all right if she referred reporters to me? She really didn't have time to deal with the members of the media.

It was more widely held than I'd thought that I was Charlotte's best friend on campus and the one most appropriate to speak on her behalf. I wondered what lies Charlotte had told those she didn't consider her friends.

I left all the messages on the machine to deal with later. Or not at all.

What to do next? Heed Virgil's warning?

But what if Virgil had dropped the information in my lap as a subtle way of asking for my help? I smiled. My mother always told me that even as a little girl I had a sneaky way of twisting things my way while sounding perfectly reasonable.

Did Virgil want me to do a search on the names on Charlotte's rap sheet and put the whole picture together for myself? Not knowing which crime went with which name and which city, I'd be flailing around for a long time. It was a job for a super-computer, not a math teacher.

Aha! Virgil was giving me busy work.

Even to myself, I was beginning to sound like a mad woman.

I'd gone from feelings of grief for Charlotte Crocker to out-rage that I'd spent so much time with a woman who was a pro-fessional criminal to a commitment to find the person respon-sible for her death.

I decided not to call Ariana. I needed a long, solo drive.

It might as well be to a convenience store in Bailey's Landing.

My car CD player was set up with the music of my college days. New Order, Tears for Fears, Duran Duran, U-2, Howard Jones, plus a late eighties mix Bruce had put together for me. Comfort music. I thought it fitting that the first cut I heard, an odd-ball choice of Bruce's, was "Don't Look Back" by the Fine Young Cannibals.

One of my father's favorite quotes came into my head at the same time, from Gottfried Leibniz, who some thought invented the calculus. "Music is the pleasure the human soul experiences from counting without being aware that it is counting."

I doubted either Leibniz or my father had in mind the three-man British band, but music was music.

I drove Route 95, then Route 1 through the towns of Sharon, Canton, Randolph, and Braintree. Winter had set in for the trees along the highway, offering a dull brown landscape, except for the occasional pumpkin patch or colorful billboard with a reminder that a special meal would be served on Thanksgiving at your favorite fast food restaurant. I'd been looking forward to spending the holiday weekend in New Haven with Bruce's cousins. I hoped my festive mood would return by then.

It would have been nice if I'd constructed a plan for when I arrived in Bailey's Landing, but it was only now that one was taking shape.

With the five other people the police had to track down from Charlotte's notes, the odds were in my favor that I'd get to Garrett first. I figured the Henley PD couldn't spare a detective to immediately drive to Bailey's Landing as I could. I'd meet Garrett and pick up some juicy tidbit of information that would lead to Charlotte's killer. Then, I'd go directly to Virgil with it and make a deal.

In return for my stellar sleuthing, Virgil would fill me in on the whole picture, how long he'd been investigating Charlotte, whether there were any mitigating circumstances that led her to a life of crime, whether at heart she was a good person. It was still possible that Charlotte had served her time, turned law-abiding citizen right before my eyes, and was simply running from people who wanted her legitimate earnings.

I was desperate not to think that I was so inept at reading people. That I was so naïve as to see qualities that weren't there.

I might also beat on him for not telling me what was now clear, that he'd been letting me hang out with her, knowing she was a felon with at least one murderous associate.

Shouldn't there be some perks in having a cop friend? If he needed help with math, I'd be the first one at his side with tables of logarithms and t-scores.

With very little traffic, I approached the Bailey's Landing city limit in a little over an hour. Kwang Ho's gesture toward giving me an address, "on the edge of town," wasn't sufficient so I'd have to check all four of the Shop At Ease sites, one at each edge, north, south, east, and west.

I approached from the southwest and saw the first neon green Shop At Ease sign right off the highway. The way my weekend was going, I shouldn't have been surprised that it was the wrong one. No Kwang Ho and no Garrett ever worked there, and the gum-chewing teen behind the counter wasn't exactly working there either. I met with similar results at the next two stops, where I interacted with friendlier but equally clueless clerks in dingy stores. I was glad I wasn't hungry.

Each store in the chain advertised the availability of lottery tickets, both inside and out. The sign on one store window read "You Have to Play!" In another, a large, grotesque, animated finger pointed to what looked like a slot machine and announced, "Your Dreams Come True Here!" Ads for the lottery were embedded in neon outlines of the commonwealth of Massachusetts and in simulated scoreboards for Boston's football, hockey, baseball, and basketball teams. Brightly lit dollar signs flowed freely around ticket-buying displays.

How come I'd never noticed all this hype before today?

The final Shop At Ease site was on the northern edge of town, near Quincy. I had a sinking feeling that Kwang Ho had given me the wrong shop name entirely. He might have been talking to me from a liquor store or a strip mall for all I knew.

Nevertheless, I had to finish my rounds and check out this last store. I repeated the pattern I'd used in the first three locations. To show good will, I took a bottle of water to the high counter near the door and paid for it. In this shop as in the others, I wanted to use my antibacterial lotion on the bottle and on the rest of the merchandise. I was used to the convenience shops at rest stops along the turnpikes of New England and New York, which were neat and orderly, inspiring confidence in the snacks I bought. The shelves in the Bailey's Landing Shop At Ease stores were dusty and crowded, with a container of bleach sitting next to the beef jerky and the hairbrushes side by side with green apples.

The only signs prominently displayed in their own corner, with the ease of access the store's name implied, were those for the lottery.

My working theory was that Kwang Ho, who sounded like he was past his youth, was the boss of whichever store I'd called and everyone who worked in his shop would know him, whereas a clerk like this kid could be so new or work such odd hours that he'd never heard of Garrett.

"Is Kwang Ho in today?" I asked the pimply guy whose car-magazine reading I'd interrupted. We'd all have been better off if he'd used slow times to mop the grimy floor and wipe down the sticky shelves.

"Okay, yeah, Monsieur Ho. He's not here right now. He's on lunch break." He rolled his eyes. "Like I get one." His gaze returned to his magazine. "He'll be back whenever."

"You don't get a lunch break"—I looked at the name on his shirt—"Warren? Isn't that illegal?" Establishing rapport, sympathizing, both highly recommended when attempting to extract information from an unsuspecting young person. Years of teaching had helped me polish this technique.

"Yeah, well, who cares, right?"

"Someone should," I said.

Warren removed his cap and repositioned it on his thick brown hair, which, like the cap, could have done with a wash and rinse. "You got that right."

"How about Garrett? Is he here?"

Warren grinned, showing perfect teeth. Someone had cared enough for Warren in his early years. "Garrett is not here."

"He gets a lunch break, too?"

"No, he's not here, like ever again."

I managed a shocked look, as if Garrett and I went way back. "He was fired?"

"No, no. You didn't hear? Oh, my God, I. Am. So. Jealous." Warren leaned over the tacky counter and whispered, though there wasn't another soul in the store. "He won the lottery."

I gasped, only half faking. "Oh. My. God. When?"

"Like, a week ago, but he couldn't get his money right away. He had to go to some college down in Henley to pick it up. That's like an hour away."

I cleared my throat as an image of convergence theory came to mind, all roads leading to my campus. "Wow."

I wished I knew for certain if I'd actually beat the Henley PD here. They had quicker ways of finding people. They could have traced Garrett's number directly instead of relying on the likes of Kwang Ho to tell them which store he was in.

Still, it had been only a few hours since I'd given Virgil the stack of notes that included Garrett's name and number and, unlike me, the cops had a lot to do.

I decided to take a chance, and worked out the phrasing of my next question accordingly.

I met Warren's gaze. "You know, I heard something kind of weird from mutual friends." I lowered my voice. "That some cops were trying to contact Garrett. I can't imagine why since Garrett is so by-the-book, you know? But maybe the police get involved when you win big in the lottery?"

Warren chewed on his lips, thinking. "Okay, well, they didn't come while I was here, but it wouldn't be that weird. Garrett can be extreme."

Extreme what? I pictured the extremes of a calculus problem and bemoaned my poor slang vocabulary. I needed to hang around Henley's dorms more.

"Really?" I asked.

"Yeah, so I wouldn't be surprised if the cops are looking for him. But not for the lottery." Warren laughed in a way that said he wished he were the one living Garrett's exciting life, sought after by men in uniforms.

"But, as far as you know, no cop came by today?"

Warren shook his head. "Unless they came when the old man was here. If so, I feel sorry for them. Monsieur Ho is not the most cooperative guy, you know, whether it's cops or Mother Theresa."

Good to know. It wasn't just me he didn't like. "Well, I guess that's it, then. I'll just have to wait for Garrett to contact me. I lost the last number he gave me and I'll just have to take the consequences."

I had no idea what I was talking about, but my words had the desired effect. Warren gave me the once over, screwed up his nose, and scanned my innocent-looking face.

"I probably shouldn't do this, but you look like good people," he said.

I gave him a demure smile that said, "Gee, thanks."

Warren reached in the back pocket of his jeans and pulled out a slip of paper. He copied numbers from the paper to the corner of a page in his car magazine, which I hoped he owned, then tore off the scrap and handed it to me.

"Garrett goes, 'I'll be at this number if something comes up.' I go, 'What can come up when you're rich.' Am I right?" Warren asked.

"You are right," I declared.

I wanted to know how rich Garrett was or would be, but didn't want to push my luck. I took the paper and checked out the number. A five-zero-eight area code, followed by a number that looked familiar.

I stared down at Martin Melrose's phone number, which I'd dialed this morning. Garrett was staying with Martin? I'd had no idea the reach the Henley College treasurer had.

Was Garrett another victim, lured to Henley to collect on a bogus win? I doubted it. If I were a scam artist—say, Charlotte or Marty—I'd never want my victims to see my face or where I lived. But if Garrett was on the other end of the con, a rich scammer himself, what had he been doing working in a low-end Shop at Ease with the likes of Warren and Kwang Ho?

I hoped I'd soon find out.

I waved the tiny scrap of paper at Warren. "Thanks for this. Garrett will be glad you helped me out," I lied.

I'd reached the door when I heard, "Lady?" from Warren.

There being no other lady in the store, I turned. "Yes?"

Warren held out my purchase. "You forgot your water."

"Thanks."

I carried the bottle—was that syrup along the side?—to my

car and threw it on the back floor with the three others I'd purchased from the Bailey's Landing Shop At Ease franchises.

I looked around for an ice cream shop. It was going to take more than water to get me through a conversation with Martin Melrose.

# Chapter 9

I sat in my car in the Shop At Ease parking lot. Three o'clock in the afternoon and I had a long drive home ahead of me. I should have been relaxing in a Swan Boat on the lagoon in Boston's Public Garden, except that their season ended two months ago. I'd have settled for a wooden bench in the Faneuil Hall shopping plaza. Anything would have been better than the weekend so far.

I dialed Martin's office. I suspected it would prove fruitless, as it had this morning, but this time I waited until the "You have reached—" message played through.

"Martin, this is Sophie Knowles," I said to the tiny speaker in my phone." I was wondering if we could meet sometime. If you get this over the weekend, call my cell. Otherwise I'll see you on Monday." I repeated my cell number in case he didn't have caller ID.

A wishy-washy message, but I didn't want to scare him off with the alternative, "Hey, I found your name in a duffel bag full of cash. I hear you're in deep in this lottery scam business. Maybe scamming innocent people in other ways, too? Does it have anything to do with Charlotte's murder? How's Garrett, by the way?"

My ice cream search had come up empty. I was now hungry and lonesome. I needed to talk to someone about what I'd found out. Or even about a shoe sale in downtown Henley. I wanted to call Bruce but we had an agreement that he'd call at the base of his climb, which he had done, and then again if he could get a connection when he could afford to have both hands free and his attention on something other than staying alive, that last phase being my version of his situation.

Sometimes he and his climbing partners stayed in a nearby

hotel, depending on whether camping was allowed at the site. Unfortunately for me, this was a luxury-free trip for the guys.

Maybe Ariana was free to talk. More like, listen. She had weekend help at the shop and I hadn't heard of any plans she'd made with Luke.

*Beep beep. Beep beep. Beep beep.*

Uh-oh, the sound of charge leaking from my phone. I checked its screen and saw a black outline where an image of a solid green battery should be. I fished around the console but the only car charger I had with me was for the Bluetooth device on my visor. I remembered now that I'd moved my smartphone charger to my overnight bag to use in Bruce's SUV. I pictured the spare charger I'd bought for just such occasions, resting comfortably in the middle drawer of the desk in my home office.

It seemed ages ago that I'd anticipated a Saturday better than this one had turned out to be.

I couldn't believe I'd used the last bit of cell phone charge on a voicemail message to Martin Melrose, aka Marty.

I pulled out of the lot. Without the security of a phone, I was anxious to get home before dark. It didn't make sense—I'd been driving a car for decades without a phone, but in the last couple of years, I'd come to depend on having one available at all times. If I found myself away from home without a phone, even to run a quick errand, I felt vulnerable, worse than if I'd left my purse behind. With a phone and a credit card, I could take care of anything.

Bruce called me a nomophobe and I had to agree. I had a new, twenty-first-century phobia, the fear of being out of contact. I tried to come up with a parallel word for Bruce, at the opposite end of the spectrum, choosing a hobby that left him so far out of contact that no one could reach him for days or weeks at a time, except the guys with whom he shared a rope and a package of granola bars.

I turned up the music and caught Bon Jovi, *So far away from everything, you know it's true. Something inside that makes you do what you got to do.* Very insightful, those singers from New Jersey.

I was on my way, phone or no phone.

The drive was easy enough that I could accomplish a few hands-free things on my to-do list. I started with mulling over an example for Friday's advanced calculus class. I pictured two intersecting curves on a simple two-dimensional plot. I'd start with an easy problem, both curves in the first quadrant, and show how to find the area between them.

My pedagogical stand-by technique was to do the calculation step by step on the blackboard, actually white these days, then call for a show of hands. Who thought that was too easy? Who thought it too hard? I'd adjust my next example accordingly and ask for a volunteer to work it out. It was an old-school strategy, but it worked for me.

During the scandalous Milli Vanilli's "Girl, I'm Gonna Miss You"—who said only country music was about broken hearts?—I thought out a plan for a unit on Hypatia, fifth century A.D., for my Mathematics History seminar group. I was determined to present a mathematician with a more exciting personal life than Mobius the next time my department hosted the Friday bash in the Franklin Hall lounge. And what was more thrilling than a gruesome death, being brutally tortured and killed because you loved mathematics and refused to abandon your evil, pagan studies? Yes, Hypatia would do nicely.

Though I was close to Henley, my stomach rumbling had reached a point where a stop was necessary. Besides, I knew there was nothing good waiting for me in my fridge. I detoured slightly to Norton, the home of Wheaton College, which I was familiar with from intercollegiate meetings. I felt better already, knowing that any campus town worth its salt could be depended on for good coffee and sandwich shops.

Smaller than Henley College, Wheaton had gone from a women's college to coed in the eighties, twenty years before we ever considered it. As far as I knew they were thriving. I parked on a busy street that dead-ended at the campus, and walked to a coffee shop. I couldn't help a longing glance at the campus, similar in architecture to Henley, except that Wheaton had cleaner lines—light brick buildings with colonial white trim instead of the darker brick, Gothic look of Henley.

As much as I wanted to stay and absorb the atmosphere of

a school without a fresh murder to solve, I ordered my food to go. Turkey and Swiss on wheat, a bag of chips, a chocolate chip cookie, and a latte. The basic requirements for a nutritious meal.

While I was waiting for the sandwich, I broke open the chips and bought a newspaper. I took a quick look for anything about Charlotte Crocker or any of her akas. Nothing. It was too soon for even a word, which suited me fine.

Driving while eating wasn't illegal yet in the commonwealth, so I managed both for the next twenty minutes and finally saw the Welcome to Henley sign. A strange feeling came over me as I wondered what had happened in the town since I'd left. How many more crimes had been committed? Had Virgil and his colleagues on the force been working on Charlotte's case all this time or had there been a more important one? A mass murder, perhaps, or a serial killer on the loose. Or did they simply take Saturdays off?

I had no idea if Virgil would be interested in what I'd learned about Garrett. My plan to strike a deal with him by serving up Charlotte's killer had gone awry after the fourth Shop At Ease stop failed to produce anything earthshaking, but I might have more than he did. Once I closed the loop with Marty, maybe I'd have more, a bigger bargaining chip.

I wished I could drive to the police station and compare notes over a cup of coffee, as if cops and citizens alike were all legitimate investigators. I knew the criminal justice system didn't work that way, but why not?

I turned onto my street and was struck by the sight of a small group of people and the lights of three police cars. I immediately thought of Mr. Gold, the pleasant, ninetysomething-year-old man who lived two houses from mine, alone, except for a part-time caregiver. I hoped he hadn't had a medical emergency, or worse. I slowed down, not sure how far I could get on the street. I saw no ambulance, a good sign.

Not as good as I thought, it turned out.

I drove far enough to see that my front door was wide open.

Old Mr. Gold stood on the sidewalk, upright and healthy as ever. I spotted Ariana among a group of my neighbors, all seeming in good health also. And, walking away from the group were four people who looked like Henley College students.

Was that Chelsea Derbin? It was almost too dark for me to be sure. Did I see Daryl Farmer? A third student looked familiar, also, but I couldn't place him. The fourth was unidentifiable also, until he passed directly in front of a small lamppost on my neighbor's lawn. From a quick glance when he looked back over his shoulder I was almost sure he was the unkempt young man I'd seen with Martin near the library yesterday.

There were three or four others, running ahead. There was no hope of identifying them.

Why were these people on my street?

I was glad to see Ariana, but I knew she hadn't planned this welcoming committee.

My stomach clutched, the taste of salt and mustard returning to my mouth in a sickening way as I realized the significance of my open front door.

The hulking figure of Virgil Mitchell strode into the middle of my street and waved at me to back up and park across from my house.

Something definitely had happened in Henley while I was gone. And at my address.

The first few words from Virgil's mouth didn't compute. A break-in, he said, about an hour ago, and I might want to take a minute before entering the premises.

Mr. Gold, my alarm company, and Ariana, all seemed to have had a part in the drama at my little cottage while I'd been out playing detective. Within moments, they surrounded me.

Virgil let them tell their stories.

"I thought you and your boyfriend were away for the weekend," Mr. Gold said, clutching his thin sweater around his stooped body. "I was keeping an eye out and I saw this kid sneaking around. He went in the side door of your house, so I called your alarm company."

Mr. Gold seemed pleased with himself until a uniformed man spoke up. He was wearing a windbreaker with "STA" stitched across his chest. My alarm company representative and casual friend, Randy. "Next time, you should call the police directly," Randy told Mr. Gold.

Mr. Gold would not be reprimanded. He pointed to the wooden sign at the edge of my lawn. "Then why do you put your telephone number in big print there on the sign?"

Randy moved closer to Mr. Gold. "Listen, old man ..."

Before an unequal fight could break out, Ariana gave up the tight hug she had on me and chimed in, addressing me. "The alarm company tried to get you but couldn't reach you, Sophie."

"My battery's dead," I said, as if that were important.

"Then we tried Bruce," Randy said.

"But, of course, he's incommunicado, so next they called me," Ariana said. She hugged me again and patted my back. "I'm so glad you weren't home, Sophie. Can you imagine?"

I still didn't know the extent of the break-in and exactly what it was I should or should not imagine.

"So, finally, the alarm company called the police," Mr. Gold said.

"The alarm didn't trip till long after this guy called," Randy said to me, ignoring Mr. Gold.

"That alarm was ten minutes too late. The kid was already in there," Mr. Gold said. "You should fix your equipment. That's why I don't even bother with an alarm."

"We'll talk later, about your password and other matters," Randy said to me.

I knew my password was too simple, and I was sure the "other matters" had to do with my neighbors and my call list.

I'd been following the movements of the cops out of the corner of my eye. Virgil had gone off to talk to the most recent officers to exit my front door and then waved two of the three police cars away, thus giving the gathered crowd no reason to hang around. The remaining two officers escorted Mr. Gold to his home.

Mr. Gold turned and waved at me before the officers ushered him inside. I waved back and mouthed a thank you. I was sure I'd hear my neighbor's version of events as soon as I wanted to know.

Virgil came back to where Ariana was holding onto me and explained, as if to a trauma patient, why I couldn't go into my home yet. His "men," he said, needed one more pass before they were finished, another walk-through, looking for likely places to lift fingerprints or footprints, checking again for blood.

"Blood?" I asked, swallowing hard.

Virgil shrugged. No big deal. "Sometimes intruders injure themselves getting in or out because they're in unfamiliar territory."

"We can only hope," said Ariana, my pacifist friend.

I gave her my first smile since re-entering Henley.

With all the hoopla outside, I was ready for the worst inside. At first I was remarkably calm about the degree of upset that met me as I entered my home, Virgil by my side, Ariana trailing behind.

In the kitchen, the bottom cupboards around my center island were open, but only partially emptied of my oversize pots and bowls. Furniture in the den had been moved, but the computer and workstation in my office looked undisturbed. A pile of class folders was in place, weighted down by my calculus textbook.

"Let me know if you notice anything missing," Virgil repeated in each room. "Or something out of place."

I shook my head each time. "Nothing that I can tell."

"At times like this, it comes in handy that you keep such a neat place, so you can tell if something's been moved," Virgil said at one point along the route. "Most places I see, you'd never know. Including mine."

An awkwardly placed compliment, but I was grateful to Virgil for his solicitude.

It was funny what people settled for at times of stress—I was grateful that my tables hadn't been overturned, my drawers hadn't been flipped upside down, and my sofa cushions hadn't been slashed to bits, as I'd seen in movies.

The areas most in upheaval were the closets in my den, my office, and two bedrooms. All the closet doors had been left open and the contents laid on beds or chairs. In each case, the back wall of the closet was now exposed, as if the burglar were looking for a safe. Boxes on the top shelves were taken down and placed on the floor, uncovered but not tipped over. My lovely lavender dust ruffle had been folded up onto the bed the way I positioned it when I vacuumed.

The burglar might have been a friend, looking for a certain item, not wanting to disturb things in a drastic way.

I didn't keep cash in my house and my jewelry had more sentimental value than monetary worth. I'd read that in cases like that, the burglar would be angry and take out his frustration by vandalizing the property. Not this burglar. Lucky me.

Virgil, Ariana, and I stood in the middle of my bedroom. "He was looking for something specific," I said. It was much too slow in coming. "The bag of money."

"Hey, pretty good. We might have to give you a badge after all," Virgil said. He covered his comment with a slight cough. "Sorry, Sophie, I don't mean to be flip. I know this must be very upsetting."

I nodded.

"It's okay," I said, by way of forgiveness.

"The good news is, nine will get you ten they're not coming back," Virgil announced.

"How do you know that?" Ariana asked, eyes narrowed.

"They were careful undoing things. My guess is they had every intention of putting things back the way they found them, but Mr. Gold's call interrupted that plan."

Something about Virgil's version of the timeline didn't fit, but Ariana's comment interrupted my thought.

"Maybe they didn't finish looking," Ariana said. "They don't know the money's not here anymore."

"They've covered everything. They got to every room. Now, they might go after ..." He looked at me.

"Sophie? They're coming after Sophie?"

Ariana spoke on my behalf, which was good, because I became more and more disoriented and unable to process the words I was hearing and the reality in front of me. As the minutes ticked by and Virgil's voice came out of the fog, I finally grasped the picture—my clothes out of place, spots on the carpets, furniture pushed toward the middle of the rooms. My home had been invaded. Fingerprints seemed to glow from the surface of my dresser and bedside tables and enormous foot-prints appeared spread across my hardwood floors.

My initial reaction of "this isn't so bad" was replaced by fear and repulsion that someone might have sat on my chair or my bed. And I wasn't quite buying Virgil's cool reasoning about why they weren't coming back.

"You keep saying 'they,' Virgil. Didn't Mr. Gold say he saw only one kid?" my spokeswoman asked.

"I'm keeping an open mind."

"I don't understand the time sequence," I said, my logical mind kicking in again. "Mr. Gold didn't call the police when he saw the kid. And Randy didn't call you until about ten minutes later, according to Mr. Gold, when the alarm tripped. So what interrupted them? The police or the alarm? We know Mr. Gold didn't come running over here himself."

"Don't take this the wrong way, Sophie, but Mr. Gold—the only one of your neighbors who claims to have seen anything, by the way—is not the most reliable witness."

"He's very sharp for his age," I said. "He cooks for himself most of the time and he still drives short runs."

Virgil wasn't going to argue with my defense of my neighbor, though his eyebrows went up at the mention of a nonagenarian behind the wheel of a car for any length of time.

"Or, it could be that he saw just one of the kids, the others were ahead of him," Virgil said. "And, remember, a lot of time was lost because Mr. Gold called the alarm company instead of the police. Then, since STA didn't get a trip, they didn't treat it as an emergency."

"And STA called Sophie, then Bruce, then me," Ariana said, still processing the timeline. "Losing even more time."

"I think Randy was wrong not to take Mr. Gold seriously," I said, still speaking up for my neighbor. "And the question remains, why didn't the alarm go off at the same time that Mr. Gold saw the kid enter my house?"

"That's my point," Virgil said. "Which is why we have to weigh everything Mr. Gold said. Unless you've given out your password?"

I shook my head. "Just to Bruce and Ariana."

"Bottom line. We don't know how many intruders. Could be one kid, or ..." Virgil said.

"Or a whole gang could be coming back," Ariana said, causing me to utter a "No," that came out as an embarrassing whimper.

"They know the response would be much faster next time, Sophie," Virgil said. "You don't need to be afraid here." He spread his arms around the bedroom, and waved his hand toward the hallway and the other rooms.

"So, they'll be following me when I leave? Grab me on the street? That's comforting."

"My guess? They've already been following you."

"Oh, no," Ariana squealed in a voice higher in pitch than she'd ever reached in my presence.

Virgil didn't need two women on the edge. He looked at Ariana. "Can you give us a minute? I'm going to talk to Sophie in the kitchen."

"I guess. Sure."

Ariana let go of me, but not without a final squeeze. "I'll be in the den," she said.

For some reason, I was as reluctant as she was to part ways.

"Are you okay to talk for a few more minutes?" Virgil asked from a step or two in front of me. Walking abreast was out of the question since he took up nearly the width of the narrow hallway. "I'd like to hang around a little while anyway."

As far as I was concerned, Virgil never had to leave.

# Chapter 10

Virgil and I stepped into my country-blue kitchen, which now looked like the intruders had come back while we were at the other end of my house, upsetting things even more.

A new trick of my mind.

Virgil held a chair for me, indicating that I sit at the table opposite him. Three police interviews in one day. A new record. I sat on the very edge of the seat and kept my hands on my lap, as if I'd been taken unwillingly to a restaurant that had been found to have too many rat hairs and had been condemned by the Massachusetts Department of Public Health.

"Is there any reason for anyone to think you kept a lot of cash in your house?" Virgil asked.

I shook my head. "I never keep cash around." Except for Charlotte's, I amended mentally. "There are ATMs on every corner. There are even a couple on campus. And if these guys were following me, wouldn't it have been clear that I took Charlotte's duffel bag down to the station?"

"It doesn't mean you turned in all of it."

I started. "What?"

Virgil had no qualms about leaning his arms on my kitchen table, which, in my mind was disgustingly sticky, worse than a Bailey's Landing Shop At Ease. "I'm a crook," he said. "I'm somehow involved with the money in that bag, and I know you now have possession of what I think belongs to me. I follow you for a while. I watch you take it to the cops."

I was with him so far, though the part about a crook watching me wasn't sitting well with my turkey and Swiss.

"That's my point," I said. "You, the crooks, saw me take the money to the cops. Why wouldn't you hijack my car then, for example?"

"Were you alone when you drove to the station?"

"No, Ariana stayed with me overnight and we drove off together in the morning. But I don't see how Ariana was a threatening presence."

"Doesn't have to be a bodyguard with you. Any other person in the scene doubles the risk." He paused. "They're asking themselves, did she really turn in every dollar?"

"They thought I kept some of the money?"

Virgil shrugged. "It's what they would do in your circumstances. For all they know, you appropriated a chunk for yourself."

I blew out a breath. "Unbelievable."

"Did you?"

This time, I forgot about the contaminated table in front of me. I pushed myself up. "You're not serious."

"I have to ask, Sophie. Maybe Charlotte owed you some money and you figured, why not—"

"You really do think like a criminal," I said. "No, I did not keep one single dollar of that money. And if there had been coins in that bag, I wouldn't have kept one penny."

I almost asked Virgil if he'd grabbed a fistful of cash for himself when he took possession of the bag, but I caught myself. I knew him to have the highest standards of integrity. Apparently, the feeling was not mutual.

But he was the guy who was my best hope of safety and living for another day.

"Thank you for that 'no' so I can put it down like that," he said. "It will look a lot better on my report than, 'since Dr. Knowles is my good buddy's girlfriend, I didn't follow protocol.'"

I sat down. "Okay, I get it. I'm sorry. I'm a little frustrated. I'd feel a whole lot safer if you'd just tell me what you know. What you already knew before Charlotte was murdered."

"Let's go back to the money. Other than you may have held some back—in their minds, not mine—can you think of another reason they came looking for money? Did you tell anyone, or talk about it where someone could have overheard or misunderstood where it was?"

I thought of the people who'd contacted me in the last twenty-four hours. Daryl, Chelsea, and other students, all of them good and hard-working. Fran, my colleague and friend. Paula, annoying, but solicitous. It was an awful feeling, imagining the worst of people I trusted. I was angry anew at Charlotte, whom I held responsible for all that had gone wrong this weekend.

I had to consider Virgil's question. Had the word gotten out to my students and colleagues that I was in possession of a large bag of money? I couldn't imagine how. There was still the matter of what Daryl and the other students were doing at my own home crime scene when I arrived, but I hesitated to mention them to Virgil. I didn't want the police on their backs if they were genuinely trying to be helpful. Maybe they'd stayed around long enough for the officers on the scene to have gotten their names and the issue would be officially resolved without my input.

I reviewed my history with Charlotte's bag for Virgil, how she'd brought it to my office on Wednesday, how I'd let it sit in the corner where she dropped it, how Bruce picked it up.

There it was. Bruce had picked it up, along with my overnight bag. "It's about my own duffel bag," I said.

"Okay, what about it?"

"When we left campus that day—"

"Yesterday?"

I blew out a breath, as if I'd lived ten years in one day. "Yesterday. Bruce carried out my duffel bag as well as Charlotte's. I was using it as an overnight bag for our trip to Boston. Maybe they thought that one was full of money, too?"

A shiver ran up my spine as I pictured Bruce and me, walking toward his SUV and then to what we learned was a crime scene, all the while being watched by Charlotte's killer, now out to get us.

It would have been better if he, or they, had simply rushed us then and there, grabbed both duffels and run. In my hindsight version of events, I wouldn't even have filed a stolen property report.

Virgil tapped his fingers on the table where I imagined the intruder's greasy hands had been. I squeezed my palms shut on my lap.

"A definite possibility," he said, unaware of the more preferable scenario I'd created. "Where's that duffel now?"

"In my garage. Empty, except for travel items. I'll get it for you."

"No need."

But I had to. I couldn't stand even the tiniest loose end about whether I'd withheld money from Charlotte's duffel. It was silly to think that showing Virgil my duffel would remove me from suspicion, but I was on my way.

Virgil followed me to the garage.

To the corner where my red and gray duffel should have been.

I gasped. "It's gone."

"Well, what do you know," Virgil said.

"They stole my duffel?"

"They didn't know it was empty."

"Actually, they're now the proud owners of a host of, uh, travel-size feminine products."

"Serves them right," Virgil said.

"Good one."

Virgil's eyes landed on Bruce's wall of equipment. "Lot of expensive stuff there. And I see some empty hooks. I don't suppose you'd know if anything's missing from here?"

I nodded. "I can tell. What's missing is just what Bruce took with him. He has a list of things according to what kind of terrain he expects." I pointed to an ice ax with a three-foot handle. "Such as, this is what he uses like a walking stick for easy snow and ice. On this trip he took the short-handled axes, and that's why those hooks are empty. That means the ice is steep and hard. Or soft. Or medium. I forget."

Virgil laughed. "Who even knows what that means, right?"

I shrugged. I thought I'd take advantage of his good mood. "I take it you're not going to give me any more information about Charlotte's case, though I've been nothing but cooperative and honest with you."

"Really?"

I thought of my trip to Bailey's Landing and the sliver of information I had on a guy named Garrett, no last name, no physical description. I told myself if I had anything useful, I'd have shared it. I had to admit, also, that I was still trying to maintain some measure of control.

I prodded Virgil again. "It's obvious she was involved in lottery scams," I said. "What else? I read about others on those sheets you left me, but there aren't really details to speak of. What other kinds of scam did she pull? So I won't fall victim." That sounded lame even to my ears.

"The less you know the better, Sophie."

"So you say."

"I will tell you this, because it's kind of funny. You know that … uh … bunch of papers I left with you?"

For some reason, Virgil didn't want to admit to giving me an official "rap sheet." I let him off the hook.

"Uh-huh."

"You know the famous story of how Al Capone got away with murder and a few hundred other violent crimes, but what put him away was he got caught cheating on his taxes?"

"Uh-huh," again, though I couldn't imagine the connection.

"Your friend got a speeding ticket in a small town in Vermont."

"I remember that time. She was very upset."

"Yeah, well, she had reason to be. Some guys up there must have had nothing better to do, because someone recognized her license picture from a poster and checked her out. That's when we found out she'd moved here and changed her name. Never underestimate the power of a small town sheriff's department."

"I'll keep that in mind. Why was she on that poster in the first place? Was she on the run?"

At last, a chance to find out Charlotte's official status when she came to Henley.

But Virgil had divulged all he was willing to.

"I'm going to leave this form with you. Even if it's just trivial stuff in that duffel, write it down and report it. Same with anything else you realize has been taken. You never know if it will turn up somewhere and give us a lead."

I looked at the form, dreading the chore. I couldn't be sure whether I'd left conditioner as well as shampoo in the bag. Was there a small packet of shoe polish also, for Bruce, the fastidious shoe person? It was going to be tedious and I couldn't imagine any return, but I did want to cooperate.

"I see a URL here. Can I do it on line?"

"Sure, it'll get in the system even faster, if you know how."

I gave him a "You've got to be kidding look."

He grinned in a "Gotcha" way.

A very satisfying nonverbal communication.

"Now, let's find Ariana," Virgil said. "I'm going to put a car out here with a couple of guys, but you'll probably still want some company tonight."

Indeed I did.


It was tough to convince Ariana that I didn't want to leave my house.

"You haven't slept over at my place for ages," she said, implying that her invitation had nothing to do with my home invasion.

"I need to stay here or I'll feel like I've been driven out of my home and I'll never recover. Also, I need to clean up this mess."

"Clean? Why didn't you say so?" She pushed up the sleeves of her tie-dye jersey and marched to my broom closet, which had everything necessary for a deep cleaning, except a broom.

I should have remembered my friend's love of housework. She had some theory of the parallel cleansing of the soul. I thought of it as simply "Out, damned spot! out, I say!"

Together we pulled out every form of cleaner from the broom closet and from under all the sinks. We found carpet cleaner, bleach, foams, and sprays. We dug out soaps in the form of powders, liquids and tablets. We lined up mops, sponges, dust cloths, rags, and wet wipes.

Two hours passed as, hardly talking, we scrubbed places that probably hadn't been touched by the intruders, and certainly not by me in years, but I was taking no chances. Ariana, taller by several inches, went high, dusting and neatening items before returning them to the now-spotless top shelves of my closet. I went low and took care of every corner of every floor, dust mopping the hardwood, washing and waxing the linoleum, vacuuming the carpets. In the middle, we shared the furniture polish and wiped down every chair and table.

We washed all the bedding and any table linens and towels that had been exposed. We stopped short of washing everything in my closets. Ariana indulged me in checking each piece to determine if there was extra grime or lint, but convinced me it was unlikely the guy had gone through my pockets if he was looking for wads of cash, and it was impractical to run absolutely everything through the washer.

Exhausted, I was finally able to lean my elbows on my kitchen table and sip tea without feeling muck.

"Takeout?" Ariana asked, her head barely lifted from the tabletop.

"Pizza with the works," I said.

"Sushi," she said.

Two calls later we retreated to the den to wait for two deliveries, California sushi rolls, which I thought was funny in itself, for Ariana, and pizza with everything except anchovies for me.

"Tell me a paradox," Ariana said.

For years this was our version of "tell me a story." Tonight it was a thinly disguised way to distract me, now that my entire inventory of cleaning solutions had been depleted.

I was up for it. "What kind of paradox do you want? The kind that involves a contradiction? Like 'All Cretans are liars.' Maybe a rhetorical paradox, like Oscar Wilde's 'I can resist anything except temptation'?"

"Something more complicated."

"How about a philosophical paradox, like the chicken and the egg?"

"We've been through that one and I know it's the egg, but don't ask me to explain it. And I don't want to hear Zeno's, going halfway to the wall, then halfway again, and again always having halfway left, so he never gets there."

"Unless—?" I prodded.

"Unless you include the wall in the set, and then he gets there."

I pumped my fists in the air. "Excellent."

"It has to do with divergence," she added.

"Convergence," I said.

Ariana's face fell. "I should have quit while I was ahead."

"Here's one that might be new to you. The unexpected hanging paradox. A warden tells a prisoner that he will be executed next week but it will be a surprise. He won't know which day he'll be killed until they actually come for him."

"We did that a long time ago. The prisoner reasons that he won't be executed at all. First, it can't be on Friday because then on Thursday if he's still alive, he'll know he'll be killed on Friday, but then it won't be a surprise as the warden promised, so therefore—"

"You love saying 'therefore,' don't you?" I interrupted.

Ariana smiled. "I do love saying that. Therefore, he can't be killed on the Friday. The same applies to Thursday, which sort of becomes the last day, like Friday was, so it can't be Thursday either or he'll know on Wednesday, and so on and so forth, back through all the days, and so he can't be executed at all under those conditions."

Ariana's expert reasoning was accompanied by elegant arm waving and many different facial expressions, all expressing delight. It was clear that I needed to seek out some advanced puzzles for our next session.

*Buzzz.*

"Finally! Food," Ariana said and leapt off the couch.

There was no question that puzzles and reasoning exercises made the time go by more quickly.

How many puzzles would it take for the events of the weekend to fly out of my memory?

My mother would have called us two old maids. Having consumed our meals, tasting all the better for having been delivered, we sat in my den. Ariana, bent over the coffee table, worked on her latest beading project, a black evening purse with bling here and there, and a thin, beaded strap. I was comfortable across from her, with a book of puzzles and brainteasers, a pencil in my mouth, my face now and then screwed up in concentration, but not so rigidly as to exclude chatting. Like old maids, indeed.

As we worked, we talked out all our favorite topics, including frivolous gossip in the worlds of beading and higher education. I filled Ariana in on my trip to Bailey's Landing and my suspicion that one of the suspect names in Charlotte's duffel bag was staying with Martin Melrose.

"The guy with the thick glasses?" she asked, holding her thumbs and index fingers in front of her eyes.

"The same."

"I've met him at a couple of your faculty parties. Not that he's really there. He kind of slinks around and doesn't look you in the eye."

"That's Marty."

After running through several scenarios that had Marty as a scammer, then a victim, then a killer, all with no earthly evidence, we moved on to questions of love and romance. Did I think the age difference between her and Luke, eleven years younger, was too much? We ended with cosmology—Will we ever be able to detect dark matter, and if so, will it still be called dark matter?

We might have gone on like that for another couple of hours, except that Ariana sat up to stretch her back and in the process knocked over a tin of tiny beads.

Not one to curse, Ariana let out some kind of low-frequency mantra meant to soothe her as she got down on all fours to gather up her supplies. I joined her, but not until I finished writing in the last few numbers of a Sudoku puzzle.

"This is funny," she said, from under one end of the table. "What's this thing?"

I crawled around my newly cleaned carpet to her side to see what she was talking about. Under the table was a wide piece of masking tape holding a black object to the underside.

I tore the tape off and saw what she'd found.

A small black box, about four centimeters on each side and as thick as the stack of cards in my wallet. Two small wires came out from one end. I laid the assembly gently on the carpet under its original position.

I put my finger to my mouth to keep Ariana from exclaiming, which I could tell she was about to do.

"It's from a toy Bruce's nephew brought over. I'll save it for him," I said.

I hoped I was fooling whoever had planted a listening device in my den.

After a few deep breaths and a reminder to myself that the box was much too small to be a bomb, I took the device in my hands and studied it carefully.

Ariana, whose eyes by now were like the biggest bead in her collection, mouthed, "Is it a bug?"

I nodded. It wasn't hard to recognize, but I wished I knew its specifications. Was it voice activated? If it was transmitting, what was the range? It could be simply a recording device, in which case someone would be back for it.

A shiver wove its way around my body at the thought of a return visit from an uninvited guest.

I wished I'd paid more attention to the speaker at the computer science seminar last month. He'd been an expert on surveillance equipment and would have known in a minute what had been taped to my table. I thought of calling Daryl Farmer. Our new computer science program was said to have attracted the best and brightest from high schools all over New England. Maybe Daryl and his friends could take my bug as a project.

Ariana opened a drawer in my end table and pulled out a pad of paper and a marker.

"Listening now?" she wrote.

I shrugged and took the marker. "Maybe recording only," I wrote in answer. Then I wiggled the wires and wrote, "Maybe listening, too."

"Call Virgil?" she wrote.

I looked at my watch.

It was close to ten o'clock on a Saturday night. Any self-respecting adult, even a cop, would have a date. Though I doubted Virgil fit that pattern, I hesitated to bother him. I had his cell number but I knew he didn't text. How could I be sure the little bug in my den wouldn't pick up my voice even if I walked outside?

Another minute and I came to my senses. I'd had enough for one night of being a victim. I felt around the device for a battery cover, hoping I'd come to the universal ridges that identified a way in to the circuit. So what if the culprit who'd planted this figured out that I found it.

Bring him on.

A one-of-a-kind feeling for me.

Suddenly, before I could slide the cover and reach the battery, Ariana jumped up and down, unmitigated delight on her face.

"Cops on street," she wrote.

Of course, Virgil had put a car on my house for the night. A good thing, too, since my enthusiasm for being a heroine was fading fast.

I breathed out and uttered a nearly silent laugh. I hugged her and whispered a thank you.

We grabbed our jackets and headed out the door. I carried the electronic bug the way I'd seen Ariana carry a real, organic bug when she released it to the wild of her back yard, holding it in one palm, and supporting that palm with the other.

# Chapter 11

An hour later, Virgil and a man in jeans and a fleece-lined windbreaker stood on my welcome mat.

"I brought the expert," Virgil said, his usual deep voice more resonant at this late hour. He was still wearing his suit, but it bore traces of a nap. I wondered if cops even bothered to own pajamas. He scraped his shoes on the mat, as if he'd walked up a snowy driveway.

"You could have waited till morning," I said, addressing the new guy especially. He was young and I wouldn't have been surprised if he'd been at the high point of his date. He carried a box similar to a toolbox, but cleaner looking than any handyman's I'd ever seen.

"Zeke," he said, holding out his hand. "No problem."

"Don't worry. He gets double time," Virgil said, slapping Zeke on the top of his cap-covered head with his thick hand as they entered my house. I hoped they were friends.

We made our way to the kitchen island, where Ariana was ready with coffee and tea, pouring mugs for all of us.

Zeke got to work immediately, leaving his mug on the counter. He extracted a metal box from his case, with a familiar readout panel on the front. He also pulled out what looked like a screenless cell phone with two protrusions that were thicker than the wires on the bug we'd found. Next came headphones, which he wrapped around his neck, and a number of smaller devices that he stuck in his pockets.

"I wanted to be ready for anything," he said. "Though your bug wasn't very sophisticated. A mucho short-range RF transmitter with a recording function. Very low battery power. Your voice wouldn't register a signal from much more than about twenty-five meters away."

I did a quick calculation, my specialty. Twenty-five meters was about eighty feet, or the length of my house.

"Someone's twenty-five meters away, listening?" Ariana said.

Zeke shook his head. "No, the listeners are most likely pretty far away, out of sight. They'll call in from a phone and get a recording of what's been said. I can tell you more later, but right now I want to get to work."

With our okay, Zeke disappeared down the hallway with his tools.

"Zeke's going to sweep your place," Virgil said, missing the irony that Ariana and I had already swept in a different way for two hours. "We'll see if there's anything else here without your having to search high and low."

"Thanks," I said, with mixed feelings about the situation. Grateful that I had a friend where I needed one, sorry that I needed him this way.

Virgil, Ariana and I drank our beverages of choice and talked about things unrelated to the break-in, though it was the reason we were gathered at my kitchen counter when we should be asleep or having fun.

"Bruce should be down off the mountain by now," I said, refraining from whining that he should have called me by now.

"Or thousands of feet up, on ice, where no one ought to be," Virgil said.

"No argument there," Ariana said.

"Remember the time Bruce went to Wyoming?" Virgil asked.

"To climb at Grand Teton," I filled in. "That was before I met him, but I heard about it."

"He fell on some ice and slid fourteen hundred feet into a big rock," Virgil said, in case Ariana didn't know.

"You mean, like a quarter of a mile?" Ariana asked.

"Hard to imagine, isn't it?" Virgil said.

"He told me he broke eight ribs that time," I said.

"I didn't know we had that many ribs," Ariana said.

"Bruce and his partner were in a tough spot. It was too windy for a helicopter extraction. They did a self-rescue and hiked out. And that was one long recovery before he was back to normal," Virgil said.

"Normal meaning he went back as soon as he was healed and climbed a higher mountain, right?" I noted.

"Right," Virgil said. He laughed. "I'll never forget the time he told me how a certain route was very popular since the weather was so nasty that it was a real challenge getting up the mountain before getting snowed in."

Ariana shivered. "Like that's a good thing."

"Then there was that close call when he was at over fifteen thousand feet on the Pink Panther route. I think that was on Mount Foraker in Alaska, and—"

"No more accident talk, okay?"

I hadn't meant to sound so cranky. Even though the absent Bruce was a likely topic of conversation among his friends, and better than a murder case, I'd had enough disasterspeak.

Virgil showed me his palms. "You're right. Sorry, Sophie."

"Why would someone plant a bug in my house?" I asked.

"Oh, that's a happier topic." Ariana smiled and nudged me.

Virgil stepped in. "I'm assuming they're hoping you'll casually mention where you stashed the money you skimmed off the top of the duffel."

I gave Virgil a look, then relaxed when I saw his "gotcha" smile and realized he was teasing.

"What if we set a trap?" I asked.

"Brilliant," Ariana said. "Give them an address where the money is and then lie in wait for them."

Virgil wasn't as enthusiastic. "That's harder to pull off than you think. It's very seldom that the real guy will come to the pick-up. They're suspicious by nature. So you've cornered a dupe and the real guy leaves town. Or they come guns blazing and that's even worse."

I wanted to hear more, but Zeke was back.

"You're clean," Zeke said, packing up his equipment.

I pointed to the bug that had been under my unsuspecting coffee table. "Are they coming back for that?"

"Nah, they'll just call it from a phone, like I said, whenever, and when it comes up empty, they'll figure either it failed—it's a cheapie—or you found it. They know we can't trace it."

"Call it how? From a regular phone?" Ariana asked.

Zeke was happy to explain things. "You use an untraceable cell phone, with a preprogrammed number. You call the number and that switches the device they planted on, remotely."

"And some people laugh at remote sensing," said Ariana, who, on alternate days, was a devotee of all things paranormal.

"Yeah, you got it. Remote sensing is the thing these days," Zeke said.

Virgil and I looked at each other, not sure if either new-age Ariana or futuristic Zeke realized they were operating on two different planes with two different meanings of the word "remote."

Zeke picked up a hand-held device about the size of a Swiss army knife, with a ring of red lights at one end. "This little goodie? It's a scanner that can find hidden cameras."

"Did you use that here?" I asked. I'd never thought there might be a hidden camera in my house. We'd gone from bad to worse. I pushed each hand into the opposite sleeve. Hiding. Protecting myself.

"Yeah, I used it just now. I like to cover all bases," Zeke said. "You never know who you're dealing with. Amateurs? Pros? You have to be ready for anything." He cradled the camera with a look close to one of affection. "The nice thing about this baby? You can find a camera whether it's on or off, since it's an optical device. It's looking for a reflection from a lens. It used to be for government use only, but for the last couple of years it's been available to the general public."

What was happening when the general public would have a need for such a device? I didn't voice my pessimism about the state of the world out loud.

"I guess we're done here," Virgil said, carrying his mug to the sink.

"We are done," Zeke said. "If you have any questions, ladies, give me a buzz. Virge has my numbers."

"Thanks," didn't seem to cover it, for both Virgil and Zeke.

I hope they caught how grateful I was.

"No problem," Zeke said. "Have a good weekend."

We all smiled.

Unlike me, Ariana fell asleep easily, even after our overly eventful evening. We made up the guest room with linens fresh out of the dryer. When I stopped in a few minutes later to ask what time she needed to be up, she'd already left for her own private dreamland.

I envied her. I was a bad sleeper, unable to let go until there was absolutely nothing left for me to think about. Unfortunately, tonight there was a long, distracting list of things on my mind, and nothing as entertaining as the last clue in a puzzle that was due to one of my magazine editors.

I looked out the window near the front door several times at the unmarked beige sedan that was my supplemental security for the night.

Once Ariana and I ran out, taking the bug to the officers, their cover was blown, they informed us. As if the most boring car on the street, with a man and a woman in the front seat with a box of donuts, hardly talking, didn't give it away in the first place. I added to the obviousness of the setup by taking them coffee and snacks a couple of times. If a burglar was lurking about my house, it was just as well he knew he wouldn't have an easy job of it.

I changed into my oldest sweats and a robe and settled in my den to read a few chapters of the new biography of abstract algebra pioneer Emmy Noether. The equations were too interesting to work as a sleep-inducer. I had the same results with twisting the pieces of metal that made up a puzzle my eager friend Paula Rogers had given me for "no special occasion." Working the puzzle reminded me that sooner or later I'd have to either bite the bullet and give her a chance as a friend, or gently tell her I was booked for the rest of my life.

I went to my computer and found myself sitting in an office that was cleaner than it had been since I moved in to take care of my ailing mother six years ago. My home page came up with links to The New York Times, local and national weather, my calendar, a list of movies opening this week, and a riddle of the day.

The riddle, which grew in difficulty through the week, was easy since it was now Sunday.

*A cowboy rides into town on Friday and leaves three days later on Friday. How is this possible?*

"His horse's name is Friday," I said to the empty room, wishing Bruce were here to appreciate it.

One thing on my newest to-do list was to fill out that stolen property report. I entered the URL from the form Virgil gave me and filled in the basics, name, address, approximate time of break-in. When it came to writing down what had been taken, I nearly backed out of the task again. Did I really want to reveal what kind of feminine products I used? Or make a claim for an old pair of white crew socks? My travel toothbrush and my pocket sewing kit? The clock on my computer jogged my memory about an item that was less frivolous—I'd left my travel alarm clock in the duffel, a too-pricey accessory that Bruce had given me with an inscription about traveling together. It was high end for its kind, but not as valuable as, say, a diamond ring, which I could never see myself wearing.

I moved on to my email, a low-key activity that might bore me to sleep.

I ran through notes from students, asking for extensions on next week's statistics problem sets or wondering how many pages their research papers had to be. "Long enough to cover the topic," never worked as a response. I'd finally learned to give them a word count for the paper. With the advent of word processors, if I asked for ten pages, I was likely to get a manuscript with three-inch margins and fourteen-point font from some, and single-spaced, tiny font from others, depending on how much content they had to begin with.

Hannah Stephens, Charlotte's assistant and the student who'd discovered her body, wrote again to ask to talk to me. I decided there was no reason to punish Hannah for the sins of her boss and agreed to meet her some time on Sunday. I figured she wasn't sitting at her computer at one o'clock on Sunday morning and expected the date wouldn't be confirmed until a more reasonable hour in the day.

I had e-mails from fellow teachers with agenda items for the next faculty meeting. Who was going to take charge of the evaluation of our first year as a coed institution? Fran Emerson wanted to know how much money I thought our department could afford to contribute to the recruiting effort for the incoming class. It was a trick question. As past Mathematics Department chairwoman, she had a good idea of our budget and a strong opinion on how much we should offer.

"Nothing, unless they agree to put in photographs of our students, and not just the arts majors," she'd advised.

The English Department chairman, now president of the Faculty Senate, was looking for volunteers to replace him. Two members of the History Department faculty wanted to revisit the question of required humanities courses. My two cents on that topic: we should be considering requiring everyone to take at least introductory calculus. I wrote a response about how little science and math our arts students graduated with, as opposed to how many arts courses my majors needed. I ended up deleting without sending. A good move.

Too many of the e-mails were variations of, What are we doing for a memorial for our dear Charlotte Crocker?

I remembered that I was supposed to be working on Charlotte's service, but I had no heart for it. At this point, I was the last one who should give a eulogy. I had no idea if other faculty knew of Charlotte's past but I had a strong feeling that Martin Melrose was aware of it. Maybe I was the last to know.

What else could I do to lull myself to sleep? Shopping might work. Both paper and online catalogs had been pouring in since Labor Day with reminders of how few shopping days were left till Christmas. I'd already ordered a beautiful framed print of Stonehenge for Ariana, which I knew she'd love, but I hadn't done much else. I browsed through sites with food and candy and chose a couple of baskets for college friends with whom I still kept in touch. It was nice to do something practical.

The satisfied feeling didn't last long.

*Geerogherr. Geerogherr. Geerogherr.*

A noise invaded my space.

A car noise that I'd learned to recognize as brakes grinding to a halt, right outside my house. Followed by car doors closing. One car? Two?

I checked the time on my computer screen. One twenty AM. This wasn't the first time I'd been working here at this hour, nor the first time I'd heard late-night car noises on my street, especially on the weekend. But now my insides pinged and my ears perked up. Despite Virgil's assurances to the contrary, my first thought was that the intruders had come back for me.

I went to the front window and cracked the blinds slightly.

The two uniformed officers were standing on the sidewalk addressing two people. From their stances, I could tell no guns were drawn. Okay, so far. I hoped that in their zeal to protect me, the cops weren't harassing my neighbors.

I opened the blinds farther and recognized the visitors. Daryl Farmer, with his hand on his hip, his blond hair catching the rays from the officers' flashlights, and Chelsea Derbin, wrapped to her chin in fleece, as usual these days. What were they doing here? A strange way to end a date.

I shrugged off my robe, grabbed a corduroy jacket from the coat closet, and threw it over my sweatshirt. Without a further thought, I went out to join the group.

As soon as my motion sensor light switched on, three feet from my front door, one of the officers, a young woman, hustled up the driveway to meet me.

"It's okay. They're my students," I said.

"We haven't determined their business," she said, putting her thick body between me and the new arrivals. "Please go back inside, Dr. Knowles."

"But—"

The next "Please, Dr. Knowles," was accompanied by a gentle but unmistakable shove toward my front door.

I recognized she had a job to do. I complied by returning to my hallway window. I raised the blinds all the way. Surely that was allowed.

The two officers and my two students engaged in conversation for another ten minutes, during which one of the officers took notes.

As soon as Daryl and Chelsea were allowed to leave, I called the number I had for the unmarked police car.

"What was that all about?" I asked.

"No worries, Dr. Knowles," said a female voice. "Apparently a couple of your students heard about the break-in yesterday and wanted to be sure you were okay. Typical, huh? Don't they ever sleep, these college students?"

"Did you by any chance ask them if they were here earlier, right after the break-in?"

"Uh, no we didn't."

I guessed I'd have made a better detective than either of my uniformed, armed protectors.

Back in my office, I tried to work on a new puzzle to send to one of my monthly magazines. Maybe I could get ahead of a deadline for once.

That was one failed plan.

Next I logged onto a library site to research a section of a paper I was preparing for submission to a statistics journal. That didn't work, either.

I found myself distracted by the appearance of Daryl and Chelsea at my home, twice, on both the day and the night of the break-in. Of the two, Chelsea was the weaker link. She'd grown up in Nebraska, the daughter of the pastor in a town with a population accommodated by four digits.

I'd met Chelsea's parents during her freshman orientation.

"Don't be surprised if they start writing you notes, asking you to look after me," Chelsea had said, and she'd been right.

It always took clever strategizing to get the parents of the incoming class to leave their darlings to the care of the college, but Reverend and Mrs. Derbin had gone beyond clinging. They'd talked their way into events specifically marked "for students only" on the program. They'd insisted on sitting with their only daughter instead of on the designated parents' side of the gym for President Aldridge's official welcome. From comments they made about Chelsea's roommate that year, I was sure they'd had her fully vetted.

Chelsea had seemed embarrassed then, but docile.

Someone who was easy to take advantage of.

Which I was about to do.

I dialed Chelsea's number from my call log. I hardly gave a thought to what I might be interrupting.

"Hey, Dr. Knowles."

"Am I catching you at a bad time, Chelsea?"

"No, I just got in."

"Daryl dropped you off?"

"Uh, yes."

"I'm curious about what you and Daryl were doing at my home, let's see, what was it? About a half hour ago?"

"Oh, well, uh, we heard about the break-in and we wanted to see if everything was okay."

"You were planning to knock on my door and ask me?"

"Yes. No." A breath." I don't know. I'm sorry if we bothered you."

I could hear the growing tightness in Chelsea's voice and felt slightly guilty at how pleased I was that my strong-arm technique was working.

"No bother, Chelsea. I was just curious."

"Oh, okay."

Feel her relax, then move in again.

"What were you doing in the crowd earlier in the evening, when the break-in happened?"

A small gasp, followed by a throat clearing. I waited.

"Earlier?" she finally asked.

"Yes, when the emergency vehicles were still here?"

"Oh, you mean earlier?"

"Yes, Chelsea, I mean earlier. Immediately after the break-in."

I heard a heavy sigh. "Dr. Knowles, I should probably talk to you, like, in person."

A breakthrough at last.

After making a date to meet Chelsea at the Mortarboard Café, the campus coffee shop at noon, I returned to my computer, re-energized. Not necessarily a good thing when what I needed was a few hours sleep.

A new thought occurred to me. It was clear from the bag of cash and the "fraud" reported on Charlotte's rap sheet that she'd been an expert in scamming people. I sensed that Virgil wasn't about to clue me in on the particulars of Charlotte's crimes, but I could certainly find out in general on my own what such scams might involve.

In other words, just how hard was it to be as sleazy as my friend?

Once again I thanked that defense agency crew who had invented the Internet. I hoped the FBI and the Department of Homeland Security weren't watching and collecting data on my browser history, because I was about to learn all I could about scams.

The first hit gave me a step-by-step guide on how to avoid scams, which, of course, worked just as well as a blueprint for pulling one off. Much like building a bomb, or poisoning someone. The Internet was the new personal life coach for people who didn't have a life.

If I wanted to scam people, as Charlotte apparently did, I'd first need a database of victims. Anyone who's ever entered a contest or answered a sweepstakes ad for a free TV or a week's vacation was vulnerable. Scammers mined names, email addresses, and physical addresses from dating sites, Internet chat rooms, game sites, call centers, and social networking sites. I felt like unplugging my computer then and there, but even a check sent through regular mail could be intercepted and my information co-opted.

Some of the warnings against lottery scams in particular seemed pitifully obvious and I wondered who needed them. "If you did not buy a lottery ticket, you cannot win the lottery," I read. I couldn't believe this was news to someone. Another piece of advice pointed out that "If it seems too good to be true that money is on the way, it is!"

Once the scammers had pegged a victim, they'd send a letter or email with fake letterhead informing him that in order to collect his winnings, he'd have to pay taxes on the amount. They'd ask for a small percentage of the alleged millions of dollars the victim won to be released to them, the "official" lottery notifiers. I thought of the small bills in Charlotte's duffel and wondered if the twenties were hard-earned wages from unsuspecting workers.

I thought no one could be so gullible as to send money on the anonymous promise of receiving more money. But Virgil had verified that there were too many cases of people who fell for this and other mail scams, like one I got recently, offering me a large sum of money I'd supposedly inherited, for just the cost of certain bank fees and handling.

I'd started out looking for general information on scams to help me understand what Charlotte and her crew had done, and ended up making a list of things I could do to avoid being scammed myself in other ways. It pained me to think I might have to freeze my credit and hold back from conveniences like putting outgoing mail in my own mailbox to be picked up.

At the bottom of the screen was a number to call the Secret Service if you suspected you'd been a victim of a scam.

But what if the scam site was itself a scam?

I latched onto the paradoxical nature of my question, which sent me in the direction of the village with the barber who shaves only those who don't shave themselves. Who shaves the barber?

Finally, I was ready to sleep.

# Chapter 12

I woke up to what seemed like an ordinary morning. It wasn't unheard of that Ariana would stay overnight now and then. The last time had been a month ago when her house was being tented for termites. The time before that we'd decided we needed a slumber party with popcorn and our favorite period movies, the one category Bruce eschewed. We'd never had armed security right outside before tonight, but no one said life would be normal all the time.

This morning Ariana was at the breakfast table with an assortment of food, reading the newspaper. She was already dressed in one of the tops she kept at my house. Today's was a rainbow-hued tunic that she wore over black tights. I'd chosen a daring combination of black jeans and a navy jersey.

Ariana scanned my outfit with a questioning look.

"I'm going to meet one of my students on campus around noon," I said, by way of excuse for the business casual outfit, though really it was my mood that kept me from adding the funky layers that I favored.

"Poached eggs? French toast? Blueberry pancakes?" she asked, a brightness in her voice that could be irritating if you didn't know that it was natural for her.

"You know I don't eat until I've been up a while. And where did you find blueberries?" Sophie the Ungrateful couldn't seem to help herself.

Bruce knew enough not to be too cheery or energetic around me in the morning, but Ariana had a hard time with the concept of low key.

Undaunted by my ugly mood, my houseguest hummed a

tune while she poured coffee for me. I recognized the drinking song from "La Traviata." I had to smile and let the music and the rich aroma from my French press work its magic.

"I can always hope." She pushed a plate of pastries in front of me.

I turned my head away. No solid food yet. "You've been out grocery shopping already?"

"Uh-huh. Thus, the blueberries, also. I slept really well. No bugs in the house. Two buff young cops outside."

"Still? And isn't one of them a female?"

"It's a new pair. Both guys. I brought them breakfast."

"I think that defeats the purpose of 'unmarked'."

Ariana shrugged. "They seemed grateful."

"Unlike me. I get it."

"And I might meet up with one of them later. The dark one. He's interested in seeing my shop."

"I'll bet he is."

To show my gratitude I gave in and picked a cinnamon roll from the plate. I broke off a corner and dunked it into my coffee. Maybe there was something to this idea of eating as soon as you got up. I rifled through the Sunday paper for the puzzle section. Today's contribution was a variation of the classic tree riddle. I read a couple out loud, hoping to stump Ariana.

"Which tree is least selfish?"

"The yew."

"Which tree is the dandiest?"

"The spruce."

"We've done this riddle before, haven't we?"

She nodded. "They're peachy."

"You're good," I said.

I picked up the main section of the newspaper and scanned the front page. I should have stayed with the benign puzzle page. A small piece at the bottom announced, "Henley College Murder Victim."

There went the normal morning. I remembered that our president had asked me to deal with the media and wondered if she'd intended that I initiate contact or just wait until they contacted me. Just wait, I decided easily.

Not that I'd forgotten that my friend had been killed, that she was really not the friend I thought she was, that my house had been broken into and bugged, and that a couple of my best students and an esteemed member of Henley's administration might be involved in all of it.

I read the notice quickly. There was no mention of anything but the "beloved librarian at Henley College" who was "very brutally murdered" on Friday afternoon while at work on campus. No mug shot or akas, no sample page from her long rap sheet. No further comment from the investigators who were "working diligently to find her killer."

I turned away from the article and caught the weather at the top of the page by the banner. "Severe Winter Storm. Blizzard Headed for New Hampshire."

"Severe? A blizzard?" I said, hardly able to believe something else could go wrong this weekend.

"I read that whole weather piece. It's not a problem. The storm is headed for the New Hampshire-Vermont border," Ariana said.

"Bruce is in Franconia Notch. That's practically on the border."

"I'm sure it's okay," Ariana said, without giving any data to support her claim.

I'd never broken our agreement. I needed to trust that Bruce would initiate a call when he could, if he had reception when he was on the mountain, or once he was safely off. He'd never said it in so many words, but I got the picture that if he wasn't in contact, he was hanging by a thread, leaning backwards from a straight up and down icy face and couldn't spare an iota of attention for a phone call.

That's how it usually worked.

But this was no usual day.

I grabbed my cell phone from the counter and pushed the icon for Bruce.

No answer. I tried three more times, so close together that I got a busy signal once.

I put my elbows on the table and my head in the cradle they made.

Ariana came up behind me and rubbed my neck and shoulders. "This whole weekend has got you all disoriented, Sophie. I knew I should have brought my massage table and lotion case. I do have some oils with me, though. There's a new sweet almond concoction I've been wanting to try. How about it?"

"Not right now." I didn't want to be soothed until I had more information, preferably from my boyfriend himself.

"You have to remember, dear, Bruce is used to all kinds of weather," she said, maintaining a steady rhythm on my shoulders and back, matching the cadence with her words. "He's an ice climber. It always snows this time of year. That's why he goes there."

I sat up. "I know that. But it's one thing to climb an icy mountain before an incoming storm, and an entirely different thing to actually be on the mountain during the storm. Who knows what point they reached before the blizzard hit? What if they didn't have any place to retreat to? No ledges or caves? They may not even be able to hear or see each other. Remember when that friend of Bruce's was visiting and told us how he was caught in a storm and couldn't communicate with anyone for nine days? He barely made it out alive. He almost starved. He had hypothermia and I forget what else."

"I think he was trying to impress us," Ariana said, pushing my upper body into position for further massaging.

"He was definitely trying to impress you, but that doesn't mean he was exaggerating."

"Anyway, that was more than ten years ago. Things were different. It wouldn't happen now, with all the cell towers there are. I read that there's hardly any place to be alone anymore."

"Then why can't I reach Bruce? By now the three of them should be having breakfast in a warm coffee shop or driving home already. Why hasn't he called back? He knows I'd worry about the storm and if he could, he'd call."

"Sophie, you know how little to trust a weather report in the newspaper. It's old, for one thing. Weather changes by the minute."

"You're right. I should look on line at the climbing sites."

"That's not what I meant," Ariana said, but I barely heard her as I made a dash for my computer.

My desktop computer was overloaded with bookmarks for puzzle pages, so Bruce had set up some of his favorite climbing sites on my laptop. I carried it to the den, which might not have been the best move, given the framed photograph that dominated one wall.

A poster-size rendition of Bruce on his favorite ice-climbing trip to Washington State. Not that you could tell it was Bruce, just a body in red, smack up against a vertical wall of sheer ice that looked like a waterfall had frozen in place and dared anyone to scale it.

The figure I knew to be my boyfriend was the only body in the photo, though the long rope coming from his harness told me someone was below him with a belay device. In each hand was an ice ax, one with a hammer on its head, the other an adze. The pick ends of both were stuck in the ice, as were both of Bruce's feet, thanks to the sharp metal spikes protruding from his crampons. The effect was of a four-legged creature making its way up the iciest, steepest cliff on the planet.

I turned my head away and logged in to one of Bruce's bookmarked URLs.

Unlike my pages of math games and brainteasers, Bruce's sites came with a warning. A sort of "don't try this at home" for casual visitors. A message at the top center of this site read:

*Participation in ice climbing involves significant risk of personal injury and death. No amount of skill, equipment, and experience can make ice climbing safe.*

No kidding.

I took a breath and clicked on a live webcam. Things looked surprisingly calm in the White Mountains. I was relieved until I noted that the camera was facing the mountains, not on it. The peaks were off in the distance. I peered at them, moving my face closer and closer to the screen, as if I'd spot Bruce and his buddies if I looked hard enough. The whole upper half of the image was white. Bruce's vacationland of choice was shrouded in fast moving clouds and blowing snow.

Thumbnail sketches showed webcam images of more than thirty other New Hampshire sites. Lakes, rivers, parks, and significant peaks. Why couldn't my boyfriend be cruising around the calm waters of Lake Winnipesaukee right now, or skiing on Loon Mountain, which looked civilized, with patches of grass and a handsome lodge?

I turned my laptop toward Ariana, who had joined me in the den and sat beading next to me.

"Look at this lovely area in Dixville Notch," I said. "Why didn't I fall in love with a simple skier?"

"Heavy," Ariana said.

I figured she meant the concept of falling in love and not the beading needle perched between her lips.

Bruce and I had had "the heavy conversation" more than once. I knew from the first day I met him what his passions were and, while "take it or leave it" sounded cold, it made sense to the two logical people we were. I guessed I'd been lucky that this was the first time my logic and commitment were being put to the test.

Clear-headedness and understanding were one thing in theory, another in practice.

I went back to my search.

It was harder than I thought to find information on the weather, hidden by ads, special offers, and promotional material.

I inadvertently downloaded an ad for two sizes of ice screws, and another one for helmets, followed by the writer's hot picks for ropes and harnesses. I learned that New Hampshire was the best place in the country for ice climbing, that is, according to New Hampshire itself. Mount Washington boasted the highest point in the northeast at more than six thousand feet. And so on, with praise for the terrain, multi-pitch ice, and alpine climbs.

I shared all this with Ariana, who kept on beading. A pair of blue crystal earrings on silver wire was taking shape. At least one of us would have something to show for the morning.

"I'm just trying to find out if people who climbed the mountain yesterday are safe today," I said. "I'm going to see if there's a ranger station I can contact."

"You know he hates that," Ariana said.

"Tough."

*Whirrrr. Whirrrr. Whirrrr.*

I picked up my cell phone before a second round of whirring could begin. Not Bruce, but another man I wanted to talk to.

"Hey, Martin," I said. I came close to calling him Marty, but he would have known something funny was up.

"Sophie. I didn't want to disturb you on a Sunday, but I see you've tried to get me. I've been so stunned about what happened to Charlotte."

"I still can't get over it all," I said. He could decide for himself how many levels that sentiment applied to.

"It makes you think, doesn't it? You can't get too complacent and assume you're safe from violence, even at a place like Henley," he said.

"How true."

"I tell my staff all the time, to lock themselves in if they're staying late. It's foolish to leave yourself at the mercy of anyone who can walk in off the street."

"Of course." I got why Martin would like to think the bad guy was a townie, not a member of the Henley community. So would I.

"So is there anything special you wanted?" he asked.

I could have sworn our Director of Finance's voice held a bit of concern that wasn't due to a murder on campus. It was unusual for anyone in the administration to return a call on a Sunday. Had Warren, my new friend at the Bailey's Landing Shop at Ease, called Martin's number to warn Garrett that a short, thin, lady was on his tail? I smiled. That would scare him.

Now that I had Martin on the phone, I stumbled over what to say. "Did you have a reason to murder Charlotte?" would have been a good start, but I didn't have the nerve to ask.

I came up with a diversion. "Olivia asked me to put together a memorial for Charlotte. You knew her pretty well, from that special lottery group, didn't you?"

"I was one member of a group who pooled our money for that one activity, yes."

"You were a member? Not anymore?"

"It's a long story."

I bet it was, so to speak. "I thought you might want to participate in the service."

"Oh, sure, sure. As I say, I didn't know her all that well, but sure. I'll be glad to contribute. What did you have in mind? Are you taking donations for flowers?"

Not that easy.

"I'm looking for help with the program itself. Some readings. Music. A eulogy."

"Oh … uh … I may not be your man for that. I—"

"It's hard to talk over the phone, Martin, and also I'm trying to keep the line open for Bruce. He's on a mountain in New Hampshire right now."

"One of his climbing excursions? I hear it's snowing pretty heavy up there. That's a good thing, right?"

"So they tell me. Are you free for a quick meeting tomorrow? I can show you what I have so far."

Which was nothing, but it didn't matter since I had other things in mind for Marty.

"My schedule is pretty tight. Eight to five with an hour for lunch. Not like you professor types with hours of free time between classes."

Martin laughed, but I knew most non-teachers, even college administrators, really believed that teachers magically appeared, prepared for each class, with no work in between. Now was not the time to ask how much prep work he did for every hour of work he put in at his office.

"Let's use the lunch hour, then. In or out?" I asked.

I heard a resigned sigh. I was proud of myself for sticking it out and getting Marty to agree to a meet. "I usually brown-bag it. Does that work for you? Noon, my office?"

"See you then. Oh, one more thing," I said. "Do you think Garrett would like to be part of it?"

Silence.

"The service for Charlotte. Do you think Garrett would like to be part of it?" In case you didn't hear me the first time.

I was now much too pleased with myself. I pictured Marty at home, but neatly dressed, maybe with a cashmere sweater instead of pinstripes, perspiring under his button down, wondering how I knew about the guy crashing on his couch.

"I think we need to talk," Marty finally said.

My thoughts exactly. "Oh?" I said.

"It's not what you think."

"And what would that be?"

"I'll see you tomorrow," he said, and hung up.

Ariana, who'd been paying close attention, high-fived me. "Nice going."

"Not too Columbo?" I asked.

"No such thing. But what was that about a memorial service? I didn't know you'd been working on something for Charlotte."

"I haven't."

"Then you'd better get busy."

"Do you know any hymns and prayers?"

Oops. As soon as I asked, I knew I was in for it.

"You've come to the right place," Ariana said, and sang an eastern-sounding tune while doing a kind of snake dance in my den. I caught a phrase or two. Golden pathways. Chain of memories. I could almost smell the incense.

What had I gotten myself into?

Whatever else came of Ariana's performance, the moments of laughter it brought both of us were worth it.

Ariana and I set out before noon, heading in opposite directions. She was on her way home in her yellow hybrid; I drove my smokestone Fusion toward the campus to meet Chelsea in the coffee shop.

I'd let Ariana think she'd convinced me to stop worrying about Bruce, otherwise she wouldn't have left me alone. There was only so much new age dancing and chanting I could take at one time. Bruce would call when he could, Ariana reminded me over and over. He was probably having the time of his life. She was willing to bet on it. The more challenging the conditions the better, and he'd come home completely safe and refreshed.

I wanted to believe she was right.

As if to emphasize the importance of weather everywhere today, rain poured down on the lowlands of Henley. The sound of my windshield wipers, usually background noise that didn't affect me at all, now seemed like labored breathing. Bruce's breathing as he trekked through a storm.

I'd almost forgotten that Eduardo, more experienced than Bruce, was with him, and that was a plus. But the third member of the team, Kevin, a relative newbie, was a minus, who might get himself in trouble if the weather panicked him. I punched the Bluetooth device on my visor and dialed Bruce's cell. Nothing.

I remembered that I had Eduardo's wife's number in my address book. No harm in calling a fellow stay-at-home to say, hey. So what if I'd never met her.

No answer from Jenna, either. I didn't leave a message, though I feared caller ID would tag me as a clingy, worry wart girlfriend.

One more thought brought me some consolation. Both Eduardo and Kevin were flight nurses at MAstar. Eduardo had been an ER nurse for many years before his air rescue career, and Kevin had just returned from duty at an American medical station in the Gulf.

That counted for something, and brought me a few minutes of peace.

I tuned to a classical music station, the music my parents loved. If it didn't put me to sleep, it would calm me down. According to my mother, my mathematician father was a great musician and could have been a professional pianist. "Music and math go together," she'd say. "I can't do either."

I fell somewhere in between, good at math, but talentless in music.

Thinking of my parents and listening to their music relaxed me as I drove through the rainy streets of the town of Henley. I took comfort in familiar melodies and the routine of Sunday shoppers on its one main street.

I headed for the Henley College campus for the first time since it had been a crime scene.

# Chapter 13

I arrived on campus shortly after noon and parked in the lot next to the dormant, rain-soaked tennis courts. The Henley campus was beautiful, even in a downpour, when the old red brick buildings took on the look of sentinels guarding the pathways and lawns.

I made a point to look east, away from the library. I pulled my cell phone out of my spare charger and checked the battery capacity—fully charged, waiting for a call. The one time I'd been caught without a charged cell phone, my home was broken into. If I were a superstitious type, instead of a mathematician, I'd have resolved to never let that happen again.

I made a dash to my meeting place with Chelsea, only a few steps away, and entered one of the oldest buildings on campus.

The combination bookstore, to the left, and coffee shop, to the right, was brick inside and out. The wooden bookshelves and tables that filled each retail establishment had probably been there since the Ice Age.

Funny I should be thinking of ice.

The music seemed just as old, with elevator versions of sixties tunes. The Rolling Stones's "Jumpin' Jack Flash" put into a blender and turned into a smoothie. And there was no question about how old the odors were. Grease and onions from the Pythagorean era, I guessed.

Who had chosen this venue for our meeting, instead of an upscale downtown cafe? I had, I realized with dismay.

I stomped my way through the lobby, shivering from the chill and shaking water from my shoes, jacket, and purse. A right turn took me into the Mortarboard Café where the smells originated and where a student with disheveled hair was wiping down the counter.

"Nasty out there, huh, Dr. Knowles?" I regretted that I didn't know his name, too, but he kindly bailed me out. "Nick," he said. "Freshman, of course. Aren't we all? The Henley guys, I mean. I'm taking biology this term." He waved his stained white rag in the direction of Ben Franklin Hall. "Love those Friday parties you put on in your building."

If I were in a better mood, I'd have enjoyed a joke about my owning the building, started a chat about Mobius and his surfaces, asked Nick if he had any ideas or special requests for scientists or inventors he'd like to see honored, inquired about what he might choose for his major. I was known as a student-friendly professor. When I was in a good mood.

But "Nice to meet you, Nick," was all I could drum up today. "Can I get a coffee?" I asked, walking away from the counter, to the area with table service. "I'm going to take a seat and wait for someone I'm meeting."

"Sure thing, Dr. Knowles."

I wished he wouldn't keep calling me by name—it brought out the fact that I hadn't known his and that I should be more accessible and engaging. The way the Henley College brochures and website promised, with its fifteen-to-one student-faculty ratio. It was hard to be anonymous on a small campus.

"Thanks," I said when he brought the coffee without a word. Sorry to say, Nick had gotten my unfriendly message.

I wrapped my fingers around the warm ceramic mug, which is the only reason I ordered the drink. I had no intention of ingesting coffee from the Mortarboard Café, where the students called the drink "mortar," like the lime-based bonding cement used in bricklaying. The times I met students here I stuck with a cold drink from the dispenser and a bag of chips.

I got past the shivery stage, settled at an interior table in the otherwise empty shop to wait for Chelsea.

I was on my way to completing the solution to a puzzle, a four-by-four grid with A, B, C, D along the vertical, and the numbers from one to four across the top. Clues were in the form, D1 is C3 divided by A2, and so on. What would I do without busy work?

With the rain pounding on the window, the too-loud music, and my concentration on the puzzle, I didn't hear Chelsea arrive. She'd pulled the chair out quietly, either not to disturb me or because she was hesitant to talk to me at all. She had taken the waif look to the max with a huge gray muffler and an oversize sweater that was probably Daryl's. Only the tips of her fingers were visible between her chin and her knees.

"Hey, Dr. Knowles," she said, barely above a whisper, sitting on the edge of the chair.

"Hey," I said, with a smile I hoped made her comfortable. "I'm glad you came."

Nick appeared, with his hair combed, I noticed. "Lunch for you lovely ladies?" he asked mostly Chelsea.

I thought we'd better order. I wanted Chelsea well-nourished while I quizzed her for the next hour.

I gave Nick a smile, also. He returned it tentatively. "I'll have a grilled cheese and a diet cola," I said, playing it safe.

"Me, too," Chelsea said. She didn't make eye contact with the poor guy who clearly wanted it.

I started on her as soon as Nick left. I didn't want to scare off my bright sophomore major, but neither did I want to miss an opportunity to learn something about the principals in recent events.

"Chelsea, I sense you're having a hard time right now, but I need to know why you were at my house yesterday."

Chelsea's eyes took on an innocent look. She shook her head, freeing long, loose curls next to her face. "I wasn't— "

"Look, I saw you." I cut her off with my sternest tone. "I saw you with Daryl. I don't know who the others in your group were, but I know you and Daryl were in the crowd in front of my house right after it was broken into. Now you can tell me right here, right now, or we can march down to the police station and talk it out with the cops."

I hoped this small-town girl didn't realize I had no authority to march her anywhere. She could stare me down or walk out of the building and I'd be helpless to stop her.

Chelsea made sobbing noises, wiping her eyes with her limp hands. I glanced at Nick, busy grilling. He had his back to us, fortunately for me, and missed a chance to rescue this damsel from an evil math professor.

Chelsea's sympathy ploy didn't faze me. I was running out of patience. The smell of melting cheese overloaded my nostrils, and not in a good way like at home with gourmet cheese.

"You can cry all you want, Chelsea. But one way or the other the police are going to find out what happened at my house. Did you and Daryl break in? Is that why you were hanging around?"

Chelsea gasped. "No, no, Dr. Knowles, I swear. Why would I do that? I would never do that."

I believed her. Whatever she was hiding, that wasn't it. "What about Daryl?" Would he do that? I meant.

A telling pause. "It was kind of a date."

"What kind of a date?"

"Daryl has a scanner and he hears police calls."

Could it be that simple? Daryl was a crime junkie? An ambulance chaser in the making?

A noisy group of students entered the coffee shop, flicking rainwater at each other. This activity was a source of great amusement to them and to Nick, who finally had some good company. He brought our drinks and set them down with a quick, "Here you go."

I had questions galore for Chelsea, but I let her go on about her dating life with Daryl.

"Daryl and I have been sort of hooking up, you know, the whole semester. Actually, I met him in August when we had that big orientation week for incoming freshman. I volunteered to tour kids, and that's when we met."

"And you've been sort of hooking up ever since?"

"Well, more than sort of." She giggled, which was only slightly less annoying than her sobbing. "He's such a cool guy and he started flirting with me right off. I was surprised, because the guys? The freshmen? Well, look at the boy-girl ratio, Dr. Knowles." She sat back, and made lecturing hand gestures. "They can just about pick any girl they want. It'll never be this good for them again."

"Ratios. I'm glad you're paying attention to the math," I said. Lighten the mood, soften her up.

She smiled, relieved of her burden, thinking I was through with her. "And Daryl's older because he traveled all around Europe before coming to college, so that gives him even more girls to choose from. Like, juniors and maybe even seniors."

At my advanced early-forties age, I'd almost forgotten what college was all about.

An uproar from the group of students, seemingly caused by a spike-haired newcomer to the table, served to bring home further the nonacademic life of my charges.

"So, did you and Daryl have a date yesterday?" Or does he just wait for police activity? I added to myself.

I had to raise my voice to accommodate the overflowing table two rows over. They'd become louder as they greeted the new guy and decided what to eat. Nick, taking their orders, was having a well-deserved good time. We might never get our sandwiches, which would have been fine with me.

I leaned across the soda-ringed table, the better to hear Chelsea's answer. I'd never been so eager to hear about a date my students had been on.

"We were supposed to go a movie at eight, but around four-thirty he calls and says, hey, there's some excitement over at Professor Knowles's house. You should come over."

"He knew this because of the scanner."

"Uh-huh."

"How did he know the address was mine?"

"I don't know. I guess from the directory."

Chelsea's answer was plausible but still didn't tell me how Daryl recognized my address right away when he heard the announcement on the scanner. I let it go for now as Chelsea continued.

"I didn't really want to go to your house, Dr. Knowles. I wanted a real date for once, but Daryl is Daryl." She threw up her hands, barely visible inside the sleeves of her sweater.

"Do you guys follow up on a lot of these calls?"

"Daryl knows all the police department codes, even for places like New Bedford and Fall River, even when it means the cops are on a coffee break or it's just a dog complaint."

"I'm asking if you go to a lot of crime scenes."

Chelsea returned to her flustered posture. "No. I don't know. Sometimes. I shouldn't have let him talk me into going to your house yesterday. But he made it sound like fun. He said to grab some other kids and we'd all go out for pizza afterwards."

Fun? Going to a crime scene, my crime scene, was their idea of fun? It was all I could do to keep myself from reacting.

"That didn't seem strange to you?" I said, remarkably calmly.

Chelsea shrugged. "Daryl's a strange guy. Like I said, he's older, and he knows stuff."

I didn't want to know what stuff. "Did you recruit some students to join you as Daryl asked?"

"No, I said I would, but then I didn't. It didn't seem right. But anyway, when I got there, there was a bunch of our friends from the dorms. I found out he called them, too."

"I saw you leave—"

"I'm so sorry, Dr. Knowles. I didn't even ask you, was your house okay? Did you lose stuff?"

Chelsea and her stuff. "Everything's fine, Chelsea. No one was hurt. That's the important thing."

We both seemed to realize at the same moment that someone had been hurt only a short time ago.

"You had enough to deal with, with Ms. Crocker," Chelsea said. "I still can't get that out of my mind."

"Did you have a lot of contact with Ms. Crocker in the library?"

Chelsea gave a sad nod. "She counseled me on some personal stuff, too. She seemed to really care."

If Charlotte had been smart and caring, she would have warned Chelsea about Daryl and his ilk. But that wasn't my business and I had more of my own than I could handle.

"Why did you and Daryl come by my house again after one o'clock this morning?"

"I don't know. Daryl said he wanted to see if anything else was going on. When the cops stopped us, he told them he wanted to be sure you were all right. We thought it was just a parked car sitting there or I'm sure he would have driven right by. The cops must have been stooped down or something."

Daryl and Chelsea must have been the only two people on the street who didn't spot the unmarked receiving special delivery food and drink.

"Does Daryl know you're talking to me?"

"No, I'm mad at him. I stayed in my friend's room the rest of the night. He's been calling all morning but I haven't picked up. What if those cops arrested us for trespassing or something? How would I explain that to my parents? They're already worried that I'm away in a big city."

I held back a smile at the characterization of Henley as a big city, though it was physically close to cities bigger than Chelsea was used to. Most of our students took advantage of the fact that Boston was only about forty miles north, and Providence, Rhode Island, twenty miles south.

I knew that Chelsea talked to her parents every morning without fail, before classes. When she'd told me about this strict monitoring of her college experience, I hadn't been able to tell if it was okay with Chelsea. I'd been surprised to learn that the ritual continued into her sophomore year.

I wondered how long a girl like Chelsea, with her upbringing, would stay mad at an alpha male like Daryl, with a manly swatch of blond hair on his chin. A soul patch, though Daryl didn't exactly fit the soul profile I was familiar with.

When Nick brought what the Mortarboard Café considered grilled cheese—two pieces of warm white bread with a mustard yellow spread in between—I thought Chelsea was going to faint, or worse. Her face turned as pale as the bread. I pushed both plates to the side and covered the sandwiches with paper napkins. I couldn't do much about the greasy odor.

"Do you care if Daryl knows we're talking?" I asked her.

Chelsea bit her lip. "He might not want you to know about the scanner. Like, is it even legal? I asked him and he says, yes, as long as you don't commit a crime with it. But I'm not sure."

I knew I could find out with a quick call to Virgil, but I didn't need to tell Chelsea. No need for her to get too comfortable.

"Does Daryl live in the dorms?"

"Uh-huh. He's in Hawthorne, with all the guys. It's a party

house, for sure, but Daryl doesn't hang out there a lot or go to their keggers." She put her hand to her mouth. "Oops, not that they drink illegally or anything, Dr. Knowles."

"I was young once," I said, but Chelsea didn't seem to get the humor. She nodded as if I'd told her something she didn't know.

"Anyway, I think they're too young for him."

Whereas Daryl was so mature.

"I have one more question, Chelsea. I need you to think back. When you met Daryl at my house on the first trip, when the crowd and all the emergency vehicles were there, was he carrying a duffel bag?"

Chelsea scrunched up her face, thinking, cooperating. "No, I'm sure he didn't have anything with him. He had his arm around me and I would remember if he was carrying something."

"Okay, thanks."

"Am I in trouble, Dr. Knowles?"

"Not with me."

"Can I go?"

"Sure."

"Thanks."

I pointed to the sandwich, a mean thing to do. "Do you want to take your lunch to go?"

Chelsea put her hand on her stomach and breathed deeply, in and out, with her eyes closed.

"Kidding," I said. "You can go. I'll take care of this."

She turned and headed out. To the restroom, I figured.

I hated that I'd taken advantage of Chelsea's timidity, letting her think I had more authority over her than I did. What kind of teacher/mentor was I? I should have been trying to help build her confidence. Chelsea was a good student. What she needed was a good, challenging advanced calculus problem that she could do on her own. I could help with that.

I couldn't wait to put the sounds and smells of the Mortarboard Café behind me. Was it always this bad, or were all my senses on alert from the strange and unsettling weekend?

Nothing seemed to bother the group at the other table,

which had grown to at least ten students, practically on each other's laps, sharing platters of hamburgers, fries, unidentifiable sauces, and enormous paper cups with long straws. And, by the way, simultaneously texting.

As I hurried by them on my way out, one of them waved and shouted, "Hey, Dr. Knowles."

I smiled and waved back, recognizing Kelli, a young woman who took my class last summer, math for nonmajors. Translation: no calculus.

"Have a good weekend," I said, extending the wave and the greeting to Nick, for whom I'd left a generous make-up tip.

I sat in my car for a few minutes, checking email. Hannah had responded that she could meet me around four o'clock in the lobby of her dorm, the Clara Barton. She wasn't up to meeting at the library, though the building had been released by the police. I wasn't up to it either.

The driving rain hitting my windshield made a much more pleasant sound than the Mortarboard had provided. What spoiled it for me was the thought that this moderate storm was the tail end of one ravishing the New Hampshire-Vermont border where my adventuresome boyfriend was trying to have fun.

I didn't know a whole lot more than I did before this meeting with Chelsea, except that I'd gleaned a little insight into my students' extracurricular lives. Daryl Farmer had such a psychological hold on the meek sophomore, I wasn't sure I could trust anything Chelsea had told me. I hoped my meeting with Martin Melrose tomorrow would be more fruitful.

One thing I did accomplish was an hour of not worrying about Bruce. But he was back now, in full force, in the stressed out part of my mind. I tried to give the thought a positive spin, picturing him sitting around a campfire, who knew how many thousands of feet up, with his two buddies, talking about how mild the storm had been and how delicious the provisions were.

It didn't matter that not even Eagle Scouts made campfires in a blizzard.

# Chapter 14

Ordinarily, with just a couple of hours between meetings, I'd go to my office in Franklin Hall and peck away at paperwork, catch up on filing, and do some leisure reading in a new math text. I hoped it wasn't fear of being alone in the math and sciences building that motivated my decision today to make a quick trip home instead. I shoved aside the little voice that accused me of being a wimp and told myself I needed a real lunch before seeing Hannah, that eighteen minutes home and eighteen back was worth the trouble, even in the rain.

As I pulled into my driveway, I congratulated myself on being able to argue both sides of any issue. Crafty, my mother had called it, and Bruce had followed suit. Win-win, I called it.

Even leftover pizza looked better than the Mortarboard Café's pseudo grilled cheese sandwich I'd left behind. I took a slice and a mug of good coffee to my office computer.

I remembered the earlier days of personal computers when I was in college. Neither I nor any of my friends would allow a crumb of food or a drop of liquid within three feet of the electronic workspace. We were all very blasé about it now that computers, small and large, were ubiquitous, came with cleaning kits, and were better constructed to withstand accidents. As often as not, when Bruce was on night duty, I ate dinner here.

I logged on to the webcam I'd been following. Instead of the hazy photo I'd seen earlier today, I was hit with a solid black rectangle. There was no explanation for why a proper image was missing. I tried general weather sites and got only generic, quick snippets of information about cold fronts and temperature. Useless.

I checked thumbnails for other New Hampshire spots. The webcams for Loon Mountain and Percy Peaks were up and running. I saw the campus of Plymouth State University, covered in a thick blanket of snow, looking picture perfect, as Henley's would in a month or so.

What was wrong with the webcam I wanted to view? Bruce's webcam, as I thought of it? Shouldn't there at least be some note about a broken camera cable or poor visibility?

Worrying about Bruce wasn't a rare occurrence for me. As far as I was concerned, his daily job was hazardous duty. Fortunately, I wasn't present in the MAstar trailer day and night when the alarm sounded and he went off to pilot a helicopter into tricky territory. He might be maneuvering his aircraft onto a freeway one day and onto a mountain ledge to rescue someone who shared his hobby the next. But, from the comfort of my home, I could indulge in fantasy and imagine that he spent his time at work simply waiting for a dispatch call that never came, playing cards and watching videos with his crew.

Ariana had been correct, however, that the events of the weekend had me on edge and Bruce's being out of contact was more upsetting than usual.

I refreshed the computer screen and saw the terrain for the Ammonoosuc River in Lisbon, New Hampshire, and for a lake in Barnstead. Still nothing but monochromatic black from Franconia Notch.

For many years, Cannon Mountain in New Hampshire had been home to the famous Old Man of the Mountain, a forty-foot granite formation comprising five ledges that together resembled the face of an old man in profile. In spite of the poems written about him, the magical powers attributed to him, and the fact that he appeared on the New Hampshire state quarter, The Great Stone Face, as it was also called, collapsed a few years ago.

"Doesn't that mean the whole mountain is probably unstable?" I'd once asked Bruce.

"All mountains are unstable," he'd said.

"Nice."

Bruce Granville was not one to pull punches.

Wandering around a spotless house wasn't doing much for me. I was caught up on class prep and puzzle deadlines and even the laundry was done, thanks to the deep cleaning inspired by my intruder.

After straightening posters here and there—a Women in Mathematics poster in the guest room, an attractive blow-up of the periodic table from my brief fling with a physicist—I settled in my home office.

The male who was most on my mind after Bruce was Daryl Farmer. I wondered what he was up to with his police scanner and what he'd done before enrolling at Henley. I started with search engines and networking sites, but Daryl was not to be found. It seemed it was going to take a hacker like Daryl to uncover facts about Daryl. That wouldn't do.

What was better than a good Internet search? A friend in the right place. One of my regular tennis partners when the weather permitted was Lori Tilden, Henley's Dean of Admissions.

A Sunday afternoon call between Lori and me could have meant an impromptu tennis game, even in the fall, but not in today's weather.

After a quick catch-up on friendly matters, I admitted, "This is not just a social call."

"I figured as much. What's up?"

I sat forward on my office chair, elbows on my desk, pencil and paper at the ready. My business-conducting position. "A favor. It's about one of my students. I need some info off his application."

Lori's "Uh-huh," sounded more like "Aha."

"I don't want you to do anything you're not supposed to, of course, but it would help me to know a couple of things about him."

"Such as?"

"His birth date and any transcripts or work experience. Anything about his life before he entered Henley."

"Hmm. Why do you need this?"

"I'm just—"

"Is he a student of yours currently?"

"Yes."

"Good. And did you say you need it for purposes of evaluating his semester's work in your class?"

"Well, I—"

Lori cleared her throat, unnecessarily loudly it seemed. I imagined her looking over her shoulder before she spoke, softly this time. "What was that reason you gave me again?"

Not that I was too dense. "I need it to evaluate his work in my class this semester."

"Fine, then, no problem. I'm going to campus this afternoon for a meeting of a dumb committee that can't get its business done during regular hours. I'll dig out his application and fax it to you."

"Thanks, Lori," I said, and gave her Daryl's name and my fax number. "I owe you one."

"How about this weather, huh?" Lori said, and we signed off.

Fifteen years at Henley College, and I still had to be tutored in its political formalities.

I realized I was forming a suspect list for Charlotte's murder.

It was unclear to me why I cared at this point. I no longer really thought of Charlotte Crocker, or whoever she really was, as my friend. But by dumping her bag of money with me, she'd dragged me into her scheme, whatever that was. My house had been broken into and seriously messed up, my duffel bag stolen, and I couldn't accept all that as coincidence.

Maybe I'd feel better if I knew the reason she felt she couldn't be honest with me. Thanks to Virgil's closemouthed approach, I still didn't know whether Charlotte was technically considered a fugitive, but I knew she was as close to one as I'd ever come in contact with.

I needed to know more.

Finally, nothing Charlotte had done warranted her cold-blooded murder, and if I could help in any way, I was going to. My plan was to continue my intelligence gathering for another day and then hand it over to Virgil.

Won't he be thrilled? I thought.

Daryl seemed to be number one on my list, by virtue of his

strange behavior concerning my break-in, and his somewhat oddball nature in general. I knew there were people who followed firefighters and police officers as groupies, and that could have been the only factor in Daryl's eerie presence last night. I was glad I'd have some data in the form of Lori's faxes soon to help me decide.

Martin Melrose was on my list simply because he played the lottery with Charlotte and a piece of paper with his name on it made its way to a duffel bag containing a million dollars, give or take. After our meeting tomorrow I'd either highlight him in yellow, figuratively speaking, or rule him out. Marty hadn't mentioned having been contacted by the police, other than the routine interview on Friday night, but why would he tell me?

I thought of Garrett, whom I'd never met. Where did he fit in? Maybe he was simply a friend of Marty's and Charlotte had his name and number as an alternate way of reaching Marty. Or vice versa.

I assumed Virgil was tracking down the four Jane and John Does in Charlotte's notes. What else had the cops done? Did their suspect list look like mine? I wondered if they'd share, if I asked nicely.

Somehow I didn't think it would be that easy.

The whole exercise in police work made me tired enough to plop into my comfortable reading chair for a well-deserved rest.

*Beep. Beep-da-beep. Beep. Beep-da-beep.*

The sound of my fax very close to my ear woke me up. Apparently the whole three hours of sleep I had last night weren't enough and I'd fallen asleep on the easy chair. Things were bad when I couldn't remember having moved from my desk chair to the reading chair in the opposite corner.

Thank you, Lori, for such fast service, I said to myself, as I pulled the sheets from the tray.

I looked at the time stamp and then at the clock.

Three-thirty. As much as I wanted to get to know Daryl Farmer better, I'd have to delay that gratification. I freshened up and gave Bruce's icy bookmarked URL one more glance before I headed out.

The rain had stopped and I let myself believe there were also clear skies thousands of feet up.

I barely made it to the Clara Barton dorm on time to meet Hannah. I used my passkey to enter the foyer where no one was on duty on a Sunday afternoon.

On the eastern edge of the Henley property, the Clara Barton was the oldest, and therefore the most rundown, of the residence halls. Cracked plastic chairs and couches lined its foyer, left over from when orange was a popular color for furniture. The funds had been in place for a facelift for years, but no workmen had materialized. Even with a cleaner, more modern décor, however, I wasn't sure anything could be done about the high-pitched humming noise heard throughout the building. If the sound signaled that something in the infrastructure was broken, I hoped it wasn't anything serious, like an electrical connection that had gone awry.

I used the old-fashioned phone on the desk to call Hannah's room. She picked up immediately and within minutes entered the foyer from the interior of the building. A tall, heavy young woman, Hannah tended to wear wide pants and dramatic tunic tops during her shifts in the library and now she was dressed the same way. The turquoise threads that formed the peacock feathers on her top fought horribly with the orange décor and added to the overall wretchedness of the scene before me. Hannah herself looked a mess. She'd have done better to skip her makeup routine today; her runny mascara contributed to the sad picture.

Hannah rushed over to me and caught me unawares in a bear hug. My head flopped a bit and ended up just at her bosom, my nose crunched. I wanted to say "There, there," and pat her back, but my mouth was buried and my arms were pinned to my side.

"Dr. Knowles, I've been dying to talk to you."

Poor Hannah. She'd put in several calls to me, all of which I'd ignored. I regretted my dismissal of her. I'd never had her in class but knew her from my frequent trips to the Emily Dickinson Library, our recently released crime scene. A senior

English major, Hannah worked with Charlotte and hoped to go to grad school for library science.

She continued to talk over my head, literally.

"I can't believe she's gone. She was so good to me, trying to build my confidence and all."

"We all miss her," I mumbled, breaking away gently as possible. "Shall we sit here?" I asked, pointing to one of the less worn orange couches.

"I don't know. It's not that comfortable down here. Too bad the Mortarboard is closed by now."

I gulped. "Too bad."

"How about the upstairs lounge. It's not busy on my floor."

I knew what the residents called lounges—nondescript rooms on each floor, with a small kitchen area, vending machines, an ironing board, a bulletin board, and a hot plate. Plus whatever any student chose to add because it didn't fit in her dormitory room and she didn't mind the risk of losing it forever. This included odds and ends of furniture, clothing, and food.

"It sounds perfect," I said.

Hannah nicely dismissed two students who were about to settle at the table with soft drinks and bags of chips that were a match in color to the foyer chairs.

"This is kind of private," she told them. "And my room is, you know ..." Hannah rolled her eyes and shuddered. The students seemed to know what she meant and left willingly. I figured the gesture could mean anything from "really messy" to a tiny, working pot farm.

"Can I treat you?" I asked Hannah, offering the contents of the vending machine. I was pleased to see a few healthy selections—fruit, juices, yogurt—among the candy bars and assorted salted munchies. I dared not inspect the contents of the small fridge under the counter.

"I'm good," she said.

"I know it's tough to lose someone close to you, especially since you were the one who found her."

"I can't get her face out of my mind, Dr. Knowles. She looked so sad. Not even pained, but just sad. And her legs were all tangled with the ladder. As soon as I opened the door to the stacks, I knew. The place was trashed. And I got this funny feeling, and I looked over and ..."

"I know it's hard but you have to try not to keep picturing that scene." I wished her luck since I couldn't stop myself and I hadn't even been there. "Give yourself time to adjust, Hannah. Don't be hard on yourself."

She fell onto a folding chair, so hard I worried about both her and the chair. "It's like I killed her."

I stifled a gasp and took a long breath before I responded. I sat down and put my hand on hers across the grimy table. "What makes you say that?"

"That night? We had a lot of books to put back in the stacks and that means getting up on that old ladder. I'm afraid to go too high on it. I'm afraid of heights and also, well, look at me"— she waved her hand north, south, east, and west of her upper torso—"I'm not exactly the climbing type, am I?"

An unfortunate question. I wished she hadn't mentioned climbing, which distracted me for a moment as I remembered my missing-on-the-mountain boyfriend. I hoped it was only to me that he was missing and that the reason I'd had no contact was that all three guys had accidently dropped their phones into their campfire. I wondered if I should bother Jenna Ramirez again, and decided to try her after my meeting with Hannah.

Hannah, who had just confessed to killing Charlotte. Not that I believed it for a minute.

I picked up on her story. "You left Charlotte to finish up in the stacks by herself. Is that what you're saying?"

"Uh huh. We usually leave and lock up together. But since I was going to be useless on the ladder and that's all there was left to do, she said I should go." Hannah paused to dry her face. "So Chelsea and I walked over to this party in Nathaniel Hawthorne. If I'd stayed—"

"You might have been killed yourself, Hannah. And that would be a whole lot worse than the situation right now."

"Maybe I could have scared him away."

"Not unless you had a gun. I don't think anything short of that would have scared him."

"Maybe not. But I'll never know, will I? And that's not all, Dr. Knowles. I'm not even positive I locked the door."

Hannah placed her hand on her heart, worrying me.

"Are you okay, Hannah? Do you need some water?"

She shook her head, removed her hand, and started to speak again. "I thought the police were going to arrest me when I admitted that, about the door. Like, they thought I deliberately left the door unlocked for someone to come in and murder Ms. Crocker. But I was just muddled when I was leaving because Chelsea was in a hurry. I know that's no excuse, though."

Another flood of tears came as Hannah continued to beat herself up. I had the feeling she did it often.

I let her regain some measure of composure and then backtracked to her comment about leaving the library with Chelsea and Chelsea's being in a hurry. I seemed to be running a beat behind her conversation this afternoon.

"Chelsea was with you?" I asked.

"Yeah, Chelsea came by to see if I could go to the party early. I think Ms. Crocker knew we wanted to go together and that's why she let me go. Chelsea and Ms. Crocker were close and she probably wanted to do us both a favor by sending us off for the evening. I think there was some beef lately, though, because the two of them argued a lot this last week."

Interesting. I wondered why Chelsea had never mentioned having arguments with the librarian-counselor she was so attached to, or, what could have been more important, seeing Charlotte shortly before her murder.

"You and Chelsea were together at the party the whole rest of the evening on Thursday?"

"Well, technically. You know how dorm parties can be. Like, mobbed. The boys are trying to get the Nathaniel Hawthorne accredited as a fraternity, so they want everyone they know to sign the petition. They're going to call it Beta Omega Gamma, which is, like, Greek for 'Boys on Campus.'"

Not exactly. "So you didn't stay with Chelsea?"

"No, you'd never be able to keep track of who you came in

with. I guess that's the idea, right? Meet new people. I didn't really see her once we squeezed through the front door of the dorm."

Note to self—Chelsea doesn't have an alibi. Check with Virgil. Another suspect? About as likely as Hannah, I thought.

"One more thing, Hannah. Do you know what the beef between Ms. Crocker and Chelsea was about?

"No, Chelsea wouldn't say, but it might be the same problem I had."

"Which was?"

"Ms. Crocker was terrific in everything. If you needed reference material that was missing she'd look through the shelves with you and call around to see if some faculty member was hoarding it." Hannah covered her mouth and uttered an "Oops."

"That's okay, Hannah, I know we're notorious for checking a book out and keeping it for years. What was it that Ms. Crocker wouldn't do for you?"

"The one thing was help with my career plans. I thought maybe she could advise me on what to take for the best shot into grad school in library science, or maybe she could use her contacts and put in a good word. But she just said I should do it all on my own, it would be better for me. But we all know that having an in is what really gets you started on the right track these days. Maybe she acted the same with Chelsea and Chelsea kept after her."

I thought I knew the reason Charlotte wouldn't share her contacts in the world of library science. She didn't have any. My guess was that Charlotte never did graduate from Simmons in Boston, the premier school for a Masters in Library Science. If she could fake identities, she could fake a degree. She was smart enough to bluff her way around a computer and help undergrads with term papers, but beyond that, she hadn't a clue.

My fingers hurt from their clenched position as I thought about the deception that had been heaped not only on me, but on Henley's student body, who deserved better. This was my cue to take a breath. Every time I remembered something phony about Charlotte Crocker, aka a dozen other C. C.s, feelings of anger rose in me. I felt betrayed all over again, and that was pointless.

"Is there anything I can do for you, Hannah?" I asked.

Hannah's eyes teared up, again. Not my intent. She half stood, leaned over, and nearly lifted me from my chair with her long, thick arms.

"Thank you so much, Dr. Knowles. Just knowing you're here …"

I regretted again that I hadn't responded to Hannah's request for a meeting sooner. She'd simply needed a friend to grieve with her. So far, she seemed the most genuinely upset by Charlotte's death.

She'd also given me something to think about regarding Chelsea's relationship with her librarian counselor.

*Whirrrr. Whirrrr. Whirrrr.*

Hannah released her hold on me and retreated to her chair while I checked my phone screen.

Jenna Ramirez. Eduardo's wife.

My heart seemed to stop.

I clicked on, looking out the dormitory window at the sky over Henley College.

It had started to rain again.

"Sophie?" Jenna's voice. "It's not good."

I knew Hannah had no idea why now it was my eyes that teared up.

"The storm?" I asked Jenna, my voice cracking.

"A storm, yes, but then there was an avalanche. Someone in the group above them knocked some rocks down, or some snow, too. Ice? I don't know exactly."

I wished Jenna would calm down so she could tell me what she'd heard, but I knew I'd be no better if I was in her place.

"Did you speak to an official? A sheriff or a ranger?"

"I think he was the ranger. One of the inexperienced climbers—not one of our boys, I don't know who—was able to call down to the station but he was cut off pretty quickly so the details are sketchy."

"Is anyone hurt?" I heard my voice as if from a distance.

A sniffle from Jenna, and a child's voice in the background. I'd forgotten that she and Eduardo had a toddler. I realized Jenna would have to contain her anxiety.

"It's not clear yet. The ranger who called me said he lost contact before he could get anything but a location. They have to wait until the storm subsides before they can start a rescue operation." Jenna had adopted the tone that a reporter might use at an accident site. The child's voice persisted though I couldn't understand his words.

Poor Jenna. How do you share this with a two- or three-year-old? I wanted to comfort her. But I couldn't breathe. Suddenly all the contents of the vending machine seemed to drop away from the supporting wires, slide down the glass, and break open on the floor.

Of all the times I worried about Bruce when he was called to an emergency operation, nothing was as bad as his being on the wrong end of a rescue operation.

# Chapter 15

As I pulled into my garage, my eyes landed immediately on Bruce's wall. It was all I could do not to sweep every piece of ice climbing equipment off its peg and into the trash. I couldn't decide who had angered me more, Bruce or Charlotte. I knew I wasn't being fair to my boyfriend who was free to choose his hobbies and the way he spent his time, but I didn't care. They'd both left me and I wasn't happy.

Hannah had done her best to forget her own distress over the death of her mentor and comfort me, but I'd raced out of the Clara Barton dorm as soon as my legs were steady enough to move.

I entered my house and immediately checked my messages on the landline phone in my kitchen, though I'd already accessed them from my car every five minutes on the way home. There was nothing new now on Bruce.

I listened to them again, in case I'd missed something. And also to take my mind off Bruce.

The first message had been from President Aldridge, wondering how I was faring with Charlotte's memorial service. Did I think that one week was appropriate, putting the date at next Friday? That way we'd have time to alert the press. Did I know of any relatives who should be invited?

Sure, I thought, she has a nephew, Noah.

I wondered about the press, and how soon we might expect a revelation concerning the dear departed librarian of Henley College. I didn't imagine Virgil and his department would be able to contain the information much longer.

Fran had called, wanting to know how I was doing and

offering to take my statistics class tomorrow. The gesture was so grand that I called her back.

"Thanks. I really appreciate the offer, but I'm fine for tomorrow," I said.

"You don't sound it," Fran responded.

The tears I'd held back while I was with Hannah, and then while driving home, poured out now on the unsuspecting Fran Emerson.

"It's not just Charlotte," I said, recovering my balance. Rather than reveal to Fran the whole Charlotte-as-Thug story, which she'd eventually read in the newspaper, I told her about Bruce's plight, or disappearance, or accident.

"No wonder you sound stressed."

"If something happens in New Hampshire"—I paused to breathe—"then I might need you to cover for me," I said, not spelling out what the something might be.

"Of course. Of course. You know I'm here."

"I don't know what I'll do, Fran … "

"I understand how worried you must be, Sophie. But Bruce is an experienced climber."

I wished everyone would stop saying that. Then again, I'd probably worry more if they didn't.

"If anyone knows what to do in an emergency, it's him," Fran added.

"He knows how to pilot a helicopter in an emergency," I said. "Not much else. He squeezes his eyes shut at the sight of blood."

I remembered first learning from Bruce how pilots and nurses had very specific and separate duties at an accident scene. While the nurses were tending to the victim, bloody or not, Bruce's job was to plot the route to the right medical facility for the situation, and in a way that avoided interaction with trees, buildings, and utility poles. A bloodless but critical task, he'd called it, defending his choice not to learn first aid.

"What about his companions?" Fran asked, bring me back to the crisis of the moment. "Didn't you tell me a minute ago that they were flight nurses? How are they with blood?"

I couldn't help a small laugh. "They're good with blood," I admitted.

"Okay, then. Let's just assume they're having a little adventure, which is why they went in the first place, and they'll be home with great stories for your grandkids." She paused. "Oh, never mind. Make that my grandkids."

I felt much better after talking to Fran, who was a grandmother to several children though she looked too young for the title.

I wasn't completely ready to give up my ill humor, however.

I turned it on Ariana, who wasn't ready and waiting when I called her. I left messages on her home and cell voicemails, briefly explaining my pressing need for good karma and special prayers, or whatever it was that sent healing vibes to the tops of mountains.

Otherwise, I was helpless as far as Bruce's welfare was concerned. He would either come back or not, and I already had a lot of practice missing him.

I needed some of the karma for myself, too. My body and soul were overloaded with worry. Jenna and I had promised to keep in touch if either of us heard anything. Neither of us knew who Kevin's contact was, whether he had a wife or a partner of either gender. I wanted to call Jenna simply to talk about our foolhardy men, but I hated to seem like the clingy girlfriend. I decided to wait at least another hour before checking back with her. Maybe by then I'd have a message directly from Bruce, who, I now told myself, would soon be home noisily rummaging in my fridge for a palatable leftover.

The pendulum I'd experimented with in my one and only college physics class didn't have as wide a swing as my moods today.

Wandering from room to room had become a habit over this stressful weekend, but it offered little solace today.

The very fact that my house was so clean was a reminder of yesterday's break-in. I was about to sit in front of the special coffee table in the den, which had been my grandmother's, when I remembered how it had been sullied by an electronic bug. I felt like tipping it over and scrubbing the bottom.

I left the den and walked to my office, where posters and photographs of Bruce and his buddies clawing their way up mountains made it no safe haven from worry, either. The room had its share of other photographs, on the mantel and on the tables, but today the happy faces of my parents and friends were dwarfed by the images of my boyfriend who was in trouble.

One framed picture of Bruce on the way up Green Mountain in Vermont was especially disconcerting as I looked at it now. The mountainside was clear rock, no ice, except for a wide patch down the middle, made by a waterfall frozen in place. In the photo Bruce and Eduardo, two helmeted creatures joined by a rope, are climbing the icy strip. Apparently the dry rock on either side of the strip of ice wasn't slippery enough to give them the thrills they were seeking.

I blew out an exasperated breath and moved on.

The guest room was no better. Bruce had appropriated one of the bookcases and kept back issues of magazines he subscribed to. One periodical, "The Accident Review," was an annual compendium of accident reports from climbers. It was a very bad idea for me to pick up a copy now and glance through it, but the perverse part of my nature reached for it automatically. Like when I couldn't stop poking an already sore tooth with my tongue.

I read a few lines about a four-man team of climbers who had to be rescued from Scud Wall in Wyoming because they'd been "surprised by nightfall." How were four adults shocked when daylight ended?

On California's Mount Shasta, one member of a private expedition of six struck out on his own without enough provisions. Even after an intensive air search, the man was never found.

On Long's Peak in Colorado, an ice cliff collapsed and killed

...

I slammed the magazine shut, imagining the next issue of "The Accident Review" featuring the threesome from MAstar who died trying to climb a steep and challenging route in New Hampshire in a snowstorm.

I allowed myself one more brief crying jag and finally called a halt to the depressing tour of my house.

I took a mug of Ariana's special blend tea to the den, determined to ignore the underside of the coffee table and enjoy a puzzle of someone else's making. I'd just begun solving a measuring puzzle—two pieces of string each take thirty minutes to burn, etc.—when I remembered the fax sheets that had come in from Lori Tilden earlier in the day. Daryl Farmer's application for admission to Henley College.

Maybe there was something useful I could do after all.

I retrieved the fax sheets from my office. Lori had come through big time. I now had a folder full of material on Daryl Farmer, including his high school transcript, letters of recommendation, and a writing sample.

The first number that stood out for me was Daryl's birth date. If I hadn't lost my subtraction skills, Daryl was born in Seattle, Washington twenty-six years ago. He was more than just a year or two older than Chelsea, as she thought. At this stage of their lives, six or seven years made a huge difference, especially given the basic naïveté of Chelsea, the Midwest pastor's daughter. I felt a song coming on, about the Midwest farmer's daughter, which, corny as it was, constituted a definite improvement in my mood.

I called up a mental picture of Daryl. His somewhat round features gave him a youthful appearance, but something in his manner had always struck me as more mature than most of his peers at Henley.

From his application materials, it seemed Daryl had not been traveling around with his backpack, enjoying the museums of Europe as he'd told Chelsea. He'd worked for a software company in the famous Silicon Valley of California. It wasn't impossible to work in the software industry without a degree, so why did he want one now? Of course, he had about eight years to get a degree somewhere else, not something he would have included on his application to enter the freshman class.

Which left wide open the question of why he was in Henley College's freshman class in the first place.

Was Daryl another con artist, like my deceased pseudo-librarian friend? I had to admit that Charlotte's many names and long rap sheet had poisoned my trustworthy nature, but there was no doubt that either Daryl had lied to Chelsea or Chelsea had lied to me.

Did no one tell the truth anymore?

I thought of the class of riddles that never failed to interest me: "Everything I tell you is a lie," being the trademark sentence.

It didn't make sense that Daryl would downplay his age and experience if he was trying to attract Henley coeds, Chelsea especially. Maybe he'd figured out exactly the right formula to impress her as worldly, but not scare her away as too much man for her.

At least he had no record, I mused, or none that I knew of. His use of a police scanner was certainly creepy, but legal. And, anyway, who was I to judge Chelsea's choice of boyfriend? Mine was showing anything but responsible behavior at the moment.

I was only slightly tempted to tell Chelsea Daryl's true age and past, but I knew her mother and father tracked her movements and her choices of friends carefully even from Nebraska. I wondered briefly if they micromanaged their sons the same way. Chelsea had daily contact with her parents by phone; she didn't need a local nag.

But lying was never a good way to start a relationship.

*Whirrrr. Whirrrr. Whirrrr.*

Another wake-up call, at seven pm, from my cell phone.

I couldn't remember a time since cramming for finals in college when I'd had such crazy sleeping patterns. Even as a child, transitions from sleeping to waking up and back were tough for me, which was why I'd never been a fan of napping. Each time I woke up from the involuntary naps in this latest spree, no matter the length, I was groggy all over again.

No wonder I felt a week had passed since Charlotte's murder. Since Bruce left for his climbing trip. Since my home had been invaded and bugged and my duffel bag stolen.

"Hey," Ariana said. "I just got your messages. I'm on my way."

"Your phone was off." A completely gratuitous comment, but just another sign of my lack of coherence when I first woke up.

Ariana cleared her throat. "Luke just left."

"Got it."

*Buzzz.*

My doorbell.

I clicked off with Ariana and tucked the folder of fax sheets under a large coffee table book on the history of mathematics, just in case my visitor wasn't cleared to see the material on Daryl. If President Aldridge dropped by, for example, she might have questions about how I came to have the files. I smiled at the thought of Olivia's stopping by for tea.

My amusement turned to amazement when I looked out the peephole at a tall, fiftyish woman in designer rain gear.

"Olivia," I said. "Come in."

Olivia kicked off her fashionable burgundy boots before I could tell her it wasn't necessary, and walked into my humble abode. Though the president was very formal at school, I knew her to be quite the opposite in a social setting. She'd been to my home only one other time, when I hosted a faculty party here and, as I recalled, she'd all but led a conga line.

"Sophie," she said, in a tone that was half reproachful and half best-friendish. "I assume you know."

"And didn't tell me" hung in the air. That was the reproachful half.

No sense playing dumb. "I haven't known for long," I said, following her to my den. I was impressed that she knew her way, and that she maintained her presidential bearing in the face of a college scandal; that is, she wasn't hysterical as I might have been in her shoes.

While damage to the reputation of the college had slipped through the cracks on my list of concerns around Charlotte's murder, Olivia couldn't afford that luxury. I realized now that I should have gone to her with the information, but I'd had no way of knowing if Virgil intended it to be public at that time.

Olivia plopped into an easy chair in the den, thankfully not near the buried fax sheets, and helped herself to a chocolate from a candy dish on the end table. "How in the world could we have let this happen?" she asked, working her mouth around the truffle.

I didn't know whether "this" was Charlotte's murder or hiring her in the first place, so I responded generically, "We couldn't have known."

"It's hopeless to raise anyone in Human Resources on a Sunday, but I need to know how an ex-convict could have made it past all the supposedly foolproof screens we have in our hiring process. We buy all this expensive software and still ... " She blew out an exasperated breath and took another candy. "You read about this all the time, like that man who forged a Harvard law degree and was Attorney General of some southern state for a while."

"You just don't think you're going to be conned yourself," I finished, glad to share my sense of betrayal and humiliation with my boss.

While I made coffee, I texted Ariana and called her off until later in the evening. My antiestablishment friend did not mix well with the upper levels of management.

"Nothing personal," she always said.

For the next half hour, over coffee and a modest plate of snacks I put together, Olivia and I commiserated and reminisced about a woman we both mistakenly thought we knew.

I felt it was about time I shared the highlights of what I'd learned from Charlotte's rap sheet. Olivia would be facing the press soon, as well as the campus community, and she needed to know at least as much as I did.

She took it all in with as much equanimity as could be expected.

"The memorial service," Olivia said at one point, as if she were announcing an agenda item at an all-hands meeting.

"I haven't done anything about it," I admitted.

"I should think not."

"What are you thinking? Skip it altogether?" I asked, hopeful.

Olivia took another deep breath; I'd stopped counting how many.

"This news about Charlotte's past is just out on one of my Internet news services. I imagine by tomorrow it will be in every paper and on everyone's tongue. I suppose I'll call an assembly and just put it out there with some weasel words about how no one is perfect, et cetera. She was a member of our staff and she was murdered on campus. I can't just dismiss that."

Olivia seemed to be brainstorming with herself. I let her talk. She'd been in office about four years and was one of the more forward-looking administrators in Henley's recent history. I was confident that she would do us proud.

"I did reach Martin today to get his take on it," she said.

"Martin Melrose?" Apparently he was taking calls from the president, if not from me.

"Melrose, yes. He's on the hiring committee. I wondered if he remembered any red flags when she was being considered for the job. He says he can't recall what her application looked like but would check her file in the morning. He says he's hardly seen or talked to her since she was hired two years ago."

"Is that right?"

Shame on you, Marty. Lying to the president. At the moment I didn't feel compelled to explain the lottery pool to Olivia. She had enough to think about without worrying that her money guy might have some shady past of his own. But I planned to grill him intensively at our brown bag lunch date tomorrow.

Olivia stood and picked crumbs from her skirt and deposited them on her plate. I followed her as she carried it to the kitchen. Nice manners.

"We should close the loop on a memorial service soon, but I'm inclined to have a simple moment of silence for her sometime this week," she said, retrieving her boots from the entryway. "Would that work for you? In lieu of a formal ceremony?"

I pretended to consider the idea for a few seconds and then nodded, rejoicing inwardly. "Whatever you think," I said.

It had been a stress-free visit, with some faculty-administration bonding and a decision that got me off the hook for eulogizing a woman I'd lost all respect for. It felt good.

Why did Olivia have to spoil the moment? Her gaze landed on one of the framed climbing photographs of Bruce that hung by the front door.

"That looks very dangerous," she said.

"Bruce is an experienced climber," I said, echoing what all my supporters had been telling me.

I realized I needed to get some new photographs. Maybe one of Ariana in her shop and a couple of the Friday Ben Franklin Hall parties.

I hoped Bruce, the experienced climber, would be around to help me mount them.

# Chapter 16

My landline rang the moment Olivia drove off. If I didn't have caller ID, I wouldn't have answered. I'd been keeping both phones next to me all evening, waiting for a call from Jenna, or Bruce himself.

"Hey, Virgil," I said.

"I'm soaking wet. I hope you have something stronger than tea," he said.

"Where are you?"

"Two houses down, walking in the rain."

"Were you waiting outside for Olivia to leave?"

"Uh-huh. I pulled up right when she did. I didn't think she'd stay that long."

"You could have joined us," I said, rummaging in the fridge for a beer, which is what Virgil meant by "something stronger."

"I figure you had private college business to discuss. And I didn't figure her digging into the pizza I brought."

"I'm starving."

"I'm clicking off."

By the time I pulled out a beer, Virgil arrived on my doorstep, dripping wet and loaded down. He held in his arms a large moving box and, on top of that, a pizza box wrapped in a waterproof sleeve.

"Where did you get this cover?" I asked, relieving him of the food, enjoying the aroma of tomato sauce and the works even through thick, dark plastic.

"Badges are still good for something," he said. I couldn't imagine how Virgil had managed to carry the boxes and talk on his cell at the same time until I noticed his Bluetooth earpiece.

"I suppose you're going to comment on this thing on my ear," he said.

"Since you brought food, I'm letting you off the hook, but, congratulations and welcome to a technology that's only about twelve years old."

"Smart alec." Virgil removed his Bluetooth device and put it in his jacket pocket. "They gave them out to everyone. I intended to accidently lose it, but I have to admit it's pretty handy. 'Scuse the pun."

I'd waited long enough. I faced Virgil, my back to all the boxes. "Not that you're not always welcome, but are you here because of Bruce?" I was amazed I got the whole sentence out without falling apart.

"Bruce? Should I be?"

Of course not. Only in a state of extreme anxiety would I assume that a homicide detective in Henley, Massachusetts, would have a hot line to a park ranger in Franconia Notch, New Hampshire.

I gave Virgil a short version, as calmly as I could, of the storm, the avalanche, and Bruce's status as missing.

"Sophie, Bruce is—"

I held up my hand. "Please don't tell me that Bruce is an experienced climber."

"Okay, I get it. I'm sure you're tired of hearing that. But who says he's missing? Is that the term the ranger used?"

"I don't know for sure. Jenna used it."

Virgil walked around me and took a seat at the table, forcing me to do the same if I wanted to maintain eye contact.

"So there's nothing official," he said, settling his bulk on the chair. "Waiting out a storm is not the same as being missing."

"It sounds the same to me. The ranger said they couldn't rescue the guys until things got calmer."

"'Rescue' is another one of those words. You have to ask yourself, did the ranger use it or was that Jenna's interpretation?"

I desperately wanted to adopt Virgil's perspective. "Okay, you have a good point."

"Bruce has been 'rescued' many times. And he's been more annoyed each time than the one before."

"I know."

"Then you know it just means he needs help getting down, and he hates that. He'd rather slide down a thousand feet with a broken leg, and he's probably waiting somewhere until the right time to do that."

"You think he has a broken leg?"

Virgil blew out a loud breath. "Come on, Sophie."

"Kidding," I said.

"I'm glad you got back your sense of humor. But, look, if you want to be alone with this right now, I'm out of here. You want me to leave?"

Virgil was kindly giving me the option of wallowing in my distress over my non-missing boyfriend. He looked concerned enough even to leave the pizza behind if that's what I wanted.

I finally noticed the label on the large carton Virgil had brought in and placed on my kitchen island. The handwritten label read: PROP., C. CROCKER.

Besides pizza, he'd brought me a box of Charlotte's things.

I said, "Of course I don't want you to leave."

Virgil promised to review the contents of the box with me as soon as he was a little drier, and had a few hundred calories of food and drink in him.

I handed him a towel and he headed first for the bathroom.

I headed for the box.

The top flaps weren't sealed, but simply folded over each other. An invitation to dive in, which I did.

I moved the carton to the floor for easier access and dug through the contents. It wasn't obvious how or why these particular items had landed in this box. I found a mixture of things, some from Charlotte's office and some from her home. An engagement calendar and a wall calendar, both with a rare book theme. A small bobble head doll of a librarian, which I was sure she hadn't bought herself. A velvet pouch with reading glasses on a beaded chain that I'd made for her, with Ariana's help.

An unsealed envelope contained photographs from the library open house during orientation last summer. I sifted through them, recognizing some students and faculty. I picked out Daryl and several other students from my classes. I saw more than one of Chelsea with a badge that said, "Sophomore Volunteer." I hoped her volunteer activities were in her control.

Charlotte wasn't in any of the photographs. I never knew until now why she always refused to have her picture taken.

Various size envelopes in the box were sealed shut. I'd do Virgil the courtesy of waiting for him to open them.

Surely this didn't represent the sum total of Charlotte's belongings. Where were her clothes? Her huge inventory of shoes and purses? What had happened to her furniture?

I heard footsteps and leaned over to see Virgil coming down the hall, back toward the kitchen. He seemed to have come from the guest room, which was past the bathroom, but I couldn't be sure.

"You didn't wait to look in the box. I'm shocked," Virgil said, his hair slicked back and drier. I'd raised the temperature on the thermostat when Olivia arrived and left it there now.

"What about all the rest of her belongings?" I asked.

"Funny you should mention that. I don't know how you feel about this, but it would be nice if you worked with the lady at county who'll have to take care of that. If they can't find legitimate heirs, it goes through probate. You might be able to make her job a little easier."

"I never realized how complicated things could be for a loner."

"Can I give her your number?" Virgil gave me fifteen seconds to respond, then said, "You can think it over, decide a little later."

"Who gets her body?"

"Do you want it?" he asked.

I laughed. "Casual question, casual answer. I can't believe I asked it that way."

"Natural, nervous reactions," Virgil said. "I knew what you meant. And what I meant was, do you want to be involved in the disposition of her remains?"

I didn't need time to think it over. "No. I'm sorry. I don't. I guess I was just curious, since there's no hope of finding a relative."

"Well, then, to answer your question, first the state has to offer the body of the deceased to a school that might want it."

"You mean a medical school?"

"Could be. Or it could go to students in dentistry, mortuary science, physical therapy. Most cosmetic surgery teachers want just the heads."

I cringed. Sometimes the realities of life and death were best kept in temporary denial.

To accompany this weird conversation, Virgil and I separated pizza slices and put them on plates, two for him, one for me. I knew he was just getting started and that there would be no leftovers tonight.

"I won't be asking that question again," I said.

"Be glad someone else deals with all that for us. As for the rest of the process, there'll be notices in the paper to see if anyone shows up. If no one claims a body within ten days and no school wants it, the state will pay a flat fee to some lucky funeral director for a suitable burial, including a grave marker, a clergyman, and I forget what else. Massachusetts has more rules than most states. We have stiff requirements." Virgil shook his head, nearly blushed. "I guess this is my punny day."

Miraculously, we both maintained our decorum.

I kept my word and watched Virgil down half the pizza and two beers before mentioning his investigation. I stopped after one slice and a ginger ale.

"Can we share now?" I asked.

"I wouldn't have come if I wasn't ready to talk," he said. "We knew we couldn't keep things close to our vest forever. When I saw President Aldridge pull up in front of your house, I was even more sure that the word was out." I nodded confirmation. "Tomorrow's paper will have the news of Charlotte's past and everyone will know what we know."

"What was the big secret?"

Virgil shrugged. "I told you, once we figured out Charlotte Crocker was the woman wanted in several states, we were trying to figure out who her accomplices were. We knew she wasn't working all by herself."

"Did you find anyone?"

"That we did." Virgil looked pleased. "The Jane and John Does on the duffel bag notes? We had the cooperation of the lottery commission and some cops and FBI geniuses got together and found them. They're in custody and the world has a few less scam artists. Of course, their lottery scams were small potatoes compared to some big-time cons they pulled off."

"That was fast work. Was Charlotte working with them or their victim or ...?"

Virgil gave me another shrug. Whether it was an "I don't know" shrug or an "I can't tell you" shrug, I couldn't tell.

"They were already onto some key players," he said. "The notes just put the icing on the cake and told them exactly which lottery game each one was linked to."

"I'm glad I didn't spend any more time researching Powerball and—I forget the names of the other games."

"Look at it this way, now you'll know what everyone is talking about around the water cooler."

"It's true that more people I know buy those tickets than I thought."

"It's about numbers, Sophie. I'm surprised you don't play."

I shook my head. "There's nothing to calculate. It's too much like guessing and a lot of luck." I looked at Virgil and realization struck. "Do you play, Virgil?"

He assumed what Bruce and I called his amused embarrassment expression, like when Bruce asked him how he liked a new woman on the police force.

"Occasionally, if I have a spare dollar," he said.

"Good luck," I said.

I decided to take advantage of Virgil's good pizza-and-beer mood.

"Can you tell me, are you any closer to knowing who killed Charlotte?"

"I'm glad you're not my boss. We're doing our best, trying to narrow the categories."

"You mean, like criminal cohorts or victims of her scams?"

"Or faculty or students."

"Of course." But I was hoping not.

"You'd laugh at the student alibis. There was a party in one of the dorms that night."

"Nathaniel Hawthorne, the guys' residence. I heard about it."

"Well, it seems every kid we interviewed was there. It was like Woodstock, where those who claim to have been there far outnumber the actual attendance."

"Were you at Woodstock?" I asked.

"On my mother's knee," he said.

It was nice to share a light moment.

A loose end came into my mind out of nowhere. "Hannah Stephens told me she thinks she forgot to lock the library door the night of Charlotte's murder." Noting Virgil's look, I hastened to add, "We were just chatting. I was not investigating."

"I know you'd never do that."

"Is that what you figure also? That the killer was able to walk in to an unlocked building?"

"It's hard to say."

"I knew it would be. You cops are worse than scientists when it comes to actually making a statement without caveats."

Virgil shrugged, maybe pleased to be compared to a scientist. "Ms. Stephens isn't completely sure how she left the door. Security goes around and checks buildings routinely, in order, after ten or so. I'm sure you know that. The first check of the library after the students left wasn't until around eleven and the building was locked at that time."

"Meaning the killer could have locked the door behind him."

"Which is why it's hard to say."

Point taken.

I had one more burning question that had nothing to do with who killed Charlotte, but was important for my own peace of mind.

"Do you know for sure that Charlotte was still running scams here in Henley?"

He shook his head. "That we do not. What we have is the word of some lowlifes she partnered with in California who claim she ran off with a ton of their money."

"At least a bag full." In spite of the painful image of Charlotte's tainted duffel, I felt a twinge of hope for my friend. Maybe she'd been trying to turn her life around when she was killed.

"That bag was the tip of the iceberg. There were offshore accounts and stashes of cash everywhere in her wake."

I couldn't stand it any longer.

"Help me out here, Virgil. I realize you can't answer with certainty, but I need to know if there's a chance that Charlotte had reformed, or gotten rehabilitated, or whatever the word is. Was she trying to get away from bad guys and bad habits, or from the law? She'd served time. Was she free to do whatever she wanted?"

"I know what you're asking and why you're asking. She was your friend. She apparently did a lot for the students at Henley, and maybe that evens things out. I can't speak to that; I can only speak for the law and procedure."

"That's all I'm asking."

"It's a gray area, believe it or not. We'd have to be able to make a direct link between a certain check or withdrawal or pile of bills and Charlotte Crocker."

"If the bills were marked, from a sting or setup, for example?" I asked.

"That's a possibility. Doesn't apply to the particular duffel she gave you, but it could have, yes. She had a bag of unmarked money. Maybe she did odd jobs and people paid her in cash and she was saving up for something."

I pushed the box with the last slice of the pizza toward Virgil. "No more for me."

"If you insist." Virgil took a large bite. "This is what makes it hard for the victims. It's very difficult to trace back and say, 'This is what I gave so-and-so, and this is what she promised, and she took my money illegally, and there it is, right there in that bag, or in that off-shore account. Hard to do."

I was floored by how complicated it all was. Maybe there was a place for lawyers in this country after all, to sort it out. "What about the IRS? Could she have been charged for not reporting the money?"

"We don't know when she got the money. Maybe she'd accumulated it only since the last tax reporting period. If it's over a certain amount and she doesn't declare it, she pays a fine, that's all. Maybe she'd just counted it and was going to claim it to the IRS the day after she was caught."

"Or killed."

Virgil nodded. "Now, that said, does it seem Charlotte Crocker had run off with money of dubious origin? Does it seem like she was trying to get even farther away with it and not look back? Sure, but if Charlotte had lived and gone to trial, there's no way she'd have been found guilty of anything she hadn't already served time for, duffel or no duffel."

It seemed Virgil was working harder than I was to give Charlotte the benefit of the doubt.

We took a break to talk about less heavy things. Virgil had no special plans for Thanksgiving dinner so he'd probably offer to cover for someone who had family obligations. Nice guy, as I'd always known. I briefed Virgil on Bruce's cousins in Connecticut, with whom we'd spend the holiday weekend.

I didn't mind talking about Bruce with Virgil; he'd known him longer than the five years I'd been with him, and cared about him.

"I've seen him get out of more situations than you can dream up," Virgil said. "No white fluffy stuff is going to defeat Bruce Granville."

If his voice didn't sound so strained, I'd have believed him fully.

I returned to the reason Virgil was in my kitchen.

"Back to this ring of thieves Charlotte was involved with. Didn't the fact that they operated in more than one state put the case in federal jurisdiction?" I asked.

"Technically, yes, but"—Virgil put on a goon expression and lowered his already bass voice—"we know people."

"You can do that?"

"The police and the FBI aren't the adversaries television and movies make them out to be. We had a little latitude to work the case. As soon as Charlotte was ID'd and tracked to Henley after that speeding ticket, we notified them. Since it's such a small community here on the campus, the feds agreed we might have a better chance to watch and learn. You can bet it'll be easier the next time a turf thing comes up, now that we've helped seal the Jane and John Doe cases. It was their last loose end."

"Except for finding Charlotte's killer."

"Except for that," Virgil acknowledged. "But she was murdered in Massachusetts, so that part is our case. If it turns out her murder was related to a crime out of state, we'll see our agent friends again."

I liked that I was asking questions and Virgil was answering. I pushed on, giving a nod toward the carton on the floor. "What's in those envelopes that are sealed?"

"Clippings, mostly. Or, I should say printouts from the web. Newspaper reports of old scams. There's a whole pile of them on a guy who committed suicide when he lost everything thanks to our girl, who was Coleen Crawford at the time. You have to wonder if she enjoyed going over all the havoc she'd created."

"Can I look at the printouts?"

"In a minute. I know from some old Korean guy up near Boston that you've been on the tail of the 'Garrett' whose name was in Charlotte's duffel."

The Q/A power had shifted back to the cop. "It was just an off-the-wall shot at figuring out what happened," I said. Not really detective work, I meant.

I had no desire to keep anything from Virgil. My mind was stretched to its limit with second guessing a storm in New Hampshire. I told him the little I knew about the Garrett and Marty connection, based only a telephone number. I omitted only my lunch plans for tomorrow.

"Something's up with Melrose," Virgil said. "We interviewed him, like everyone else who was at the crime scene gathering, including Ms. Rogers. I don't have my notes here but I think that's her name."

"Paula Rogers, Dean of Women," I filled in.

"Well, Melrose tells us he hardly knew the deceased, but Ms. Rogers told us that he holds the lottery purse for the group on campus." He gave me a sideways glance. "But you knew that." I shrugged, noncommittal. "We checked and there's nothing that indicates he's skimming, but I felt he was holding something back."

Good for Paula Rogers, I thought, and made a note to have my people call her people and set up a lunch date.

"Have you interviewed Garrett?" I asked.

Virgil shook his head. "So far we haven't even laid eyes on him. You just gave me the first good lead with the Martin Melrose connection."

I pointed to the carton, suggesting that reading its contents be my reward for my helpful tracking of Garrett.

Virgil smiled. "We hoped you'd be willing to look through it, see if anything jogs your memory to give us a clue."

"Really? I get to work with you even though I don't want to claim her body?"

"That's the kind of guy I am. Plus, the guys are through with lifting prints and so on. There's nothing left of value to the investigation unless you can come up with something."

I licked my lips. Forgetting for a moment that a murder was involved, I felt like I'd been given a box of new puzzles, some of them brainteasers, some logic puzzles, maybe an anagram, a wordplay, and a sudoku or two. I could hardly wait to tackle them.

"Thanks," I said, casually, lest my enthusiasm work against me in the eyes of the cop.

Virgil checked his watch. "Oops. I'd better run."

I smiled because, first, I doubted Virgil had somewhere to be at nearly nine on a Sunday evening, other than out for more pizza, and second, because Virgil didn't run.

"Don't worry about the dishes," I said, sweeping the empty pizza box and paper napkins into the trash. I dusted my hands. "All done."

I thrust a baggie with the last of Ariana's cookies on Virgil as I walked him to the door.

In the back of my mind, I'd been mulling things over. About Charlotte and her life at Henley. She'd been such an asset to the college community. She'd been a good friend and a supportive colleague. I remembered hours of research she'd done for a grant proposal I had to submit, errands she'd done for Ariana when she was tied up at her shop.

What if Charlotte had truly reformed and had been counting on us to help her stay a law-abiding citizen? What if she had no control over people in her past who ultimately tracked her down and wouldn't let her turn a corner in her life?

"Can I have another day?" I asked.

He gave me a quizzical look. "For what?"

"Before you give Charlotte's body to the Commonwealth?"

"Sure," he said.

"Thanks. And there's one more thing."

"Yeah?"

"About Bruce. My perfectly safe boyfriend." We both smiled. "Is there anything you can do, anyone you know? Maybe you know a cop or a sheriff in New Hampshire? Can you make a call?"

He pointed down the hall toward my office. "What did you think I was doing back there?" he asked.

He gave me a quick hug and left.

# Chapter 17

I was carrying the information-laden carton that Virgil had gifted me to a more comfortable spot in the den, when I heard the sound I'd been waiting for all evening.

*Whirrrr. Whirrrr. Whirrrr.*

I dropped the box, pulled my cell phone from my pocket, and read the screen name. Jenna Ramirez. My heart rate quickened and I held my breath. The phone slipped out of my hand before I could click on. I went into a momentary panic that I'd lost her call.

"Jenna," I said, picking up and finally orienting the phone correctly.

"Hi, Sophie. There's no further news, so don't worry. Or, yes, worry, whatever. I've been trying but I can't get through to anyone up there."

We both broke down in a schoolgirl way that would have embarrassed me if I cared what anyone else thought.

I considered Virgil's interpretation of the state of the climbers.

"Jenna, did the ranger, or whoever he was, actually use the word 'missing'?"

"He said he knows where they are, from that one brief cell contact, but they can't get to them. I'd call that missing, wouldn't you?"

I hadn't meant to upset Jenna further. "I would, yes, Jenna. It's hard for me since I've had absolutely no direct contact with anyone up there since the storm."

"I'm sorry, I didn't think of that. And, I can't believe I've been so insensitive, Sophie. When Bruce came to pick up Eduardo, he told me about your friend. It just went out of my head. That must be very upsetting for you. Was it horrible?"

I was in no shape to discuss Charlotte's murder and all the complications of her life. I figured Jenna would hardly notice if I ignored her question and went back to our mutual problem.

"I understand why they called you and not me, Jenna. I'm not surprised that, since you and Eduardo are legally married, you'd get information before I would."

"Maybe that's it, but who knows what kinds of forms these guys sign as far as whom to call? I know Eduardo told me once he left my number for good news only, and MAstar's number for bad news. I don't think he was kidding, which is why I'm surprised the ranger told me as much as he did. I'll bet he was new."

I heard a long sigh, close to a wail from Eduardo's wife.

"Jenna?"

"I'm okay," she said, hardly sounding it. "Todd is finally asleep. I haven't told him anything about being notified and I don't want to be upset in front of him. He's a very smart little boy and you'd be amazed at how much he picks up on."

I was sure her son was very smart but the loudest word for me was "notified." I didn't like it. "There's nothing to tell your son, right?"

"No, nothing." I heard the 'yet' in Jenna's voice and didn't like that anymore than the 'notify.'

When a call waiting from Ariana interrupted, I was glad for an excuse to sign off with Jenna. I realized Jenna needed to talk, but connecting with her was having the opposite effect from what I'd hoped.

"I'd better take this," I said, rationalizing that we both needed third parties to distract us.

"Hang in there," Jenna said, and I promised I would.

What else could I do?

"Any word?" Ariana asked. "I know you'll call, but I hate waiting. I'm coming over, okay?"

"You don't need to."

I recounted Virgil's spin on the situation in the mountains, trying to make it my own. I added Jenna's report to me, and waited for Ariana's assessment.

"It sounds like Virgil's right. Missing would be where they had no idea where the guys were or when they went up. Missing would be the ranger wouldn't even have known they went up, missing would be—"

"Missing would be they can't find the mountain. I get it. Thanks, that's what I wanted to hear. I'm fine."

"See you in a few minutes," Ariana said. "Bringing a change of clothes."

I didn't argue.

I spread the contents of the PROP box on the coffee table and sat on the couch in my den. I opened each envelope and scanned the contents, setting aside items for further reading. One envelope was stuffed with newspaper reports of scams. Some of the pieces had been downloaded from a news site; some had been physically clipped from an old-fashioned newspaper. Scams of every category were represented, from the lottery to investment schemes to chain letters as a ruse to build someone's database.

I told myself that Charlotte was not the perpetrator of these crimes, but had saved the clippings for the purpose of making amends to the victims. Aha, I added, perhaps the money in the duffel was to be distributed to said victims.

And the private plane was to take them all on a holiday to Bermuda. Welcome to Sophie Knowles dreamland.

I wondered why I was bothering to go through the clippings, but decided to keep at it until Ariana arrived.

I tore the tape from the next envelope. This one was dedicated to a single victim, the man Virgil had mentioned. Robert Foxwell, who owned a small but successful flooring company in Oregon, had committed suicide after being conned out of his savings by Charlotte, operating under the name Coleen Crawford. He'd fallen for her investment scam and lost his money and his business.

As I read the details, I recognized the scheme: Foxwell gave her a few thousand dollars to begin with and received a large return very quickly. He then increased his investment, and again received a large return. I could see clearly where the game was headed, though, unfortunately, Foxwell had been oblivious to it. The money Charlotte gave him was simply cycled from other "investors." Once hooked, Foxwell invested his whole net worth the next time, and, of course, saw neither his money nor Coleen Crawford ever again.

One of the clippings described how Coleen/Charlotte was caught and sent to prison for fraud. A small amount of money had been recovered and some of it returned through lawsuits by offended parties. But investigators had no way of knowing exactly how much booty Charlotte had accumulated and stashed in cash or in accounts all over the world. With the article was an informative sidebar explaining how scammers on the run often immediately turn a check into cash so they'll leave no trial.

Good to know.

I wondered how much of what was in the duffel was from those scamming days. Unless she could also turn loaves into fishes, Charlotte could not have saved a million dollars on two years' worth of salary as a college librarian.

Another clipping in the set announced Charlotte's latest release from prison two-and-a-half years ago. Apparently Charlotte came to Henley soon after. For all I knew, all the money in the duffel belonged to Robert Foxwell, her last known victim. Why else would she have gathered and saved this complete dossier on that particular scheme and victim?

I realized I couldn't make assumptions about Charlotte's motivations for anything she'd done. I didn't know her beginnings, but her whole adult life seemed to me a series of bad choices and wrong paths taken. I couldn't fathom her reasons or those of anyone who made a profession out of taking advantage of people.

That she'd spent two years conducting herself as a model citizen was a conundrum, but not a reason to give her a pass on her prior life. And Virgil couldn't say for sure that she wasn't working a con at Henley, right before my eyes. I'd wanted to give her the benefit of the doubt, even allowing that the money in the duffel might be clean, but the Foxwell story had set me against that hope anew.

Maybe my lunch date with Marty tomorrow would set that straight, one way or another.

Meanwhile, I had more of the detritus of Charlotte's life to go through.

The clippings from the Foxwell file included several photographs of the family before and after Hurricane Charlotte struck. To all appearances, Robert Foxwell and his wife were happy shop owners before they met her. As for the after photos, David, who dropped out of college when his father died, looked despondent in one, angry in another, ready to explode in a third.

Mrs. Foxwell died a year after her husband, from an undisclosed cause, leaving David to fend for himself at twenty years old. He was quoted as saying that although nothing could bring his family back, he believed "no sentence is long enough" for Crawford.

I wondered what had become of him.

*Buzzz.*

Anger and disgust at what Charlotte had done returned in full force as I stuffed everything back into the envelopes and back into the box. I shoved the carton aside and went to answer the doorbell.

It was going to take everything Ariana had to pull me out of this recurring bad mood.

"I know just the thing to do," Ariana said, depositing her bags where Charlotte's condemning property box had been.

She lined up four clear plastic organizer trays on my coffee table, each containing an assortment of colorful beads in different materials. I scanned the array of beads of stone, glass, gemstone, wood, and metal, all of varied sizes and shapes, each one beautiful.

I plunked down on the floor to be closer to the treasures. I decided to give my loyal friend a thrill and name the more unusual shapes, as she'd taught us in one of the first classes I took with her. I touched a sample of each bead as I recited its official name. Faceted, saucer, melon, tube, pipe, chip, and—the most exotic of all, of Native American origin—heishi, tiny pieces of shell that have been drilled and ground into beads.

I'd seen a heishi necklace on someone recently, but couldn't remember the circumstances.

As I hoped, Ariana leaned over from her place on the couch and gave me a very American high-five for my fine bead-naming performance.

Ariana removed the last box from her tote, this one with the serious tools of the trade—findings, needles, cords, chains, pliers, wires, tweezers, wire cutters, and at least ten kinds of clasps.

"I guess I'm in for a work session," I said.

"We're going to make a little present for Bruce," Ariana announced. "It will send a message to the universe, that we know he'll be back soon to accept it."

I let out a long breath, wanting badly to believe as Ariana did, that there was something I could do to bring Bruce and his friends back safely.

"Good idea," I said, sounding pretty convincing, given the way I felt.

Ariana brought out a spiral-bound beading book from one of the bags she'd carried in. She had flagged several pages already and opened the book to the first floppy blue marker. I knew this organized approach was all for my benefit since Ariana didn't believe crafts books had much to offer except "to stifle our creativity," as she put it.

"How about a keychain?" she asked, showing me one made of delicate Murano glass beads cascading from a silver jump ring.

I shook my head. "Bruce is never going to carry a beaded keychain."

On to the next marked page. "How about this copper wire basket for his desk, to hold paper clips and things?" Ariana asked. "We could do it in manly colors like brown and navy."

"He doesn't really have a desk at MAstar. The guys don't have their own rooms in the trailer and they don't leave much personal stuff there. But even at home, his laptop is on a little end table by his recliner. Bruce is not a desk or paper clip kind of person."

To back up my observation, I pointed to the array of mountain-climbing photographs of Bruce on the walls of the den. Not a desk, stapler, pencil holder, or tape dispenser in his life.

"I see what you mean," Ariana said, returning to the crafts book. "Let's see what else we have."

She sorted through one flag after another.

I heard simply, "Ankle bracelet, no. Beaded pen, no. Zipper pull, no. Beaded box top, no. Beaded napkin rings, no." Then finally, a little light sparkled in her eyes. "He reads, doesn't he?"

"Uh-huh."

"We'll make him a bookmark. It can be fun and a lot more challenging than the key chain I had in mind."

"Uh-oh," I said.

"Yeah, too bad your boyfriend doesn't wear jewelry. We could make a simple necklace."

We both laughed at the idea of Bruce Granville, medevac pilot and ice climber, wearing anything that wasn't completely functional.

I had an unwelcome thought of Daryl Farmer, who was never without something decorative. Aha, Daryl was wearing a heishi necklace at the Mobius party. I'd used it, in fact, to demonstrate the value of mathematics.

The mystery of where I'd seen heishi beads recently was solved, but only partly.

There'd been another instance.

I sat up straight, struck by a set of pictures that fit together. I scrambled across the carpet to the abandoned box of Charlotte's belongings. I searched for the last envelope I'd opened and pulled it out.

"What are you looking for?" Ariana asked. "You can't get out of this project. It's for Bruce, who might need it."

"Here it is," I said, looking closely at the newspaper shots of David Foxwell. Blond, with a soul patch, and a necklace. The same muscular build, not very tall. He had one hand on his hip, a stance Daryl often took. The same initials, like someone who'd taken a new name but kept his initials. Like Charlotte Crocker/ Coleen Crawford and the other C. C.s.

Now I was really reaching. One more minute and I'd be

willing to swear in court that the shirt in the picture was one David Foxwell still owned, but as Daryl Farmer, Henley College freshman.

I showed Ariana the photographs of David Foxwell. "You've only seen him a couple of times, but who does this look like?"

Ariana stretched her neck and screwed up her face, studying the grainy likenesses. "I'm not sure."

I groaned and tapped the photo with the shot that was closest in on Daryl's upper body. "Look at this necklace. Does it look like heishi?"

Ariana pulled back. "Do you want it to be heishi?" she asked. Poor Ariana. I was sure she felt like an unsure eyewitness in front of a line-up window. "It's a great necklace, but it's really hard to tell. It could be made of saucer beads. They're almost the same size. You'd almost have to feel the texture to tell."

She gave me an apologetic look.

"You're right. There's no way to tell from a newspaper photo," I said, disappointed.

"I feel like I failed a test."

"No, no, never mind. How about the guy himself? If he were two, two-and-a-half years older? Do you recognize him?"

Ariana brightened. "Oh, I get it." She touched her smooth chin. "The soul patch? That guy in your class who hangs around a lot. I forget his name."

"Daryl Farmer. He's always with Chelsea Derbin."

"Right, that's him."

Thanks, anyway, I thought. I knew Ariana was guessing, wanting to support my imaginings.

I turned the clippings around to face me again. Maybe I was grasping at straws. How many small coincidences added up to a match?

I knew it would help me to tell Ariana the story I'd half formed in my head. Maybe if I heard it out loud, the concoction would sound as far-fetched as it truly was and I'd be able to move on.

"Listen to my theory and tell me what you think," I said. "Be honest."

"Okay."

I gave Ariana the basic story of Charlotte-as-Coleen's investment scheme and Robert Foxwell's suicide, and took off from there.

"Say, our very own freshman Daryl Farmer is really David Foxwell. I just learned, never mind how, that Daryl is really twenty six year old. Six years ago, when his father committed suicide, he was twenty, and had to leave college and go to work. His father's killer, in David's mind, gets out of prison"—I looked again at the article and verified the data—"two-and-a-half years ago. In between times, David was working in computers in California."

I paused for a reaction.

"I see where you're going," Ariana said. "Young David is very smart. He hacks around, however they do it, and finds out that the woman who has ruined his family is now a librarian at Henley College in Henley Massachusetts."

I picked up the thread, getting more and more excited that I might be onto something important. "He enrolls as a freshman. He notices that the woman he's after is very close to this young woman who's a sophomore math major. He sees that the sophomore is very naïve and ripe for the picking."

"Chelsea Derbin."

"Yes, what luck. Chelsea told me she met Daryl right off last summer at orientation. He signs up as a math major also, which is right down his alley, and he dates Chelsea to get close to Charlotte."

"Kind of a reversal of how you'd think it would work. Usually a guy would befriend the older woman to get to the girl."

"Well versed as you are in the art of romance," I said. "In this case, we have Daryl using Chelsea to gain the librarian's trust, find out her schedule, and so on."

"He wants to get even," Ariana said, covering her face while she said this, lest the universe think she approved of any violent act.

"He wants to kill her." I said, having no such limits on my relation to the universe. "And he wants the money."

Ariana gasped and slapped her forehead. "I forgot about the money."

"We don't know for sure whether he ever got back what his father lost."

"He thinks of that money in the duffel bag as his."

I smiled. I had a convert to my theory.

Things were looking up.

I needed to busy myself with a physical activity while I played with my theory in my head and figured out how to approach Virgil.

"Let's make a bookmark," I said, bringing a smile to the face of my good, honest friend.

# Chapter 18

Ariana had taken pity on me and had chosen a relatively simple idea for a bookmark, a twelve-inch long black cord with a pattern of beads hanging from each end.

"We beaders call it a book thong," Ariana explained, with a grin.

"Bruce's birthday is in June. Pearl is his birthstone, right?" I asked. Ariana knew such things.

Ariana nodded and produced a chart from the pocket of a tote. She unfolded a full color rendering of gemstones, from beautifully striated agate to a translucent blue-green zircon.

"A pearl is one choice for June," she said, tapping an image on the chart. "It's magical, created by a living organism, and said to be formed from tears of joy." She moved her finger two rows back, to the Ms. "Moonstone is the other gem for June. The Romans thought it was made of moonlight. Both go really well with black onyx, which makes its wearer brave, so I think we're on our way to something beautiful. In a very masculine way, of course."

"Of course."

Using a thin needle, Ariana expertly drew seed pearls from a compartment in one of her trays. I found four moonstone beads in the shape of ellipsoids, two onyx beads of teardrop shape, and two that were spherical.

We each took an end of the cord and worked with the beads and assorted silver findings. I approved a pewter heart-shaped charm for the top end of the bookmark. Ariana talked me out of first sketching a pattern on graph paper.

"Let it flow," she said, flapping her long arms.

I nodded, though I wasn't sure exactly what she meant. That's what made our friendship so wonderful.

Unlike most times when we worked on a crafts project together, we embraced periods of silence.

As I worked with cones, spacer beads, and pliers, my thoughts were on Bruce, picturing him using our creation to mark his place in a book on World War Two planes that I'd ordered for him. He hadn't been gone all that long, I reasoned. He'd called from the base of the mountain at about eleven yesterday morning, and now it was eleven at night. Only thirty-six hours, though it had seemed like weeks.

If he were at sea level, would the police even consider looking for him? I tried to focus on the shortness of the time Bruce had been away, but it was hard to dismiss the extenuating circumstances of an icy mountain, a heavy snowstorm, and an avalanche of rocks and snow.

I switched my thoughts to David Foxwell, aka Daryl Farmer, a less personally involving matter. As pleased as I was with my narrative, there were some loose ends to my story.

I addressed Ariana, whose bead design was flowing much better than mine was, with multicolored branches and perfect knots. I knew Bruce would have no trouble figuring out who had fashioned which end.

"How would Daryl have known about the money in Charlotte's duffel bag?" I asked.

"He probably just assumed she had a bunch, and came to claim some of it."

"Could be. Or his intention in crossing the country to find her might have been simply to kill her." I swallowed at that. "Maybe he learned about the money only when he arrived at Henley."

"Why do you think Daryl is still around if he did what he came to do? Charlotte's dead. Do you think he's the one who broke in looking for the money after he killed her?" Ariana put the end of a long string of beads in her mouth and swept her arm across my den, as if I might not know which break-in she referred to.

A montage of images came to me of Daryl Farmer, one of

which showed him as the guy Mr. Gold saw entering my home to violate it, neat as he'd been. I saw Daryl in my mind at the Friday parties at Ben Franklin Hall, sitting in front of me in class three times a week for statistics, standing near me at functions on campus. Had Charlotte been standing next to me at those times also?

Had anyone at Henley ever been safe with Charlotte alive and Daryl out to get her? Were we safe now?

I answered Ariana's question with one of my own. "What if Daryl has unfinished business?"

"He knows by now that there's no money for him anywhere, don't you think?" Ariana said. "Are you saying there's someone else he has it in for? Like—"

"Like Chelsea," I said, springing to my feet, not caring that carefully placed beads were slipping off my wire.

"Do you think he'd hurt her?" Ariana asked. "Why would he do that? I think he's a guy who was just out for revenge. He's not a serial killer or anything. I don't get that vibe from him."

I didn't ask how Ariana could distinguish serial killer vibes from the vibes coming off someone who'd murdered only one person. I figured it would be too long a story for this hour.

"Maybe Chelsea knows who he really is or he thinks she does. Maybe he enlisted her help and now he has to get rid of her. I don't know."

Ariana put down her string of beads in such a way that it stayed intact. "Let's not get ahead of ourselves, Sophie. Shall we get Virgil back here?"

"Good idea," I said. "But I need to call Chelsea, too."

"You can invite her over or something."

Something. "Why don't you call Virgil, to save time," I said. "I'll try Chelsea."

Ariana nodded and moved to the hallway and then to my office, opening her phone on the way.

I punched in Chelsea's number and took deep breaths, reminding myself that all I had was a theory based on uncon-firmed similarities. I didn't want to send the fragile Chelsea into a panic, but I'd never have forgiven myself if I did nothing to warn her of potential harm.

I waited through four rings, forming a decision tree in my head, with three branches, to account for Chelsea's being with Daryl, Chelsea's not being with Daryl, and no answer.

The winner was "no answer."

I heard the click to voicemail and debated whether to leave a message. What if Daryl heard it? The message would be on her cell phone, I realized with relief, not shouted out to a kitchen answering machine as a message to my landline might be.

I spoke as calmly as possible, "Chelsea, this is Dr. Knowles. Please give me a call at home when you get this message. I want to talk to you about your statistics paper."

Now I had to invent a plausible reason to single out Chelsea's paper for a chat. I remembered that she'd chosen the application of statistics to agricultural issues, an interesting choice that reflected her ties to her roots in a farming community. I could dig out an advanced reference to give her, or advise her to be sure to visit the site developed by the National Agricultural Statistics Service. Neither of these ideas merited a late night call either from or to my home, but it was the best I could come up with on the spot.

When Ariana and I reconvened in the den, she gave her report. She'd also had to leave a message, for Virgil. Maybe he did have some place to go on a Sunday evening.

"He wasn't picking up, but, get this, if I have an emergency I should dial nine-one-one."

"That's comforting."

"I guess that's all we can do tonight," Ariana said, yawning.

A minute later the clock in the den struck midnight and my friend, Cinderella, threw up her hands and said goodnight.

"This is getting to be a habit," I said, as Ariana shuffled toward the guest room. She waved and called over her shoulder. "You should be going to bed, too."

"Sure, right away."

I headed for my office.

It was nice to have Ariana's supportive and often cheery presence. I knew her strategy was to be here for me in case I heard from Bruce or … about Bruce … in the middle of the night.

I went on line to check the weather at Franconia Notch. I found nothing new about the storm, no new webcam graphic. It was as if New Hampshire had shut down. The number listed on the site was the same one I'd been calling, a computer-generated message about regular business hours.

How does a mountain have regular business hours?

I hadn't checked my email since early afternoon and it was now overloaded with student queries. It seemed my majors had a hard time doing without me for a whole weekend.

"I can't open the third link on your list for probability sampling examples," said Rena. I responded, "Check your browser. Any version of Firefox 3.6 should work."

"Is stratified sampling going to be on the final?" Lamar asked, insinuating that it wouldn't be fair, since I didn't spend much class time on it. I wrote back, "I'll post a study guide for the final in a week or so."

"Can I change my topic from statistics in corporate America to manufacturing statistics?" Brendan wanted to know. "As long as you don't really manufacture statistics," I answered, unable to resist.

I shot off quick replies to five other students, then opened a file with my notes for a class in about nine hours, on statistical sampling. I was ahead of the game, having anticipated a time-out in Boston.

I reviewed my intro to the session. I wanted to emphasize the importance of understanding sampling methods without sounding like a preacher. If I had my way, every voter would be required to take my class or one like it before being issued a ballot. Though it should have been obvious, I planned to remind the voters in my class that no published survey obtained data from every single person in the pool of voters. Not just in politics, but data was interpreted for us at every turn, and not necessarily by people who were objective about the results.

My electronic charts were in order, with examples from reports of so-called "trends" in climate, in sales, even in medical results. I decided I'd have time to cover aspects of sample design and introduce the formula for sample size to prepare the students for the homework assignment.

I closed the file, quit all the applications and thought about trying to sleep.

I got as far as turning back my old lavender comforter when my landline rang from my night table.

Virgil's number popped onto my screen. I sat on my bed and clicked on.

"You up?" he asked.

"I'm up," I said, wondering why, in the midst of all the serious matters of the evening, I found myself curious about where and with whom Virgil had been earlier. If he had a girlfriend I wanted to meet her. "Did you have a good evening?" I asked, not to be too subtle.

"I've been on the phone a lot, setting up some contacts in New Hampshire."

My breath caught. "Did you learn anything?"

"Not yet, but I have some avenues established, sort of like a phone tree."

Only the near Luddite Virgil would hold onto the methods of our grammar school days, when our parents communicated about days off or worked out field trip details by telephoning around in chain letter fashion, before texting and emailing were invented.

"Thanks," I said, grateful for any communication method, old or new, that put me closer to wherever Bruce was.

"What's this about a theory around our Charlotte Crocker case? Ariana mentioned there's something I should know?"

"How much time do you have?" I asked.

"Go for it."

I did.

It was hard to explain what I'd found and what I'd guessed at, without props like photographs and a nicely graphed timeline, but I did my best to fill Virgil in on the story I'd put together. I threw in what I'd learned from Daryl's admissions file, the lies he'd told Chelsea about his age and background, and his two appearances at my home at the time of the break-in.

Virgil didn't interrupt while I was talking and he didn't respond right away when I was finished, ending with my concern for Chelsea. When he finally spoke, he had a few questions.

"Do you know where Daryl Farmer is now?"

"No. Does this mean you think my little narrative has merit?"

"Anything can have merit in an investigation."

Back to unforgiving cop mode, I noticed. "Right. And I don't know where Chelsea is either," I added.

"Okay. Give me some time and don't do anything else. Got it?"

"Got it."

"If Chelsea calls you back, play it cool and let me know. Don't do anything yourself. Got it?"

"Got it."

The second time I sang the words, just to make a point.

*Whirrrr. Whirrrr. Whirrrr.*

My cell phone.

I didn't know how long I'd been asleep, only that I'd been tossing and turning. I'd left my night table light on, and both phones handy. I checked the clock—two fifteen—and the screen on my phone.

Chelsea this time.

"Hey, Dr. Knowles. Hope I didn't wake you. I know you stay up late."

Had I ever been this cavalier about calling my professors? Yes, I realized, I had, though not too often. I was sure that Janice Barnard, former Resident Assistant on the fourth floor of my dorm at my alma mater, would testify to the fact that I'd awakened her more than once. And with very little at stake, usually that my boyfriend at the time hadn't called all day.

"I'm awake now," I said, my standard line for the roughly three times a month that students woke me up.

"I figured if you called me so late, it must be important."

"Sort of, but nothing to worry about," I said, untruthfully. "I was actually looking for Daryl and wondered if you knew where he was."

Neither of us mentioned that I'd cited her statistics paper as the original reason for my voicemail message.

"Don't talk to me about Daryl. We supposedly had a date and he never showed. I'm ready to dump him."

It sounded to me like he'd dumped her, which wouldn't have been a bad thing in my mind.

"Were you going on a police scanner jaunt?" I asked, before I could curb my sarcastic nature.

"No, I talked him into a normal date, like dinner and a movie, something I could actually tell my parents about. We were going up to Cambridge to one of those arty movie houses."

Where I should have been on Friday. "What are you doing now?"

"Studying statistics."

For a moment, I bought it.

"That was nice. Thanks Chelsea."

She laughed. "Really, I did my homework. I'm just hanging out with some of the girls in the Paul Revere lounge. Sunday nights we all do our laundry and our hair and, you know, talk about boys. I mean math."

I hesitated to put a damper on the carefree laugh of one who didn't know she might be in danger.

"Do me a favor, Chelsea, and let me know if Daryl calls you."

"What's this about, Dr. Knowles?"

"I've got to go now. I'll see you in class tomorrow."

Chelsea was safe in the dorm. There was a hot line to Virgil from authorities in the mountains of New Hampshire. Bruce's new bookmark was ninety percent done and I could count on Ariana to finish it up, fixing my end of the cord, too, in the process. Though I'd been reluctant to make it, I now saw it as a good omen. You couldn't have too many good luck charms to avert disaster.

The world would probably be okay if I went back to sleep.

Ariana had left by the time I shambled into the kitchen to the smell of coffee she'd brewed, which was next to the fresh scones she'd whipped up, which were next to a paper bag marked, S's LUNCH.

I was beginning to like having a roommate.

Ariana had left a note near my mug. The message read "Force the Stress Out," a cue to me to use the mantra method she'd taught me. The exercise was supposed to send the tightness she knew I was feeling from my head to my feet, step by step, and out through the floor, until the last phrases, "The bottoms of my feet are relaxed. I am relaxed," became a reality.

Maybe later.

For now I had to take my stress to school.

# Chapter 19

Dressed in my standard fall teaching outfit of black slacks and black shirt, with a faux Victorian vest today, I drove onto campus, parked in one of my usual spots between the tennis courts and the Mortarboard Café, and walked toward Ben Franklin Hall. The well cared for lawns and small statuary on the seventeen-acre campus looked the same. The strategically placed lampposts stood straight up. Students with backpacks, cell phones, and bottles of water dotted the landscape.

It was another Monday among many, the start of a week of classes.

But I felt the whole world had changed since Friday.

My biggest challenge would be to act normal and hope the B. F. Skinner method of effecting inner change through outward behavior would work.

After a quick drop-off and pickup in my office, I stopped in at the first floor lounge for my second cup of coffee, not as good as the brew Ariana had left for me earlier. I was glad I didn't have to pay for it.

Fran, deep into her class notes at the conference table, looked up. She came over to me and hugged me, the first sign that it wasn't an ordinary Monday for her, either.

"I'm so sorry, Sophie," she said. "Charlotte Crocker is all over the news. Different identities? A record a mile long? Crimes all over the country? I can't believe it."

"Believe it."

"I need your take on it. Lunch?" she asked, checking her watch and packing up to leave for class.

"Not today," I said, though sharing a sandwich with Fran

was much more appealing than trudging over to admin and eating with Martin Melrose. Especially since I no longer considered him or Garrett, whoever he was, a suspect in Charlotte's murder.

"Earlier, then? Are you free at ten?" Fran asked.

"Uh-huh. Let's meet in my office."

Robert Michaels, chemistry department chair, walked in, apparently having just shared a joke with Judith Donohue, head of biology, who was right behind him. Both stopped laughing when they saw me, and while they didn't embrace me, they were flustered enough to drop a pen (Robert) and a textbook (Judy).

"Hey, you must be devastated to read all this about Charlotte," Judy said, with Robert nodding in agreement. "I was blown away. I find it very upsetting and I didn't even know her all that well."

"Neither did I, it turns out." I smiled as a way of accepting the sympathy of all.

In some ways it was a relief that the news about Charlotte's past, and maybe present, had spread. No more secrets, no more solitude in my grieving. And I knew that at least with Fran, I'd be able to share my feelings of resentment also.

Thirty students, give or take, fell silent when I entered the classroom just inside Franklin Hall's front door. I didn't have to clear my throat till it sounded like a foghorn, or tap on the desk and shout, "Good morning. Let's get started. Please." I half expected them all to jump up and join me for a group hug.

It dawned on me only at that moment that I might have to say something about the crime on their campus, the fate of their librarian. Even those who didn't know that Charlotte and I were friends, not simply casually acquainted as colleagues, deserved some words of explanation or acknowledgement of the crime that had been committed on their campus.

I had a fleeting memory of a story Hal Bartholomew, the physics department chairman, told us of Marie Curie. The famous chemist and physicist stepped in as professor to replace her husband at the Sorbonne after he'd been killed in a street accident. An entire auditorium of people sat in silence waiting for her first words. It added to the drama that Marie became at that moment the first woman to teach at the Sorbonne. With reporters present and all eyes on her, Marie opened Pierre's notebook to his last lecture and picked up the discussion of radioactivity from the middle of a paragraph.

Or so the tale went.

Even if the story was only partly true, it put my own little drama in perspective.

I addressed my waiting class, and, unlike Madame Curie, satisfied their need for a transition.

"Good morning, everyone. I'm sure you've heard the news of the death of our reference librarian, Charlotte Crocker. I'd like us to take a moment to remember her. She was an important part of our daily lives on the Henley campus. Let's think of her service and all the good things she did for us, and remember also those who loved her and will miss her."

It was the best I could do *ad hoc*, and maybe even if I'd taken hours to prepare.

I looked over the heads of my students, past their laptops and their textbooks at a poster Charlotte had given me featuring the prime numbers in bright colors. I hoped eventually the nice things she did would outweigh her crimes in my memory.

I was conscious of Chelsea, safe and sound in the front row as usual.

Though it had been decades since we recorded attendance in college, it was a time-honored tradition, an unwritten rule, that students took the same seats in every class session. If a brave student did try to take a different place, chances were the rightful owner would glare, face the intruder with a questioning look, and then be extra early for the next class.

The practice was a help to professors who could then map a person to a seat, and thus learn students' names more quickly. It was easy to see now that Daryl Farmer's place, one row over and one seat behind Chelsea, was empty.

During the silence, ostensibly for Charlotte, I sneaked in a thought of Bruce, imagining him safe at home. I took a breath and tried Ariana's method of pushing the stress out of my body, through my modern Mary Janes and onto the old wooden floor of the classroom.

"Thank you," I said to the class. "Now let's look at Chapter Seven."

I got through examples on sampling techniques without much of a hitch. As when I worked a puzzle, once I started on a math problem, my focus was complete. Halfway through the explanation of sample size and confidence levels, I might have taken on a confused look if someone mentioned the names Charlotte Crocker or Bruce Granville, thinking they had theorems named after them.

A good discussion of populations and probabilities could do that for me.

I knew it would be impossible to walk back to my office at the opposite end of the building from my classroom by myself.

Several students hung back to accompany me, and it would have been insulting to dissuade them. I'd been grouchy enough lately.

The overriding theme of the entourage taking me down the hallway was, "Anything new on who killed Ms. Crocker, Dr. Knowles?"

I continued to shake my head and promise that I'd let them know if I heard anything before they did.

Nothing came up about Charlotte's nefarious background. I decided that the sixties were officially over and college students didn't read newspapers, especially not before a nine o'clock class. I figured it wouldn't be too long before the Charlotte Crocker case went viral on a social network.

I was moved by my students' gestures of care and support, summed up by a senior biology major's offer, "Let us know if you need anything, Dr. Knowles. Like, we could take you to a movie or something."

How about The Eiger Sanction?

In my office, waiting for Fran, I checked all possible avenues for news of Bruce or Daryl.

A voicemail from Virgil had the simple statements, "DF is in the wind. Not official." As long as it wasn't "BG is in the wind," I hardly cared. I figured I'd done my part and it was now up to the Henley PD to find DF and prosecute him for Charlotte's murder.

An email from Martin Melrose read, "If today is still on, I'll be here." One might have thought Marty wasn't looking forward to seeing me. At this point I'd lost motivation for the lunch date myself and was tempted to call it off. If he was involved in a scam, did I really care? I felt my only job now was to help keep Chelsea safe while Virgil and his department went after Daryl.

"Knock, knock," Fran said, pushing my office door farther open than the rather uninviting crack I'd set it at.

Who would have thought that a simple "Come in," to a friend would have set me off, choking me up once again, prompting Fran to give me another hug? Her grandmother persona was working overtime today.

It was a couple of minutes before I could intelligently explain to Fran that my distress at the moment was about fifteen percent Charlotte, eighty percent Bruce, with a five percent random stress factor having to do with deadlines for the new statistics research paper and life in general. Few people other than Fran Emerson, former chairwoman of mathematics, would have understood my report.

I gave her a rundown on my Daryl Farmer-cum-David Foxwell theory, partly to test it against someone who knew Daryl and partly to spread the word that if she saw DF she should not approach, but call the HPD. I also threw in a request that she keep her eye on Chelsea, though I figured that if Daryl did skip town, we'd never see him again. At least, not by that name. Doug Finch, maybe. Or Don Fletcher. Or Daniel Fuller.

I felt a new idea for a word puzzle developing on the spot.

"I guess you never really know anyone," Fran said. She'd taken a seat and now stretched out her long legs and gazed up at a corner of my office, as if mulling over a basic issue of epistemology. "First Charlotte wasn't who she said she was, and now Daryl? A freshman with a past?"

"Not your ordinary freshman," I said.

"Not as far as computers go," said the one who would know,

the director of our new computer science major. "He's writing an advanced app for a smartphone. Way ahead of the curve."

"So you think he has the skills to hack around and track down the woman he feels was responsible for his father's suicide?"

"Let's just say he's the first one I'd call if I needed anything like that done. Hijacking, phreaking, decompiling to find exploits."

"Do I even want to know what all those activities are? When did students get smarter than teachers?" I corrected myself. "All except you, Fran."

"Ha. You should come to class sometime. He essentially took over my Java lecture. And I don't mean coffee."

"Smart doesn't always equate with good judgment," I said.

"Amen. Did you say the HPD is looking for him?"

I thought of Virgil's cryptic, "Not official," that the HPD hadn't put out any kind of bulletin on Daryl, but was simply making inquiries and trying to track him down unobtrusively. It was something, and I took the effort to mean that Virgil gave some credence to my theory.

"Unofficially," I said to Fran. "My guess is we'll never see him again."

"A guess and a hope."

I nodded agreement.

"Do you have any more classes today?" Fran asked.

"My History of Math seminar at eleven," I said.

"Do you want me to take it so you can go home?"

"Thanks, but Liz Harkov is a guest speaker today. And then I have lunch with Marty, so I might as well stay."

"Marty? You're rejecting my offer for someone named Marty?"

I'd forgotten that no one in Franklin Hall ever called our main money guy by a nickname. "Martin Melrose," I said. "Long story."

"Ah. He's another one who's been acting strange lately," Fran said.

"How so?"

"He's had this young guy staying with him for about a

week, I think. Martin's secretary, Mysti, and I got chummy last year when I was on the budget committee. She gives me the scoop even when I don't want it."

"Thanks for the warning."

"This was the whole school budget, remember, not the math budget, so you're safe. Anyway, this term I have my cognitive class and my GUI workshop in the admin building on the same floor as Melrose's office and the kid is there a lot. He looks like kind of a loser, sits in the waiting area in the hallway. It's like he's guarding Melrose, or something. Or vice versa."

"Is his name Garrett, by any chance?"

"Yeah, that's the name Mysti calls him. Do you know him?"

"Not yet."

Fortunately, neither Chelsea nor I was responsible for leading the discussion in the History of Math seminar.

Liz Harkov, from Henley's Modern Languages Department and an expert in Russian history, had offered to speak to the class. Her topic, dear to my heart, would be the socioeconomic background during the life and times of mathematician Sonya Kovalevsky, the first female member of the Russian Academy of Science. I loved cross-curriculum projects. And the timing couldn't have been better to give me a break as well as the pleasure of hearing a knowledgeable colleague speak.

Liz handled the seminar beautifully, fielding questions that covered the interaction between government and academia and the state of mathematics research publications in Russia. Some of the guys in the class tried to look bored, on principle, I assumed, during the discussion of the treatment and opportunities for Russian versus American women mathematicians.

As fascinating as I found Liz's presentation, my mind drifted now and then during the hour. I was happy that I'd crafted my own questions weeks ago when Liz and I set the date for her talk.

I hoped Liz didn't notice my distracted state and take it as a lack of interest or a reflection on her ability to engage us.

I decided I should be compiling a list of those to whom I'd owe an apology when things were back to normal.

Eating lunch in the administration building was anything but normal for me. I walked by the east wing of the Emily Dickinson Library, dodging puddles from yesterday's significant downpour, and climbed the outside side steps of admin. It was strange to find them empty, where on Friday the staff had gathered for what looked like a photo shoot but was really a front row seat to a crime scene. The same crime scene that brought me to the building now.

I entered the building and remembered, too late, that admin people dressed better than those of us in the outlying buildings. Residents of Franklin Hall were especially casual, with mathematics students and teachers all piggybacking on the excuse of the scientists above us, that lab work was messy. Never mind that the math labs involved only computers and the occasional new set of white board markers. Some of us in math even wore lab coats to cover up an especially casual outfit.

I worried that my lunch wouldn't measure up any more than my outfit did. I had no idea what Ariana had packed for me and hoped it wasn't anything embarrassing, like lotus flowers or soy soup. Not being restricted by slow starts in the morning, she might have made a quick trip to the local health food store. She'd simply mentioned that there was a surprise in the bag and not to open it before noon.

I walked by all the skirted and suited administrators and administrators' helpers, nodding when I had to, successfully avoiding any attempt to engage me in conversation. It had been a while since I'd seen so many men's ties in one spot on campus.

Since Charlotte was now beyond my reach, it was Bruce who was going to have to pay for my surly mood eventually. I patted my hip pocket where my cell phone lay in wait.

*Whirrrr. Whirrrr. Whirrrr.*

I started. This wouldn't be the first time I set off my ringer accidentally.

*Whirrrr. Whirrrr. Whirrrr.*

But it wouldn't keep ringing. This was a real call.

I dug the phone out. Virgil again.

I ducked around the corner by the elevator I'd be taking to

Marty's office and clicked on in relative privacy. The little alcove was left over from one of the many renovations the old admin building had gone through in its hundred-year history. I might be standing in what was a pantry for the nuns who taught here when this property housed a convent school.

"Hey, Sophie."

"Hey, Virgil?"

My senses were on alert, judging Virgil's tone before he said another word. Not low and sad, as if he had bad news about Bruce, but not happy either, so he hadn't heard from anyone in New Hampshire. It must be about Daryl.

"Listen, we found your duffel bag, the one that was taken from your garage. Your travel clock was still in it."

I groaned. Of all things I cared about, the duffel bag, with or without the travel alarm, was near the bottom of my list.

"Great, thanks, Virgil."

"Actually the guys found it Saturday night in a park dumpster near your house, but I wanted to wait to see if anything came of it before I told you."

"That's nice. Thanks."

I wasn't sure what was up with Henley's homicide squad that they spent so much time on a cheap duffel bag with some toiletries and an atomic travel clock. By now the bag may have been tossed around so much that the clock was broken. Surely they weren't going to drag me to the station to pick it all up.

"I know it seems unimportant, but what's interesting is whose fingerprints are on the clock."

"I assume they're Daryl's," I said.

"Nope. One set came back to your treasurer, Martin Melrose, the other to a low-level con artist, Garrett Paulsen."

I gasped. "Marty and Garrett broke into my house?"

"The whole thing doesn't compute, since there were no other fingerprints inside your house or on the electronic bug. I guess they got careless in the garage. Paulsen's prints are on the handle of the bag; Melrose's are on the clock."

"But Mr. Gold—"

"We have to throw this into the mix with Gold's statement of seeing only one intruder, Sophie. We'll talk about it. The reason

I'm calling you now is we're on our way to pick up Melrose and the kid, if we can find him. I know you're on campus so I just want to say, keep away from Melrose's office."

"You think he killed Charlotte? Or Garrett did?"

"I think everyone killed her, until further notice. I'm just saying. You never know when things can get messy and I don't want you there. I have enough problems worrying about … " Virgil coughed and I shut my eyes so tight a pain shot through my head.

"Worrying about Bruce? Is that what you were going to say? Is there news about Bruce?"

"No, nothing yet. You know I'll tell you right away and I know you'll do the same."

"Okay."

I brought my breathing back to normal.

I hung up and hit talk in preparation for calling Marty's office, right above me. I decided for once I'd obey Virgil and cancel lunch with Marty. Not that I believed him to be Charlotte's killer, but eating alone from my sack of whatever Ariana had dreamed up sounded better to me anyway.

I stepped out of my private little alcove and headed for the side entrance I'd just used, clicking the phone on as I walked.

I took three steps forward and felt a hand on my shoulder.

"Sophie," Marty Melrose said, running his fingers through his hair with his free hand.

"Martin, I was just going to call you. I—"

He pushed the elevator button and nudged me toward the car. "We can ride up together."

At least I'd be able to tell Virgil that I'd tried to stay away from Martin Melrose.

# Chapter 20

We rode up in silence in the creaky elevator that was as old as the building. Admin workers claimed it was the last passenger elevator in the country with a metal gate that had to be manually pulled shut before the machine would move. The car smelled of rust and soggy plaster, causing me to look around for leaks.

Martin cleared his throat several times, and, I guessed, was using coughing noises to mask the awkwardness of the silence.

Martin's expression was somewhere between sad and worried.

I had no reason to be afraid of Martin Melrose, I told myself. He was the one who should be worried, with his prints all over my alarm clock. The farther in time Virgil's phone call became, the less I could picture Marty rummaging in my garage. I began to think the fingerprint analysis was wrong. Virgil's warning was just Virgil being overprotective.

It was Daryl Farmer we all had to be afraid of, not a mild-mannered accounting major from the sixties.

Anyway, Marty wasn't in very good shape. He was a designer dresser, for sure, but his body was definitely low end, approaching Social Security age and badly in need of exercise. Short as I was, I could defend myself against him if I had to. And Virgil had said he was on the way.

Nevertheless, when the elevator doors opened to a bustling second floor, full of deans and vice presidents and their staffs, I felt my shoulders relax. I thought I'd never forgive Charlotte for living a life that ended in murder and thus caused me to be more fearful than at any time I could remember.

We arrived at Marty's small waiting area, free of anyone who looked like the loser Garrett whom Fran had mentioned. Too bad, since I'd been hoping I'd see at least one other person in the English Collegiate Gothic building dressed worse than I was.

I plunked my cloth drawstring lunch bag on the small round conference table in Marty's office. I waited while he pulled a soft leather sack from his desk, thus becoming the only person I knew who had a lunch bag as expensive as my best briefcase. Marty took a seat. His expression had turned sour, as if he'd already eaten his lunch and it wasn't very good.

Seeing the school's chief financial officer in such a sorry state somehow energized me, bad person that I am, and I felt I'd never have as good an opportunity to get closure on Charlotte's activities on school grounds. And maybe at a convenience store in Bailey's Landing.

Marty got ahead of me, however, opening the discussion by scratching his head and saying, "You know, Sophie, I'm not really sure why we're having this lunch. Not that it isn't pleasant to see you here at the heart of the college, mind you, where you're always welcome."

Another time I might have been miffed at the suggestion that Franklin Hall was a dispensable appendage of the college, far from its beating administrative heart. But today, with Virgil on the way and Marty about to be taken in for questioning, if not arrested, I felt confident. An impossible image came, of Marty with his bow tie and high-end lunch sack, in a prison cell for the crime of burglary against me.

"And the same goes for you, Marty," I said, working to make his name sound cute. "We'd love to see you any time out there in the buildings where the actual work of teaching and learning takes place."

I smiled, as if to say, "If you're only joking, so am I."

As I swung my head and my arm to reference the outlying buildings, I looked out the tall, narrow windows and caught a glimpse of the Emily Dickinson Library, a much newer building than admin. One of the admirable architectural features of Marty's building was the enormous size and position of the stately windows. From the outside, the array of windows resembled a beautiful block matrix.

On a more practical note, their sills were only a couple of feet from the floor. This meant than even a short person could see out to the campus below.

This short person was now able to see the door to the library. I experienced a simultaneous shot of memory back to when Martin Melrose made a comment to me about locking the doors of buildings on campus. It might have been his indifferent reaction to a murder on campus, or it might have been the remark of the person who took advantage of an unlocked door to the library last Thursday night.

Of all the things Marty could have said to warn me about security, why that one? He might have said, "Don't stay late" or "Be sure you have someone with you."

How would Marty know the Emily Dickinson Library door had been left unlocked, thanks to a couple of students who had to get to Nathaniel Hawthorne dorm's version of a kegger? If he was Charlotte's killer, what was his backup plan if the door had been locked? Did he have his own key?

I wished I'd paid more attention to the special security brochure all faculty and staff received. I remembered vaguely that it contained a list of all those who had master keys to campus buildings, by title, not by name. I'd glanced at the page and recognized that only the top tier of administrators were on the list but I couldn't remember if "Associate Vice President for Finance/ Controller," Marty's official title, was one of the trusted offices.

I couldn't let that detail derail me now.

"You gave yourself away, Marty," I said now.

"I don't know what you're talking about."

"You all but told me the library door was unlocked the night Charlotte was killed, and I'm saying the reason you knew is because you were able to walk right in and attack the person who was scamming you out of lottery money."

The accusation sounded lame to me. I had to remind myself that this was part of my plan. Let Marty think I suspected him of murder and maybe he'd confess to robbery and I'd find out why he took my duffel bag.

"You think I killed Charlotte?" Marty let out a high-pitched laugh that was at war with his pinstripes. "You are so far off the charts."

"Then put me on the chart," I said, though I had an intense dislike of sports metaphors. "And while you're at it, explain why your fingerprints are on my stolen travel alarm clock."

Marty's eyes widened. I felt an explosion coming on and surreptitiously pushed my chair back and moved to its edge for a quick getaway. I listened for noise in the hallway and was happy to hear chatter.

"It was Garrett Paulsen. All Garrett."

I didn't fill Marty in on exactly how the police had found Marty's and Garrett's names and numbers in the first place—because, good citizen that she is, Dr. Sophie Knowles turned in the money and notes immediately. Almost immediately.

"Very creative, Marty. Blame the absent guy."

"Okay, I started it, in a way," Marty said. "When Charlotte came two years ago, I sensed a kindred spirit. I'm the head of the hiring committee, so I saw her application before the rest of the committee did. Something she'd written prompted me to check and I saw that she had a record. I already had a very bad gambling habit by then, mostly horses, and I owed money. A lot of money. I thought, here's someone I can join forces with. So I made sure she was hired and that no one knew about her past."

"You kept it quiet and you blackmailed Charlotte."

"I did her a favor. I hid her past and gave her a job."

"Then used that against her."

"No, no, I would have been happy if she'd just been willing to teach me a few things. I'd never conned anyone or skimmed or anything like that."

I gave him a dubious look. Marty responded by pointing to his desk and the file cabinets that lined the room, and continued.

"Do you know how easy it would have been all these years to embezzle? Auditors these days are wet behind the ears. And they think all they need is a high-powered computer, but let me tell you, I could have gotten rich the good old-fashioned way."

"That's an interesting perspective on your profession."

"It's true. Their software would be obsolete by the time they had a clue. But I never took a penny that way."

"But you ran cons."

"I think I've said enough."

"Marty, can you help me out here? I'm not trying to point the finger at you." That was for Virgil, who'd be showing up soon, but Marty didn't have to know that. "I'm trying to figure out if my friend was still living a double, or triple, life."

"You can rest easy on that. I tried to get Charlotte to help me with a couple of simple investment scams. You know, 'Send me money and I'll quadruple it in thirty days.' Charlotte would have nothing to do with it anymore."

I wished with all my might that Marty was telling the truth. That Charlotte really had been trying to go straight. I felt a smile come to my face and hoped Marty didn't misinterpret it as being for him or his story.

In a sense I'd gotten what I came for. My friend as I knew her was not a criminal. She'd refused an opportunity to engage in unlawful activities with the financial heart of the college.

I felt a selfish sense of vindication, that I'd befriended a good person after all, though I doubted Daryl or any of Charlotte's other early victims would agree.

Marty went on and on about how so many college treasurers cook the books, a term I hadn't heard in a while. I picked up his thread when I heard Garrett's name.

"I scammed the wrong guy, however. Garrett Paulsen. Bad stroke of luck. Rather bad advice from a so-called friend. Garrett's a grifter himself and was pretty upset when he realized he'd been had. How he fell for my con with all his own experience, I'll never know."

I thought I'd show off my research. "Did you tell him he won the lottery but had to pay to collect?"

"No, no. That had been one of Charlotte's cons years ago. I went the bank fraud route. I can't believe I'm telling you this. You're not wearing a wire are you, Sophie?"

I laughed. "No, Marty. I told you why I came. I needed to find out about the woman I'd been friends with for two years."

"I'm finding this strangely therapeutic, though I can't imagine why. Anyway, I made up some title like Fraud Control

Department for a consumer group and sent a letter to bank customers. They fill out the questionnaire that's going to help them protect their identity, but of course, in the end it's what we use to steal it. Even a modest size mailing can net you a goodly sum."

Or a badly sum. I shook my head. "I don't get why, Marty. You're a smart man with a good job. I don't understand what happened. First you waste your time at Suffolk Downs and then you have to break the law to support the habit?"

This time my mental picture of Marty was of him in disguise, his wingtips and bow ties left at home, sitting in the grandstand of the horse racing track in East Boston.

"I guess you have no addictions?"

None that I could think of. None that I wanted to admit to Marty.

"None that put me in debt," I said.

"Saint Sophie. Good for you."

I let it pass. "So Garrett Paulsen came after you?"

"He must have hired someone to help him. I can't believe Garrett's smart enough to have found me. I needed to pay him back and there was no other solution than to go to Charlotte for help. I thought he might expose me or even kill me. Hard to tell which one would be worse."

"She wouldn't help?" Meaning, my friend Charlotte wouldn't do anything wrong.

"No way. She refused to even give me a loan. I figured she still had money from her former profession. She actually told me any money she had was for charity"—Marty let out a cackling laugh that annoyed me—"and she was donating it piece by piece until she could manage on her own. Legit, she meant."

I was sad to think she thought she had to flee with it instead.

"So you went to the library last Thursday night to—"

*Whirrrr. Whirrrr. Whirrrr.*

I whipped out my phone. A text from Jenna Ramirez. "I have to take this," I said.

I opened the text, my fingers sticking to the screen from perspiration, though the rest of me was chilled from the drafts in the old building.

I read,

WEATHR BETTR. HELP ON WAY.

I took a breath and imagined a whole posse of trained rescue workers on the way up the mountain to carry Bruce and his buddies down. At the same time, who was to say what the rescuers would find. I couldn't think of that right now.

I texted back,

DO U HAVE #?

I tapped my phone on my knee.

"Do you have to go?" Marty asked, hopefully, I thought.

"I'm waiting for an answer," I said. "I might have to leave in a hurry."

If things had gone differently, I might have shared my concerns about Bruce with Marty, but at the moment I needed to keep the two stressors in my life in different parts of my brain and my psyche.

"Well, as I was saying, I told the police the truth about Thursday evening. I had nothing to hide. I went to the library to talk. I found Charlotte in the stacks. We fought, but with words only, I swear. I finally realized she wasn't going to budge and I stormed out of there."

"Was the library closed at the time?" I heard my voice from a distance, what with half of me being on a mountain in New Hampshire.

"Yes, it was after nine. And she was alive when I left her."

"Did anyone see you leave?"

I felt I was on autopilot, listening, asking questions, but waiting for the *whirrrr whirrrr* of my phone. The part of me that was tuned into Marty registered that Marty had been there after Hannah and Chelsea left. But before the killer. Unless Marty was the killer.

"I wasn't anxious to be seen," Marty said. "There were students around outside. It was before the rain and rather mild, so no one was in a hurry to get back to the dorms."

"Except the party people."

"Excuse me?"

I hadn't realized I'd said anything out loud. I waved my hand for Marty to continue.

"I recognized a couple of students, but you know, I don't

know a single one by name. They're just ciphers to me."

He would say that, ratcheting my annoyance factor up a notch.

I'd been glancing out the window on a regular basis during our non-lunch, wondering when I'd see a car that told me the Henley PD had arrived, in either a marked or an unmarked vehicle. I looked now and saw nothing resembling an official car. Virgil had been ready to confront Marty almost an hour ago. Maybe, unlike us, he'd stopped for lunch.

I had another key piece of information to squeeze from the administrator in front of me.

"Marty—"

"I hate that name."

"I know. Back to your fingerprints on my alarm clock?"

Marty sighed loudly. "Garrett brought me your duffel. He threw it at me to make a statement. Made me open it up and rustle around inside. Wanted me to see how there was no money. He'd gone to your house and—I told you he's dumb—grabbed a duffel from the garage without checking to see if there was anything in it worth taking. Then when he entered the house to grab whatever else he could, he tripped the alarm. So he ran."

"What made him go after my house in the first place?"

"I … I might have mentioned …" Marty showed me his palms. If he was asking for sympathy or forgiveness, he wasn't getting either.

"You pointed Garrett to Charlotte and then to me? To save yourself and your habit? That's pitiful, Marty."

"You have to understand—"

"Maybe Garrett killed Charlotte," I said, alarming myself. "And then followed me when you told him I was her friend."

It hadn't been Daryl at all who was the murderer. It was the Shop At Ease guy whom I'd still had only glimpses of. I shivered, thinking of him, following me, entering my home.

I checked my phone for the third time in as many minutes, making sure each time that the ringtone volume was set at maximum.

Marty shook his head hard enough to dislodge his glasses. "No, no. He didn't do it," he said, but I'd lost my place in the conversation and must have looked as confused as I felt.

"Garrett did not kill Charlotte," Marty said, emphatically. "He had a gun. He would have shot her, and I know she died from a fall from the ladder."

I knew I hadn't been paying full attention, but fallacious reasoning always woke me up. "You're saying the reason you know Garrett didn't kill Charlotte is that he has a gun?"

*Whirrrr. Whirrrr. Whirrrr.*

I started, dropped the phone, and banged my head on the table when I rose. The number of phone droppings and clumsy incidents in my life had gone up about four hundred percent in the last three days.

I looked at the screen. Not Jenna. A call from Virgil.

"Hey," I said. "Are you calling with the number?"

"Sorry?"

Another casualty of my scattered brain. I'd assumed Virgil knew the storm had broken and that I'd just asked Jenna for a phone number. It's a wonder he didn't think I was playing the lottery.

"Eduardo's wife texted me that the storm was over and they're starting the rescue." I tripped over "rescue," apparently having a love/hate relationship with the word. "Detective Mitchell, I'm in the Administration Building having lunch with Martin Melrose," I sent a meaningful glance Marty's way, putting him on notice that the cops knew where I was, should anything nasty happen to me.

"I know. His secretary just informed me of the fact."

"Are you calling with a number, then? I'm hoping for a direct line to the sheriff or the rangers up there."

"I have better than that. I have a ride for you. Are you up for a trip to the mountains?"

"When?"

"Now. Just come to the east entrance to the Administration Building and look for a tall, handsome cop."

Another time I would have asked what the cop's name would be. This afternoon, I fairly screamed, "I'm on my way."

I stood and clicked off the phone. Before I could say anything, Marty picked up my unopened lunch bag and handed it to me, as if he wanted no trace of me in his office.

"You're leaving," he said. Not a question.

"I guess it's your lucky day," I said.

I caught one last glance out Marty's magnificent windows and saw a familiar beige sedan pull up to the west side of the building, not bothering to park in a legitimate space. Virgil's partner Archie O'Connell, back from vacation in time for this plum assignment, exited and headed for the outside stairs I'd used an hour ago.

"Or maybe not," I said.

"Excuse me?" I heard for the last time, I hoped, from the tight little man who thought he was virtuous because he could have robbed the college blind but didn't.

"Maybe it's not your lucky day," I said.

I left Marty's office and nearly ran through the waiting area and down the hallway to the east end of the building. Not bothering to wait for the elevator, I flew down the stairs and out the door.

Virgil leaned against the fender of his personal black Camry, arms folded across his wide chest. Except that he was hatless, the whole picture mimicked an inexpensive version of a livery service.

I knew Virgil would be taken by surprise and put off kilter, but I ran up and kissed his cheek anyway, in full of view of the passing coeds.

# Chapter 21

Virgil insisted he didn't know anything more than the one happy fact: Bruce and his buddies were on the way down the mountain. Were they walking on their own, as opposed to being carried on a stretcher? He didn't know. Were they starving? Frostbitten? No information on that. Was anyone seriously injured? He couldn't say. Anything broken? Fractured? Sprained? Nothing had been said about any of those possibilities.

I'd gone down the list in descending order, except for having skipped number one—"alive?" Virgil was patient through it all.

We made one stop before leaving campus, to my car where I picked up a jacket and bottles of water. So what if they were the dusty purchases from the Bailey's Landing Shop At Ease. If Bruce could survive on granola, I could rough it in Virgil's car.

I finally slumped down in the seat, stopped badgering the driver, and took out my phone to re-plan my day.

My first business was to call Fran Emerson and ask her to take a linear algebra study group for me at three. Fran was well positioned to help the students with homework in vectors and transformations since that was her current research interest.

I explained my new plan for the afternoon and asked if she could also cover for me at the Franklin Hall faculty meeting. Not satisfied with the full faculty meetings that ate up an evening every month, the science and math faculties gathered separately, as needed, for issues pertinent only to us.

"You poor thing," Fran said. "Missing the privilege of hearing Robert's latest physics joke. Will you give me your proxy vote on what color we should paint the walls of the lecture hall?

If we authorize the many, that is. So, first you have to turn over that vote."

"Where do I sign?"

We both laughed. It seemed a long time since I'd felt so light and nearly carefree. As long as I didn't worry about what was in store for me in New Hampshire.

I called Jenna and told her I was sorry I didn't know much more than she had texted me.

"You're so lucky you can pick up and go," she said.

The sound of Todd's voice, screaming in the background, told me why she couldn't join us. I promised to call her as soon as I learned anything.

Ariana was as excited as I was.

"Things are shifting for the better. The weekend is finally ending," she said.

I did a calculation.

Charlotte's killer had been identified, but not caught; Bruce had been located, but was not home safe.

"I'd say we're about eighty percent there," I said.

I was used to the scoffing noises I heard from my friend whenever I threw a quantitative caveat into her pronouncements.

"It's facing reality," I told her now through my cell phone.

"It's being bound by the rules of earth," she said.

A typical routine from the Ariana and Sophie friendship, the longest lasting one I had.

I checked my email and decided everyone else could wait until tomorrow for a response, though college students rarely believed that. One date gone bad, or one B+ instead of an A, was on a par with a life-threatening event to many of them.

I badly needed a review of where things stood with the investigation into Charlotte's murder. A lot had happened at the same time that my beloved was stranded on an icy mountain, and I knew details of the case had gotten lost in the pathways of my brain.

As I was trying to formulate a question in a politically correct way, Virgil favored me with current information.

"You may be interested to hear that we picked up Garrett

Paulsen this morning. He has so many priors, it's not hard to find a reason to hold him while we figure out his role in the Crocker case." Virgil glanced over at me. "Sorry, I should have said, 'in your friend's murder investigation'. We don't mean any disrespect. It's just habit."

Virgil seemed to be speaking for the whole Henley PD. I certainly understood the habit and, I suspected, the need for emotional distance when your job was nearly all about the seamier side of life.

"No problem," I said. Virgil reached into his inside jacket pocket, pulled out a photograph, and handed it to me. "Ever seen him before?"

I looked at the image of a squirrely young man with a flak jacket, dreadlocks, and a baseball cap.

"Garrett Paulsen?" I asked, realizing I'd never seen the man. At least I didn't think I had, until I caught a glimpse of his neck and the faint outline of a birthmark crawling up his cheek. I turned the photo to minimize reflections from the afternoon sun. The memory clicked in. "Yes, he was milling around with the crowd on campus, at the crime scene. He was with Marty."

Come to find out, with his stained jacket and matted hair, Garrett did look worse than I did, even less fit for an appearance in the hallowed marble halls of the Administration Building. I wondered how the dapper Marty coped with him. I guess large financial debts could make a difference in what a person could tolerate.

"Thanks," Virgil said, putting the photo back in his pocket. "Things like this always help. We can say he was familiar with the campus."

"I can't say for sure that I saw him at my house, but I believe he was in the group leaving with Daryl and some other students."

"We don't need that ID now, so it's all good," Virgil said. "The question is, is he just a small-time alarm clock thief or a killer? There's nothing really violent in his past, but that's not to say a little robbery or even a meeting couldn't go bad and put someone like him over the edge."

I gulped. What if I'd been home and the tipping point had

come for Garrett in my garage? I chose not to believe Garrett would turn violent.

I told Virgil Marty's version of things and his testimony that Garrett wasn't a killer.

"But you already know all this if you've talked to Garrett."

Virgil nodded. "The stories mesh pretty well."

"Did you confirm that Garrett planted the bug in my den?"

To my surprise, Virgil shook his head, No. "And I doubt he did. I spent about four minutes with the guy before I left Archie with him, and I could tell he's not even smart enough to follow the instructions on the bug package. I mean, who isn't going to at least unzip a duffel bag part way before he carts it off and sets off an alarm?"

"Good point. I hope he liked the hotel shampoo and conditioner. But where does that leave us? With two break-ins in my house? A house burglar and a garage burglar at the same time? What's the probability of that?"

"You're the probability girl, but that's what it looks like."

"Someone was in my house before Garrett entered the garage, someone who knew how to defeat the alarm."

"And plant a bug," Virgil said. "Are you thinking who I'm thinking?"

"Daryl," I said, and Virgil nodded.

"The scenario is looking good for your favorite old man, Mr. Gold," he said.

"Mr. Gold saw Daryl enter the house. Daryl defeated the alarm, so STA wasn't alerted. He set it again so he'd know if I came in. Then when Garrett entered the house through the garage, the alarm went off. Daryl probably wasn't expecting a second thief, and may even have thought I was the one who entered the house."

"Until the alarm keep ringing."

"Then Daryl went out the way he came in."

"It's a wonder Daryl and Garrett didn't smash into each other," Virgil said.

"What are the chances you'll ever find Daryl? If he's as good at hiding as he was at finding someone who wanted to hide, it's low probability, right?"

"We have some pretty good guys, too."

Uh-oh. "I didn't mean to insult your IT department."

"No offense taken," Virgil said, with a grin. "Even the smartest bad guy is going to make a mistake. He's going to order a phone or rent a movie or sign up for a personal trainer, whatever. The trick is to be watching at the right time and place."

"You'll get him," I said, mostly to make up for the near insult to the boys and girls of the Henley PD.

I leaned back, a little dizzy and distressed that two people had violated my home, but satisfied that we'd solved another puzzle.

"Is Marty in custody? I saw Archie headed into the admin building."

"He's there for questioning. Marty is so clean it's hard to imagine he jumped right from gambling to murder, in spite of all his debts. We can't tie him to fraud yet, either, and if we jailed everyone who was in debt, there wouldn't be enough cells in the state. We're just waiting to see what shakes out between him and Garrett."

It seemed my work might be over. But I knew I wouldn't rest completely until Daryl was in, out of the wind.

Virgil drove with his right arm hanging over the back of the seat, in the manner of the cool kids in nineteen fifties movies. All that was missing was a pack of cigarettes rolled up in his sleeve. Bruce, a huge fan of films from all eras, would have been able to quote a movie title, car, and actor-driver in a minute. Maybe I'd be challenging him with a quiz in a couple of hours.

I hoped the perfectly clear and snappy weather would continue all the way to New Hampshire.

"I'm sure the pumpkin patches are on display all the way up 95," I said to Virgil. "It should be a beautiful drive."

"Who said anything about a drive?" Virgil said.

I looked at him and then out the window. I hadn't noticed that we were still in town, having veered off to the west instead of picking up the highway due north. With any other driver in the car, I might have been frantic, certain that I'd been kidnapped. But in the next minute I saw a very familiar sign.

HENLEY AIRFIELD, 1 MILE.

"What's this about?" I asked.

"You don't think MAstar is going to let its star pilot and supernurses come home by ground transportation?"

"They're going to pick them up in the helicopter?"

"Make that *we're* going to pick them up in the helicopter. Well, not me. But you and Ernie will be in the plane. I forget, do they call it a plane?"

"Uh, no, I don't think they ever call it a plane. Planes have fixed wings. I've heard Bruce refer to his 'aircraft.' Never 'plane.'"

As if that mattered. "I'm going to New Hampshire in an MAstar helicopter?" I all but squealed. Too much time with Chelsea and her peers.

Virgil had a wide grin, clearly pleased with his little surprise. Things just went from good to better.

I held my jacket closed up to my neck as Virgil and I walked, heads down, in what always seemed like a wind tunnel between the Henley airfield parking lot and the MAstar trailer.

We passed row after row of small planes, lined up, wing tip to wing tip, on the gravel. Several aviation-related businesses and flying clubs were housed here along with MAstar. The roar in the air was as though all the planes had their engines revved, about to move up and over in formation, though I was sure they all had ignitions turned off, if that's what they were called.

The last time I was here, I was with Charlotte and a kid who'd called himself Noah. It would be a while before I'd be able to forget the real purpose of that special tour. How had I not realized why Charlotte was more interested in the outlying private planes than in the MAstar flight nurse's demonstration of a new unit for transporting critically ill newborns?

I called up a happier visit, one Christmas eve when the team hosted a party for kids with disabilities and Santa made an early afternoon appearance. One of his elves (pilot Jonathan) flew the helicopter onto the airfield, then Santa (flight nurse Rocky) jumped out with a bag of toys and a good time was had by all.

I wanted those days back.

Inside the chain link fence that defined MAstar's property, Virgil and I climbed movable orange metal steps to the door of a trailer and entered a strangely homey environment.

I'd been inside the doublewide many times and was familiar with its home-away-from-home setup. Coffee perking on a Formica counter; someone's aromatic, spicy lunch heating in the microwave; the large logo mat on the floor of the kitchen soaking up spills.

The signage throughout the trailer reminded me of dorm décor. Printed or hand lettered instructions and warnings appeared everywhere. On the microwave, the printer, the small washer/dryer set in a corner of the kitchen. Walls were covered with maps of the area's topography; computer screens showed weather maps; white boards held schedules; cork boards bled memos.

I smiled every time I read the sign above the rack that held the crew's helmets: Thou Shalt Not Whine! I assumed this was an especially pertinent warning when a call came in the middle of the night.

Pilot Ernie Sims, whom I'd met a few times was waiting for us in the den, a room with flimsy paneled walls and a mishmash of furniture, not unlike the lounge on Hannah Stephens's dorm floor.

"Hey, Virgil, Sophie. Always a pleasure," Ernie said. "Good news, huh? Going to pick up those crazy dudes?"

A woman who'd been eating a sandwich and watching an action flick clicked the TV off. She stood and brushed crumbs from her slick pants. "I'm Irene. I'll be your nurse today," she said to me, with a big smile, gripping me with a strong handshake.

Irene, newly hired to replace a nurse I'd known, was among the few females in the company. All of the pilots and technicians and most of the flight nurses were ex-military males, guys who apparently hadn't had enough excitement and emergency situations in combat.

Tall and lean, Ernie Sims was a perpetual smiler, but of the sincere kind. He and Virgil exchanged small talk that went over my head.

"How goes the ten sixty-one?" from Ernie.

Followed by "As good as your HAPI," from Virgil.

"Don't let these guys fool you into thinking they're really having a conversation. They're just showing off," Irene told me. "Ernie asked about Virgil's miscellaneous public service and Virge meaninglessly answered, 'helicopter approach path indicator.'"

"Thanks," I said. "I did learn ETOPS from Bruce."

And we all laughed at the acronym for "Engines Turn Or People Swim."

It seemed strange to be in these quarters without Bruce. I knew exactly where he slept on his night shifts, where his favorite cereal was shelved, which videos in the vast collection were his favorites. I shut my eyes for a minute and pictured him stretched out on the faux leather couch, safely leafing through a movie magazine.

Both Ernie and Irene were in their flight suits, one-piece black jump suits with purple and white stripes running down the legs and arms. Irene had "MAstar FLIGHT NURSE" stenciled on the back of her jacket, under a purple cross that was part of their logo.

"Back to work," Ernie declared. "The techs have cleared us. Ready to go, Sophie?"

I could hardly express how ready I was.

On the field, ready to board the helicopter, I thanked Virgil for all he'd done to track Bruce's status and to book me on the flight to New Hampshire.

Our goodbye was reminiscent of a Casablanca moment, with the aircraft waiting, the roar of the rotors drowning out my farewell words. I blamed Bruce for my growing tendency to make parallels with movies. When I started comparing myself to Ingrid Bergman—she was six inches taller, with about eight inches more hair, and dreamy, not ordinary, brown eyes—it was time to take stock.

The four long, narrow rotors at the top of the helicopter looked almost too thin to do the job, lifting all of us plus the craft, plus heavy equipment. But I'd been a passenger before and I knew it was up to the task.

With Irene's help, I hoisted myself from the ground onto a step and then up to the interior of the aircraft. I was privileged to buckle myself into one of the gray fabric seats, next to Ernie, while Irene slid the door shut and sat in the back.

"Thank you for flying MAstar," Ernie announced, as if to the population of a fully booked commercial airliner.

And we were off.

Though it wasn't my first time in a MAstar helicopter, the other trips were short hops, for pleasure or enlightenment about what was Bruce's office in a way. I reminded myself that "r" in MAstar was for rescue.

I understood why Bruce liked to fly. Soaring above both suburban and city life had its pleasures. Looking down on everything from SUVs to backyard swimming pools to office buildings gave an unmistakable sense of exhilaration and power. The largest, most expensive home on Boston's Beacon Hill was like a dollhouse; the highest horsepower muscle car like a child's toy.

"Is everyone going to fit in here coming back?" I asked Ernie. Rather, shouted to Ernie over the noise in the cockpit. I knew the usual working crew comprised one pilot and two flight nurses, plus two spaces for patients on gurneys. It seemed one too many for the carrier.

"I didn't tell you. Only two more on the return."

I swallowed hard and felt a shiver through my body. But it was silly to think Bruce might be the one staying behind. I wouldn't be on this flight if Bruce weren't okay to travel home. Would I? Wouldn't Virgil have warned me if this trip was simply to take me on a visit to a New Hampshire hospital?

In spite of his formidable task of piloting, Ernie noticed my distress.

"We heard a little while ago. Eduardo is in bad shape.

A leap of logic told me that meant Bruce was in good shape. I had no trouble going with that loose reasoning for now. A form of survivor guilt took over and I was on a roller coaster of emotions from great relief that Bruce was able to go home, to concern for Eduardo.

"Is he going to make it?" I asked, regretting that I had to shout out a question that should be whispered, if spoken at all.

For some reason, benign I hoped, the engine noise grew louder at that moment, or it might have been increased ringing in my ears. The words I heard were "surgery" and "neck."

That couldn't be good.

"Does Jenna know?"

The engines went back to their normal thunderous roar and I understood Ernie to say that another MAstar pilot knew Jenna best, and he was dispatched to talk to her in person.

"I didn't want to tell you about Eduardo back there," he said, cocking his neck toward the trailer far behind and below us. "Cell phones, you know?"

"Cell phones?" I asked. I spread my palms and shrugged, hoping my body language would make the question more clear.

"You might have called someone or gotten a call on the ground."

"I wouldn't have told anyone," I said.

"Not deliberately, but it's only natural that you might mention what's on your mind. Eduardo has this thing about one of us talking to Jenna before anyone else does since she's a little high strung."

I had no idea there were so many unwritten, personal protocols among the MAstar team. I'd have to ask Bruce what his were. Did he think I was high strung? If that meant feeling like my whole body had been turned inside out and its pieces needed reassembling, at this moment he'd be correct.

Poor Jenna. She had every right to be strung however high she wanted. And Todd. I shook my head in sympathy for him. I was his age when we lost my father to cancer. My mother did a heroic job, making sure I knew who Peter Knowles was, what a wonderful math teacher he'd been, how much he loved me. I had new respect for how she'd handled the challenges.

It was premature to think that Jenna might have to endure the same fate.

Another awful thought intruded.

I turned toward Ernie again. "Do you have details on Bruce and Kevin?" That you're not telling me, I meant.

"Honest. All we know is what I told Virgil, that both guys are cleared to come home."

The ringing in my head dropped to a lower, slightly more comfortable frequency.

I took a minute to check the flow of the world below me. It wasn't a famously pretty time of year in New England. Though we were a month from official winter, most of the trees were bare of leaves, their trunks a desolate gray. But the landscape was green and even ordinary features like reservoirs, ponds, woodland areas, country clubs, and state parks took on added interest when viewed from a couple of thousand feet.

About an hour after takeoff, the landing struts and runners touched ground on a helipad above the parking lot of Mercy Hospital.

As glorious as it had felt to ride above it all, Ernie's seamless landing and our deplaning felt even better.

I'd had the whole trip to prepare myself for what Bruce might look like, what shape he'd be in. Would he even be conscious? I mentally chided myself. Of course he'd be conscious. They wouldn't send an unconscious patient home. He'd be bruised, maybe, but I could handle that. Would we need help or would I be able to take care of him myself?

The automatic doors of the hospital slid open in front of us, allowing a couple with a never-before-seen-by-me triple stroller to exit and MAstar workers and me to enter.

I was about to have the answers to my questions.

# Chapter 22

The young doctor who met us in the waiting area—Dias, according to his nametag—must have thought me cruel indeed as I broke into a wide smile at the list of Bruce's injuries. A broken leg, a minor head wound, and what he called partial-thickness frostbite on some of Bruce's fingertips.

Kevin had emerged with a broken leg and a dislocated shoulder.

Plus, there were assorted bruises and rope burns for both.

I was nearly giddy. I hoped the doctor understood that compared to what I'd dreaded, and relative to the accident reports that filled Bruce's magazines, their injuries were like scraped knees on a preteen.

As was appropriate, Doctor Dias was close-mouthed on Eduardo's condition, other than to tell us he was "stable."

"Code for 'none of your business'," Irene whispered when he turned to leave.

When we finally got to see Bruce and Kevin, not even the matching blue wheelchairs could dampen our reunion.

Choruses of "Hey, buddy," and "Woo hoo," punctuated the greetings.

I leaned over and held onto Bruce as best I could, given his restraints. For all the exchanges of "I love you" and "I'm so happy to see you," we might have been apart for weeks instead of days.

"I'm going to have to postpone the climb in Nepal," Bruce said when we finally let go of each other.

I was the last to laugh.

"Hey, Sophie, got a hug for me?" Kevin asked. "I'm on my own here."

I hardly knew Kevin, the youngest member of the MAstar staff, but I leaned over and hugged him anyway, avoiding the arm that was in a sling.

"You'll have to tell me about the case," Bruce said to me.

It said a lot that I had to think for a beat about what he meant by "the case." The murder case that had consumed me as much as the trauma over my missing boyfriend had receded for the last few hours.

Bruce insisted on a summary as he reluctantly let Irene wheel him down the hallway while Ernie piloted Kevin's chair, a few rotations behind and I took on crutch-carrying duty. I suspected Bruce's interest in what had happened since Charlotte's body was found stemmed in great part from wanting to reconnect with me on a level other than his own current state.

I gave him the bottom line, that the police had settled on Daryl Farmer as the person with the best scores on means, motive, and opportunity. His disappearance put him over the top as the most likely killer.

I could see that it was a struggle for Bruce to keep awake and pay attention. The doctor had warned us that he'd given both climbers medication to ease the discomfort of the helicopter ride home.

Ernie seemed to have no compunction grilling the sleepy guys. Perhaps he thought it was his right to interrogate as he pushed Kevin's wheelchair up a slight incline.

"What happened up there, buddies?" he asked. Something I couldn't have asked in my present mood without sounding like a harpy.

"There was a team in front of us that was so slow, you'd think they'd never been on a real mountain," Kevin said. "Like, what did they think? That they could go from climbing artificial holds on a theme park wall to scaling Cannon?"

Bruce picked up the thread, his speech labored, as if heavy meds were kicking in. "We couldn't pass, so we played it slow. We thought we could still beat the storm, but it was on us like"—Bruce's weak swooping motion didn't do justice to a raging storm—"and we just did the best we could."

"Until the guys who were in over their heads literally cut

loose an avalanche onto us," Kevin said.

"Rocks and snow. Very nice," Bruce added.

"I was belaying, almost out of the way, tucked into a corner with an overhang, so nothing major happened to me," Kevin said. "Bruce was next to me, but more exposed."

I guessed a broken leg, a dislocated shoulder, and rope burns were nothing to write home about.

"Eduardo was leading and got the full brunt," Bruce said. "We figure he fell at least a hundred feet. He was over fifty feet above us when the avalanche knocked him down and ripped his axes and crampons from the ice. Then some of his gear zippered and failed as the rope went tight."

Kevin picked up the story as the two men seemed to be reliving a nightmarish moment. "We watched him slide and tumble down the ice. He came to a stop below us. Luckily I was securely anchored and the rope wasn't cut by any sharp rocks."

"He just missed them," Bruce said. "Snow was packed into his mouth and throat, but we got to him in time to clear his airway so he could breathe."

"We did what we could, put on every piece of clothing we had, and waited."

I let out my own breath.

"Bad scene for Eduardo," Kevin said. "But the doctors are very hopeful."

"And ... woo hoo ... you two are here to tell the tale," Irene said.

"Ready to climb again," Bruce said.

One of the crutches slipped from my hand and landed on Bruce's shoulder.

"Oops," I said.

As we approached the helipad, I looked around again at the unfamiliar surroundings of Mercy Hospital, its grottos and angelic statuary meant to offer respite and compassion. Having Bruce safely back gave me a small measure of hope that things could be peaceful again down in Henley, Massachusetts.

I sneaked a look at my phone to see if by any chance Virgil had reported in by e-mail. Maybe Daryl had been located and taken in. For all I knew, Daryl was among us in New Hampshire, even at Mercy, posing as a temporary IT consultant on his way to Montreal.

I wondered if I'd ever have closure if Daryl was never found. I made a note to ask Virgil the statistics on missing criminals.

I scrolled through notices of messages from Chelsea, Hannah, and Fran, all of which could be handled later. Nothing from Virgil.

One e-mail that would never have stood out before last weekend was listed with a subject line, "Unpaid Beneficiary – Urgent We Hear From You."

From a Charlotte wannabe-scammer? I deleted it immediately and emptied the trash.

I sent a quick text to Ariana and an email to Virgil with updates I knew they'd be looking for.

Two young women, candy-stripers without the pink-and-white uniforms, I guessed, loaded the climbers' gear onto the aircraft.

"Last call for Flight 896 to Henley," Ernie called.

For now it was going to have to be enough to have closure on my boyfriend's ice-climbing trip. Not complete closure, however. I knew that once all the guys woke up and were on the mend, it would be a while before we stopped hearing stories of what had happened on the mountain.

We flew back to Henley without much chatter as both patients fell sound asleep under Irene's watchful eye. From the front seat, I kept looking back to make sure both men were breathing. Every time I did, Irene gave me an understanding smile and a thumbs-up.

I'd given Virgil a quick call on the way back and he was waiting at the airfield with a van and driver. The vehicle was something between a true ambulance and a soccer mom's mini-van with a few medical embellishments. I never thought to ask how all these logistics had been worked out. Perhaps all law enforcement officers and all transportation related personnel, by land or sea or air, were connected somehow and had only to tap into a network to plan a journey.

I doubted it was that simple and once again thanked Virgil and Ernie and Irene for setting up the trip. Virgil had even thought to retrieve my car from campus and used it to lead the van to my house.

We'd worked out a plan where Kevin, who was "between girlfriends," as he put it, would stay at my house, along with Bruce, who gave me no argument. It was either my little cottage or a crowded rehab center two towns over.

Kevin's residency in my home would be short-lived, until his mother arrived tomorrow to stay with him while he recuperated in his own apartment.

Bruce's stay was another story. I knew how my mother felt when as a child I'd disappear into a bookstore in the mall without telling her. She'd be so relieved when she found me, but very cranky that I'd put her through the worry.

My mother got over things like that very quickly, but there was no telling how long I'd be cranky.

If the patients weren't ready to be awake and social, it was too bad for them, because Ariana had worked her magic and even with barely a moment's notice had put together a party of sorts at my house.

Takeout containers from the major ethnic food groups lined my kitchen island. Chinese, Italian, Mexican, and French, the last from a new heat-it-and-eat-it place in downtown Henley.

She'd also made up the couch for Kevin and the guest room for Bruce.

"Guess I'll have to sleep at home tonight," she said, adjusting a handmade banner she'd stretched across the doorway between my kitchen and the hallway.

"Welcome Home Bruce!" it read, with a hastily added "and Kevin!" at the bottom.

Virgil enjoyed passing his beer in front of Bruce and Kevin and reminding them they couldn't mix meds and alcohol. "Just one advantage of staying at sea level," he teased.

Adrenaline kicked in and overpowered the meds while the guys told their stories again to Virgil and Ariana. Fran stopped by, and they told them again. Each time I heard the tale, I picked up a few new details, like the fact that Bruce had also suffered frostbite in his toes and Kevin, to whom nothing major had happened, in his words, endured a head wound when his helmet was crushed by a large rock.

I couldn't help thinking of Jenna and Todd and wishing they were with us to celebrate a successful rescue. I debated calling her and decided to wait until she was ready to initiate the contact. I knew Bruce had other ways of finding out how Eduardo was doing.

The final event was the signing of the casts, with as many acronyms as words. Ernie informed us lay people that the NYD he wrote stood for "not yet diagnosed" and Irene's NWB meant "nonweight-bearing." Virgil said he couldn't decide between IP for "injured party" and ASB for "antisocial behavior." Ariana simply drew an angel and wrote "guarding you" next to it.

Before she left, Ariana asked me how I'd liked my lunch surprise. The goodie bag had been the victim of the impromptu helicopter ride to New Hampshire. I had no idea where the food was now, maybe being crushed by aircraft wheels on the Henley airfield.

"I'm sorry," I said. "What was the surprise?"

"No big deal. I made you cookies in the shape of dollar signs."

It was just as well I didn't eat with Marty.

Fran, who'd passed on the art project, generously offered to continue to cover for me on campus.

"You've got your hands full here," she said, pointing to wheelchairs, crutches, ice bags, a home blood-pressure monitor, and the piles of pillows, blankets and towels out of place in my kitchen. Evidence that my home had turned into a hospital ward. "On the other hand, you may need to get out of here tomorrow."

I nodded. "I'll see you on campus."

From the way the athletic Kevin hoisted himself from his wheelchair to the couch in my den, I figured he'd had some practice.

"Got my first break from falling out of my tree house at nine," he told me as I stuffed pillows behind his back. "After that, it was from football, snowboarding and skiing."

"And now this," I said. "Your mother must be very proud."

Uh-oh, cranky Sophie. But Kevin didn't seem to notice.

"She's so glad you can keep me here tonight. Thanks a lot," he said.

I gave him a smile to make up for my mood, and moved essential items—water, cell phone, tissues, and a pocket-size crossword puzzle book for good measure—close to the edge of the coffee table for easy access.

Bruce was my next patient. Though not on my five-year watch, Bruce had had his share of breaks also and managed the transition from chair to bed with apparent ease.

"Put me near the window, give me a pair of binoculars, and I can be Jimmy Stewart, huh?" Bruce noted. *Rear Window,* his first movie reference since the accident. A hopeful sign that his mental powers were not diminished.

I wanted desperately to have a long conversation with my boyfriend. Instead of listening to his adventures along with a host of other people, I felt a strong, selfish need to tell him what I'd been going through and to ask what his plans were for the future. That is, was he willing to commit to a moratorium on recreational activities that invited tragedy?

A helicopter trip, a party, plus another hit of meds had taken their toll, however, and I could tell the laid-up Bruce was ready to call it a day.

Almost in dreamland, he grasped my hand. "I'm so sorry to do this to you, Sophie." For a minute I thought this was an intro to a break-up movie, but his follow-up "I love you" put that thought to rest.

"I'm glad you're home," I said, which was infinitely true.

"I want to hear about the case. I know it's been hard for you. Tell me all the details. Is it all wrapped up?"

The next minute he was sound asleep.

I had to struggle not to shake him awake and have it out with him. "You could have died," I'd have said. "Your friend Eduardo, the father of a small child, will probably never be the same. Why do you do this? It's not a hobby, it's a death wish. When you're healed, are you going to climb back up there?" I knew the answer to that one: "No, I need a bigger challenge," but I wanted to hear it so I could properly scream my response.

I'd been through no physical trauma, but my own tension and foul mood made it impossible to do anything useful. I cursed my inability to focus on the outstanding, lucky outcome that Bruce was alive and with no permanent disability. Wasn't that all that I'd wanted, from the moment I learned about the storm?

Was I never satisfied?

I worked out some tension by polishing off an anacrostic that was someone's idea of "difficult," then getting to work on cleaning up the kitchen.

My mother had been in a wheelchair at the end and I fell back on what had worked for her. I rearranged furniture to make wider pathways. In the linen closet I found the full body pillow she'd used, and in the garage I located the special table that slid over her bed.

I reordered the refrigerator with drinks and food on waist-high shelves and dug out the picnic cooler to use for my patients' lunches. I made a list of snacks and supplies I'd pick up on the way home from campus tomorrow.

Finally I was tired enough and headed for my own bed, hoping I'd wake up in better spirits.

# Chapter 23

If anyone had asked Kevin, he'd have said the mood at breakfast was just fine. Excellent coffee, which Bruce managed to make in spite of his handicap, while, thanks to Ariana's foresight and generosity, I prepared fresh orange juice, bacon, and pancakes. A side of two scrambled eggs for Kevin and a bowl of fruit for Bruce. What was not to like?

But, polite and sweet as we were with each other this morning, the air between Bruce and me was heavy with an agenda that needed to be addressed sooner or later.

Now, however, I had to get to campus. I'd printed out cards with doctors' numbers and the contacts for physical therapy, which both men would need. They promised to make calls and set up a schedule.

I made one last check that food, water, and videos were in easy reach, and gave one last sermon about taking it easy. I reminded the men, who seemed clueless about their vulnerabilities, of the doctors' advice.

"Even if you feel fine and think you can move without assistance, do not abandon your chairs and crutches," I lectured.

Both men saluted.

What was a caregiver to do?

I was out the door for a normal, anticlimactic Tuesday, with classes and meetings.

I could hardly wait.

I started the school day in the mailroom in the basement of Admin. With a few chairs, a bulletin board, and a minimalist décor, the mailroom was the campus version of a corporate office water cooler. Besides a large wooden matrix of mail slots, the room housed two copy machines that supplemented equipment found in each department office.

Faculty and staff gathered to gossip, relive a ballgame, trash a movie or school policy, critique an outfit or a book. Rarely was there news like the last couple of days, however. First, the murder of one of our own in the Emily Dickinson Library, and now—in case you missed it—Martin Melrose had been seen walking out of Admin in the company of two police detectives yesterday.

I suspected that Marty's secretary, Mysti, had spread the word. Archie and his companion really weren't that obviously cops and I doubted they'd led Marty out in handcuffs.

I stayed only long enough to gather my mail and check the bulletin board to see if there was anything I needed to know immediately. There wasn't.

In the few minutes I spent there, I couldn't avoid the scuttlebutt.

"I'm surprised there's no notice of a memorial service for Charlotte Crocker," an art instructor observed.

"I'm not," said Henley's Shakespeare scholar. "How can you eulogize a fugitive from justice? It's repulsive."

"People shouldn't play the lottery anyway. It's a waste of money," from an unknown adjunct.

"Not necessarily," from, I assumed, a lottery player.

I wanted to defend Charlotte, to clear up the technicality that she had served her time and was not, strictly speaking, a fugitive.

Instead, I picked up my mail, left the building, and walked back to Benjamin Franklin Hall.

It was an unseasonably warm day and I took my time, sifting through the mail as I strolled. With twenty minutes to go before my Tuesday-Thursday differential equations class, I brushed leaves from a bench by the center fountain and took a seat. I mentally wrote "save" on a new catalog from a textbook publisher and "toss" on an ad with a form to order Thanksgiving flower arrangements for my friends and family.

With Bruce likely to still be disabled on Thanksgiving

weekend, I doubted we'd be making the trip to his cousins' home in Connecticut. Maybe I should think about sending an arrangement. I moved the flower ad to the mental "save" pile.

Among the notices to remit my annual dues to a professional mathematics society and to a teachers' organization, was a personal letter from Reverend and Mrs. Calvin Derbin of East Fullertown, Nebraska.

I should have expected the periodic missive from Chelsea's parents. Certainly Chelsea had told them about Charlotte's murder and I guessed this was a plea to help keep their daughter safe.

I opened the classic cream-colored envelope and read the careful handwriting, dated last Friday. After expressing words of gratitude for all I've done for their "cherished only daughter, Chelsea Ann" they wanted to assure me of their prayers for her mentor and my friend, Ms. Charlotte Crocker. Details followed of how they'd reacted when Chelsea broke the news. " ... this morning, she told us of the horrible death of Ms. Charlotte Crocker." I figured Chelsea wanted to put her own spin on the campus crime, in case the news got to East Fullertown over the tabloid wires.

The Derbins closed with their usual good wishes for health for me and my loved ones.

Not this week, I thought, as I folded the note and stuffed it in the stack.

Chelsea was present and accounted for in the front row of my differential equations classroom, having made peace, I hoped, with the fact that she might never see Daryl again. In spite of the pleasant, sunny day she was wrapped in a thick, oversize sweater that left very little skin showing. She looked pale, as she had all month.

At nine o'clock in the morning, she would already have had her morning phone conversation with her parents. Watching her pull her DE textbook out of her backpack, I flashed back to the letter her parents sent me. Something didn't add up. Mrs. Derbin had mentioned Chelsea's telling her of Charlotte's murder last Friday morning. But Charlotte's body had remained undiscovered until Hannah found her on Friday afternoon at four.

How did Chelsea know Charlotte had been murdered a full eight hours before anyone else did? Except Charlotte's killer.

Impossible.

Mrs. Derbin must have been careless with the time. But I knew better. The daily phone conversation was an eight o'clock EST, six o'clock CST ritual and Mrs. Derbin was anything but a sloppy timekeeper.

It occurred to me that I'd read the letter hastily while acknowledging greetings from students passing by and thinking of the problem sets due today in DE. I'd go back and read it again and put this ridiculous notion to rest.

I glanced again at Chelsea, whose head was on the arm of the student chair. She wasn't the only one resting, a common practice before our nine o'clock class.

Even before I called the class to order, I'd mostly talked myself out of the conclusion that had crept up on me. People made mistakes all the time writing notes, rounding off numbers and time lengths.

And what possible motive would Chelsea have? Surely Charlotte's unwillingness to give Chelsea career advice wouldn't spur her on to murder.

Was Chelsea Derbin even strong enough to overcome an adult as tall and fit as Charlotte Crocker? Lately the frail-looking sophomore had been ill so often, she could hardly keep herself upright.

Soon enough I'd get another shot at studying the letter.

For now, I needed to conduct a class without looking at the students in the front row.

I opened my notes and began. "Let's suppose Newton, Leibniz, and the Bernoulli brothers were arguing about who had invented differential equations."

Who said mathematicians had no sense of fancy?

As soon as I was back in my office, I pulled the Derbins' letter out of the stack on my desk and reread the offending sentence.

*We love starting our day with our call to our daughter, but when we talked to Chelsea this morning, she told us of the horrible death of Ms. Charlotte Crocker.*

There was no question; the news had traveled during the Derbins' regular morning call on Friday, the day Charlotte's body was found. The time difference between Henley and East Fullertown was two hours. Even if Chelsea had made a special call to her parents as soon as we all knew Charlotte had been killed, that still put the time at about three in the afternoon in Nebraska. Not the morning.

I'd have to give this idea time to settle, think about what else might support it or not, maybe run it by Bruce and Ariana, then talk to Virgil. I didn't want to stir things up needlessly, but it was possible the nationwide police search for Daryl Farmer should be called off.

I packed up and made my way down the Franklin hallway, empty now as the ten o'clock classes were in session. I didn't have office hours until one thirty and I'd planned to do some shopping in between. I called home as I walked.

"Hey, are you awake?"

"Uh-huh. Are you?" Bruce asked.

"I just taught a class."

"Is that a yes?"

I was glad the meds hadn't dulled his wit.

"I'm going to do some errands and make a grocery run. Is there anything special you want?"

"Kevin's mom called and took our order. She'll be here later with a load of stuff. I think we're set."

"Okay, I—"

*Thump.*

I was knocked into the wall, my briefcase falling to the floor, along with my purse. I managed to stay nearly upright, surprised more than injured.

"Sorry, Dr. Knowles. I wasn't paying attention."

Chelsea, all one hundred pounds of her, had rammed into me.

We bent down together to retrieve my bags. Once I had everything repositioned and closed off with Bruce, I saw how stressed Chelsea was, and not simply from having bumped into me. Her eyes had a frightened look and her voice was close to a screech.

"Is anything wrong?" I asked her.

"I was going to ask you the same thing," she said.

My imagination was working overtime as I became convinced that Chelsea was aware that she'd blown it in her phone call to East Fullertown on Friday morning. As I played it back in my head, her "sorry" sounded more like a threat than an apology.

Her distracted, almost drugged state frightened me and I was glad when biology professor Judith Donohue and three of her students entered the building at our end and engaged us in conversation about the new display case items.

I took advantage of the opportunity to rush out of Franklin Hall and into my car.

Where was the normal Tuesday?

More important, where was the normal Sophie St. Germain Knowles, supremely logical thinker who didn't jump to conclusions. Or jump when a sophomore ran into her?

I'd even had a fleeting thought to tell Virgil about the note and my suspicions. As if a couple in Nebraska could never make a mistake about a date or a time.

I hoped I'd be myself again soon.

Since I needed supplies more than food, I'd decided to skip the grocery store and stop at the enormous multipurpose store at the edge of Henley's main retail area.

There was nothing like a general discount store to put things in perspective. Aisles full of the most ordinary things, like soap and pencils and underwear, served the purpose of making everything else seem superfluous, or at least back burner material.

I remembered that my mother's favorite thing to wear was a kangaroo pouch sweatshirt that let her carry a myriad of essentials right in front of her without burdening her arthritic hands or requiring strapping on, as a fanny pack would. The pouch arrangement was also perfect for use with crutches.

I headed for the clothing department, following huge signs

that led me to the back of the store. It took no more than a half hour to find three sweat suits that would work well for my patient, plus odds and ends for his convenience in every room in the house.

As Bruce's everyday needs came to the fore, Chelsea's possible involvement in Charlotte's murder receded.

As I exited through the giant sliding doors, I looked forward to delivering my packages and having lunch with Bruce and Kevin.

There was still a chance for a normal day.

I turned into my driveway and pushed the square gray button on my garage door opener. The nicely painted white door didn't budge. I stopped in front of the door, shifted to PARK, and tried again. Nothing. Maybe a loose connection. I slapped the opener against my palm and pushed the button again. Nothing.

A nuisance that had happened before. It was probably time for a battery change. I thought of calling Bruce and having him push the button inside, next to the entry to the house, but even that trip might be a hassle for him. I'd do what I always did when I was alone, enter through the side door of the garage and push the opener on the wall myself.

I left my car in PARK and traipsed down the side walkway, digging in my purse for my house key. I couldn't help thinking of how Garrett Paulsen took this same route on Saturday when he broke in, hoping for a small fortune.

It seemed weird to me that I'd never met or talked directly to Garrett. He was the phantom to whom Marty owed money and who'd been with him at the crime scene; the guy I'd tracked all the way to Bailey's Landing and gossiped about with a convenience store clerk; the thief who'd entered the door I was about to unlock and grabbed my duffel, full of socks and travel sundries.

Garrett was in jail now for a crime of fraud completely unrelated to me and to all of Charlotte's capers. I wondered if I should visit him just to have a closer look at the man who'd rummaged around my garage and sullied my good duffel. Maybe I could thank him for tripping the alarm when he tried to enter my house, and thus sending Daryl packing.

My mind was so focused on Garrett, his dreadlocks and the baseball cap he'd been wearing in the photograph Virgil had shown me, I wouldn't have been surprised to find him pilfering through the files in my garage when I opened the door. With all of that, it didn't register in time that I hadn't really needed my key to unlock the door. It had been closed, but not locked.

What greeted me was not a thief going through my things, but a student. Chelsea Derbin stood under my disabled door opener, holding its unplugged cord in one hand and a gun in the other.

"Ha," she said, in a voice louder than I'd ever heard from her.

The cry was at once a strange laugh and an "aha," as if she was as surprised as I was to find us together in my garage.

My instinct was to turn and run out the side door, but if what was trained on me was a real, loaded gun, I didn't stand a chance.

"Chelsea," I said, as if she'd come to review the homogeneous equations of this morning's lesson. "What are you doing?"

It was as good a question as any while I wondered if I'd live to hear an answer.

# Chapter 24

Chelsea's gun hand waved back and forth in a wide arc, in synch with her hopping from right foot to left and back again. I could almost have escaped between one end of the swing and the other.

If I wasn't too scared to move.

"I don't want to do this, Dr. Knowles," Chelsea said. "I really don't."

"You don't have to do anything," I said, with surprising steadiness in my voice. It occurred to me that I wasn't shocked after all. Not after reading her parents' note and not after getting thrown against the wall in Franklin Hall.

"It was never supposed to happen. I just wanted to talk to her. Charlotte. You know she told me I could call her Charlotte that last night?"

I was grateful for the warning: *Don't try to coddle Chelsea by letting her call you Sophie. It won't work.*

I became more frightened by the minute, and more determined not to let it show. I tried to recall any tips I'd heard about negotiating, but none of the ones that came to me were pertinent to this situation.

"I know you'd never deliberately hurt anyone, Chelsea. You weren't brought up that way."

A strange smile came over her, like many new expressions I'd seen on her face today.

"You know what's funny? I was brought up that way. I was brought up with guns. My dad taught all of us how to shoot, my brothers and me. And when I came to Henley, the first thing he did was get me my own handgun, so I could protect myself in the big city."

She turned the gun and looked down its barrel as if wondering how and when she should use this gift from her father.

*Thunk.*

I heard a noise from inside the house.

Bruce! Bruce and possibly Kevin were in the house. How had I forgotten?

Did Chelsea know I had guests? What would Chelsea do about it if she knew? I closed my eyes against the possibility that she'd already done something. But the noise meant someone was alive in there.

Did my guests know my situation out here? Of all times for two strapping, fit men to be incapacitated.

I dropped my keys on the floor to distract Chelsea in case she'd heard the sound. She'd moved from the center of the garage closer to me, her back to the door to the house.

I saw that she'd gone to some other world, hardly reacting to either disturbance. I made a move to flee. But the gun was back quickly, pointed at me again, and I returned to a stock still position.

"Your dad wouldn't want you to be here now, Chelsea."

"I took the gun with me to the library that night. Only to scare Charlotte. I didn't use it, did I? I'm not a bad person, am I?"

"No, not at all. You wanted Charlotte to be reasonable and talk to you. You didn't want to hurt her."

"That's right. She wasn't even afraid of the gun. I put it in my pocket to show her all I wanted to do was talk. But we argued and then we started pushing each other and knocking things over. How stupid was that? Then she just turned and went up the ladder like I didn't matter. Do you know what she said?"

"What did she say to you, Chelsea?"

"'It's for your own good.' That's what I've been hearing all my life and I couldn't stand it. She was going to talk to my parents. I couldn't let her do that. I shook the ladder so she'd come down and talk to me."

"I understand that. And the police will understand that. You just have to explain it to them the way you're explaining it to me."

"No, I can't do that, Dr. Knowles." She threw back her shoulders. "I knew what I had to do when I saw you in class, Dr. Knowles. My mom told me she sent you a note and I knew, I knew." Chelsea pounded at her head. "I made a mistake on the phone that morning and I hoped no one would ever figure it out, but now what else can I do? It's all Charlotte's fault. Why didn't she just promise she wouldn't tell?"

"Wouldn't tell what?"

Chelsea looked down reflexively, toward her abdomen.

If I felt I had freedom of movement, I'd have slapped the side of my head or pounded the front of it as Chelsea did off and on.

How had I missed this?

Chelsea had been wearing cover-all sweaters every day. She stood in front of me now, her face pale, in a down coat that might have fit Virgil. She'd been nauseous since mid-semester, a malady I'd attributed to all manner of causes, from presentation jitters to the smells of the Mortarboard Café.

"Ms. Crocker knew you were pregnant."

Chelsea screwed up her face and nodded. "Like an idiot, I told her. I thought she'd be happy for me because she supposedly cared about me. She should have been glad because Daryl and I were going to get married."

No you weren't, I thought. Poor Chelsea.

Poor me! Was I experiencing Stockholm Syndrome, feeling sympathy for my captor, a frail, pregnant teenager?

"She was going to tell my parents."

"They would have found out eventually, Chelsea."

"Not before we were married. We were going home together at Thanksgiving. My parents would have met him and seen what a great guy he is. So smart and worldly. They would have been thrilled. But Charlotte ruined it, telling me all these lies and she was going to tell the lies to my parents."

"What lies did she tell you?"

"All of a sudden, last week, she started to rave against Daryl. She was all over him, how he wasn't good enough for me. She said he wouldn't stay around, baby or no baby."

Chelsea drew in a deep breath and held it. Her face turned red and her body shook. I thought she was going to faint. I hoped she'd faint, and stay unconscious just long enough for me to grab her gun.

She let out the breath. It wasn't going to be that easy.

I listened for movement inside the house, but heard nothing. Did Bruce know I was home? Ordinarily he'd have heard the car in the driveway and come out to greet me. But if he was stashed away at the back of the house, essentially immobile, all bets were off.

Chelsea's breathing was heavy and labored as she continued, talking as much to herself as to anyone in the real world outside of her.

"Then she told me this story about how she'd taken Daryl's father's money and he killed himself and Daryl found her and"—Chelsea threw up her hands, gun included—"I can't believe it. Ms. Crocker a criminal? Daryl using me to get to her?"

"It's all true, Chelsea," I said, risking further stress to the already frail girl, but I didn't have many options.

"Don't say that," Chelsea screamed.

Nothing like a screaming murderer to cause shaking all over one's body. My body. I knew I couldn't keep this civil conversation going forever. I had to do something.

But what?

I snuck a look around my garage. What could I use to defend myself against a gun? My treadmill, on the left, took up a lot of space and was useless to me now. So was my rack of file boxes near the door, dating back to my first year at Henley. What about the garden tools? A rake, a shovel, pruning shears, hedge clippers. But they were too far away, near the disabled roll-up door.

To my immediate right, however, was Bruce's wall, full of potential weapons. Extra crampons, ice axes, and sharp, curved picks.

He'd hate that I thought of his equipment that way, but right now a long-handled ax spelled not sport, but survival for me.

I started to maneuver myself closer to the wall.

"Don't tell me Charlotte was right. I know that," Chelsea said, seeming unaware of my plotting. She pulled at her long hair. I was sure it hurt, but maybe that's what she wanted. "Look around. Where's Daryl? Do you see Daryl? He never cared about me. It was all about him and his dad and the money."

"If you stop now, Chelsea, your baby won't have to be born in prison."

I had no idea if that was true, but these were desperate times and I allowed myself a rash promise.

I heard my voice as if it were someone else's, someone not standing a few feet from a woman with a gun. The look in Chelsea's eyes was foreign to me. Where was the docile sophomore math major I'd known for almost two years, who always handed in her problem sets on time, who was the first one to volunteer to set up for a meeting, the last one to leave when there was cleanup to do?

"I can't do that. I can't go to the police. My parents—"

*Whack!*

"Hey, Sophie, what's up?"

Bruce's voice, from the other side of the door that he'd managed to open a crack with the end of his crutch.

Did Bruce know what was happening out here? Did I want him to know?

Chelsea started, but not enough to drop her gun. She slunk back against the wall and put her finger to her lips.

I nodded. *I'll never tell.*

Relief flooded me that she hadn't known about the disabled occupants of my house. I shuddered at the thought of what she would have been willing to do to cover her tracks.

Chelsea turned to face me directly, gun at the ready. I could tell she was having a now-or-never moment, possibly thinking to finish me off, then shoot Bruce.

"Is everything okay?" Bruce, stalling, while he worked his crutch like a crow bar around the struts of the metal rack closest to the interior door.

I looked past her at the opening he'd made. The bottom end of his crutch crept through, higher and higher, until it reached a point behind the rack.

I got it. Bruce knew. He was going to provide a distraction by overturning the rack.

The rest was up to me.

I waited, my body gearing up for the coming avalanche, this one welcome.

The crutch wiggled into position. I pictured Bruce on the other side of the door, finding the right leverage to tip it over.

I held my breath, watching the rack sway.

*Crash. Thump. Crash.*

The rack fell over, dumping its contents in a heap on the floor directly behind Chelsea. Fifteen years' worth of Henley College Mathematics Department files. Tax records. Games and puzzles. Boxes of decorations.

A ceramic Santa rolled out from a Christmas carton and stopped at Chelsea's feet as she turned to face the inventory of things I'd thought worth saving.

As she swiveled and sidestepped to avoid slipping on a tennis ball, I reached back and yanked the lowest ice ax from its metal hook and swung it over and onto Chelsea's arm. Her gun arm. The curved pick with the jagged teeth on its underside hooked around her wrist, tearing through her thick down coat.

Chelsea screamed and dropped the gun.

Bruce, in his chair, still using the crutch as a lever, pulled the door open all the way. Kevin hopped out on his one good leg, stumbled through the mess on the floor, and threw himself, cast and all, on top of Chelsea.

They both screamed in pain.

After that Chelsea never had a chance.

# Chapter 25

The small television set in my kitchen was tuned to the morning news. We'd had a few days of normal life and now Bruce and I sat at breakfast listening to the reporter's version of the successful conclusion of the Charlotte Crocker murder investigation. Brief mention was made of the altercation in my garage, though I never intended for that part of the story to be made public.

"How about that?" Bruce said. "See, if I didn't climb ice, I wouldn't have had a small fortune in axes on your garage wall, and you would have been up a creek."

"Is this the conversation we're supposed to have about how you did or did not learn your lesson last weekend?" I asked.

"I thought it could be."

"Not a chance," I said.

He pointed to his leg, still encased in plaster.

"Can we wait until I can at least walk around while you rail at me?"

He and his climbing buddy had saved my life.

It was the least I could do.

"Then we can talk about how I worry about you, too."

"You mean in case there's a fire in Benjamin Franklin Hall?"

"And I suppose that's all you did since I left on Friday. Hang around home and campus, nice and safe."

"Hmmm."

"I suppose you left the police work to the cops."

There was a lot more Bruce could have brought up but didn't, starting with involving myself in a murder investigation and ending with a gun in my face.

"You have a point," I said.

He saluted, a satisfied smile on his face.

The embrace that followed was the best kind of truce.

I reached into my pocket and pulled out the beaded bookmark Ariana and I had made and handed it to Bruce.

"Ariana and I made it while you were missing."

Bruce looked closely at the beading. "Here's Ariana's section," he said, fingering the most neatly tied knots.

I faked a blow to his knee, then turned serious. "We did it so the universe would know we expected you home."

"I know," he said.

Were those tears in my boyfriend's eyes?

Plans for Thanksgiving dinner with Bruce's cousins had to be scrapped. They understood that a road trip was too hard an undertaking in his condition. Since it wasn't feasible to move the party, with the other fifteen guests, to Henley, we'd all make up for it with a Christmas reunion instead.

Ariana was sorry we had to pass up a holiday in Connecticut, but delighted at the new arrangement: Dinner in my cottage with our nearest and dearest.

"You can invite Luke," I said.

"Luke is so last month," she said, shaking her head. "Let's just have one turkey at the table."

"Clear enough."

When I called Virgil to invite him to squeeze a little Thanksgiving dinner with us into his workday, I did a little business also.

"If it's not too late, I'd like to take care of Charlotte's remains," I told him.

"Not too late. I've been waiting."

"Of course you have. The president had a moment of silent prayer for her at an assembly, but I think she deserves more than that. She really did try to go straight and she made a huge effort to save Chelsea from the pain of a guy who was just using her."

Virgil agreed and added his own observation. "And although she was keeping a load of cash for contingency, we did find a considerable number of charitable donations when we combed her current financials. If that matters to you."

"Thanks. It matters."

I thought about the contents of the box Virgil had brought me. Things Charlotte had saved for one reason or another, known only to her. I remembered seeing the delicate beaded eyeglass chain Ariana and I had made for her. Charlotte had kept it in a special pouch.

Maybe it had made her happy to be accepted by a couple of standard, boring women without criminal records.

Maybe we'd touched her life in some way that mattered. And quite possibly, the good she'd done for the Henley community mattered also.

Even with short notice, Bruce and I were able to round up a tableful of companions for the Thanksgiving table. Virgil came as did Irene and Kevin, the man who flew into my garage and crushed my attacker. The least I could do was feed him and his mother, who was happy to join us. I felt that all of them had contributed to the reasons I was alive and able to be grateful this holiday.

The best news was that Eduardo was out of intensive care and had been transported to a facility close to home. We promised to move the party to his rehab center across town for dessert.

The dinner conversation was what one would expect, given the stressful times we'd been through and the personalities around the table.

"I still can't believe the library lady's killer was a girl," Kevin's mother said. A lovely woman from the far reaches of Maine, I figured she didn't know how anyone was capable of doing bodily harm to another.

Virgil was ready with statistics. My hero. "If you want numbers, I can tell you that the Henley city jail has seven cells in the basement of the building. Five are reserved for male prisoners and two for females."

"I still feel sorry for Chelsea," I said. "She felt trapped and I believe her that she went there just to talk to Charlotte." I turned to the cop in our midst. "What are the chances that Chelsea would be able to serve her time in Nebraska, for her parents' sake?"

Virgil shook his head. "Let's say, if her daddy was the governor of Nebraska and her mother was the attorney general of Massachusetts, maybe. And even then, she'd also have to have another relative who was the Chief of Staff—"

"I get it. She stays in Massachusetts."

"What about Daryl, or whatever the real name was of that boy who disappeared?" Ariana asked.

"Nothing yet," Virgil said. "Now that we know he didn't kill the woman he tracked across the country, it's up for grabs how intense the search will be. Technically, the only crime he committed was lying to his girlfriend."

"And breaking in to my house," I said, though I had no intention of pressing charges against him. The sooner I was done with all the crimes of the past weeks, the better.

"Crime and punishment talk. This is what happens when you invite a cop to Thanksgiving dinner," Bruce said.

"One cop, two ice climbers. It hardly seems fair," said Virgil, helping himself to his third piece of cornbread, contributed by Kevin's mother.

"I have some numbers, too," Bruce said. "Did you know that of all the rescues in state parks, less than five percent are climbing related, and only three percent are related to roped climbing and mountaineering?"

No one answered directly, but there were questions all the same.

"What was it like being stranded up there?" Ariana asked the men who were.

"I was never really afraid," Bruce said. "How about you, Kev?"

"I was concerned, but not scared," Kevin said.

His mother rolled her eyes.

"I was maybe a little uneasy, but not frightened," Bruce said. We all rolled our eyes.

"Well, not to worry. We're always here to transport you," Irene said. Her comment had the desired effect as the recently missing guys moaned.

"You had to remind us," Kevin said.

I knew it hadn't exactly been a triumph for them to be picked up by their own company.

"Next time ..." Bruce began. He looked at me and cut himself off.

He raised his glass.

"Happy Thanksgiving, everyone."

"You bet," I said.

**Sophie Knowles returns in:**

# A FUNCTION OF MURDER

**Book Three of the Professor Sophie Knowles Mysteries**

# About the Author

Camille Minichino is a retired physicist turned writer. When her first book, on nuclear waste management, was popular only in academic circles, she turned to cozy mystery novels and has published 25 of them in 4 different series: the Periodic Table Mysteries; the Miniature Mysteries (as Margaret Grace); the Professor Sophie Knowles Mysteries (as Ada Madison); and the Postmistress Mysteries (as Jean Flowers). She's now working on a 3-book deal for a fifth series, the Alaska Diner Mysteries (as Elizabeth Logan). She's also written nonfiction, many short stories, and articles on the craft of writing. She teaches science at Golden Gate U. in San Francisco and writing workshops around the SF Bay Area. More information is at www.minichino.com.

Curious about other Crossroad Press books?
Stop by our site:
http://www.crossroadpress.com
We offer quality writing
in digital, audio, and print formats.